MAYHEM

MAYHEM

JEFFREY SALANE

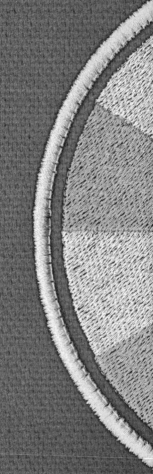

SCHOLASTIC PRESS | NEW YORK

To the counted outs who can be counted on.
And to Adrienne for being herself.

Library of Congress Cataloging-in-Publication Data available

ISBN 978-0-545-45033-1

10 9 8 7 6 5 4 3 2 1   16 17 18 19 20

Printed in the U.S.A.   23
First edition, May 2016

Book design by Phil Falco

Here's the rub . . . There's no difference between poison and the cure.

— JOHN DYER BAIZLEY

CHAPTER 1
ALARMED

M was awake.

Or almost awake. She felt herself at an edge. Perched between a dream and a nightmare that drifted into each other like clouds in the sky.

It wasn't a bad feeling. It was just another day. It was the feeling of being alive.

Slowly, M smiled and stretched out her arms, running her hands over the soft blankets on her bed. Comfort flooded in as she fumbled with the buzzing phone alarm on the side table until the silence finally came. Then she opened her eyes.

The smell of waffles hung deliciously in the air.

M sat up in her bed and let out another stretch along with a yawn that nearly cracked her jaw. Too much sleep was a dangerous business.

Her room was painted a sophisticated gray with pops of bright teal and burnt orange in the chevron drapes. A white cushioned desk chair sat empty across from her. She had picked all the colors herself. She remembered that.

M touched the carpeted floor with her bare feet and walked

over to her full-length mirror. Her long brown hair was held back with a pink headband. There was some acne threatening to come in on her forehead, but nothing she couldn't handle. Photos framed the mirror, tacked and taped around the edge. Her best friends stared back at her: Jenny, Chloe, and Emma.

"M, I hope you're up," came her mother's voice from the kitchen. "Those lessons aren't going to learn themselves, *ma petite miette*."

M climbed downstairs still dressed in her favorite pair of flannel pajamas and tracked the smell of breakfast into the kitchen. "Morning, everyone."

"Morning, love," said her mother with a warm smile. Her deep black hair was down and swept around her shoulders in its unkempt, uncombed glory, like always. She had on an over-size sweater poncho and sat cross-legged sipping her coffee. Her mother was such a hippie!

"Morning, M," said her father. He stood by the waffle iron in a ridiculous BLESS THIS MESS apron that was ghost white with flour mix. "Flaxseed waffles and agave nectar, sound good?"

"Sounds perfect, Pops," said M as she gave him a kiss on the cheek. She grabbed her plate and joined Mom at the table. The newspaper was open, so M let her eyes wander over the headlines that didn't make the front page.

"Oh boy, NASA found more comets heading our way, huh?" M said with her mouth full. She smacked her lips and mimicked a comet crashing into the table. "Maybe it will strike before school photos. My skin is doomed."

2

"Oh no, that organic papaya mask I made for you didn't work?" said her mom.

"It smelled too good," admitted M. "I ate it."

"Attagirl," said her father as he sat next to her and cut into his waffle. "If it looks good, smells good, and seems good, it's probably good. Even if it's papaya zit spread."

He let out a huge laugh, maybe bigger than the joke deserved, thought M, but his laughter emitted a happiness that cheered up any room, like an antidote to the blues.

Looking at the two of her parents together in quiet moments, M felt an itch. Not a physical itch, but more of a disturbance, like a Jedi might feel in *Star Wars* . . . a disturbance in the Force.

She couldn't put her finger on it, but there were things about her parents that felt almost out of place sometimes. Her father's green eyes and blond hair sometimes shocked her. M looked at them every now and again and thought, *How did I come from these two people?* But maybe every kid felt that way about their parents at some point in their lives? Sometimes, though, M could almost see scratches in her family story, like static, and for a split second another picture rose out of the mess. A different family, a different home, a different M. Then it would all become clear again and her dad would tell another bad joke.

These disturbances were few and far between. And they were nowhere near as dire as the Death Star. No planets were going to be harmed by these two people. These were the type who made flaxseed waffles and papaya spread on a school day.

Her father pulled out a knife and slit open a banana before dicing it into bite-sized slices for his waffle. "Mmmmm, M. You've gotta try this."

For a moment M wasn't sure if he was talking about the banana or the knife skills, but then he tossed the banana slices onto her waffle. She folded it in half like a banana-filled taco and stood up from the table.

"Thanks, Pops," she said, taking a bite. "Mime gonna finish dis upstairs. Need to get ready before the gang arrives."

"Of course, don't let us get in your way," he kidded. "We're only here to serve you."

"Paul, don't tease," her mother scolded sweetly.

Back in her room, M dressed and reviewed her homework from the night before. There was going to be an exam today on Monet and his contemporaries in Ms. Ohlmsted's class and M was determined to ace it. Sure, Art Appreciation was a blow-off course for other kids in her school, but she weirdly loved it, especially the history and study of different techniques. Maybe M had been an artist in her former life.

Like clockwork, the doorbell rang downstairs over and over again, accompanied by a flurry of frantic knocks. It sounded like survivors trying to get inside a locked door to be saved from the apocalypse.

M ran to the door with her backpack on. Jenny, Chloe, and Emma had their faces pressed up against the side glass panels, hollering at the top of their lungs.

"Save us, M! Save us!" they screamed while trying to keep a straight face.

"Mom, Dad, you know the drill. My squad's here!" M shouted over the madness. "I'll see you after school!"

"Have a great day, dear," her father said cheerfully. "And don't go changing today; we like you just the way you are."

"Har, har har," said M as she stepped outside and turned her attention to the others. "There's no hope for you jerks, especially if you keep scaring my neighbors like this." Then she called out across the street, "It's okay, Mrs. Truffle. Everything's fine. My friends were just joking."

An elderly woman sat on her porch with several small dogs darting around her front yard. She waved back with an annoyed gesture. "They're stirring up the dogs."

"Sorry, Mrs. Truffle," the girls all apologized in a flat tone.

"Ugh, let's get to school before you make the whole neighborhood think I live in the weirdest house for miles," said M as the group walked down the street. "It's bad enough we have neon-green barrels to collect rainwater and compost religiously in our backyard. I think my parents are two days away from getting livestock and starting a commune."

"Oh, please," Jenny scoffed jokingly. "You won the parent lottery, M. Sure, they're crunchy, but your parents are *cool* crunchy. I mean, my parents think I can survive on one hundred texts a month. Well, I've got news for you, Mom and Dad: I can't!"

"And what's wrong with lime green?" asked Chloe. She was

trying a new color of nail polish, *Shrieking Lime*, and the name fit. Her fingers looked like they were wearing Day-Glo green outfits.

Fort Harmon Middle School was bustling with kids getting dropped off by their parents, but M lived criminally close, like across-the-street close. All of her friends lived close, too. M remembered moving to Harmon last summer. Her parents must have known that moving to a new city would be hard for her, so they invited all the neighbors with kids her age over on their first night in the house. Ever since then, Jenny, Chloe, Emma, and M had been inseparable. They walked to and from school together every day. And they had almost every class together, too. Except for their electives. While M had chosen Art Appreciation, the others had chosen one of the wildest courses the school offered: Survival Skills. They had begged M to join them, but survival skills weren't something M had any interest in.

"M, just to make you jealous, we're going to learn how to start a fire without a match today," bragged Emma. "Are you sure you don't want to switch electives? I've asked Mr. Harch and there's a spot for you if you want it."

"Sounds like a scorching good time, but I'll stick with the arts," said M. "Besides, we can't be in every class together. Geez, stalk each other much?"

"Hey, it's not creepy. It's survival," joked Chloe. Then she shook her *Shrieking Lime* finger and spoke in a low, husky voice that mimicked Mr. Harch. "And survival is no laughing matter."

The girls burst out laughing again as they made their way inside the building to their first class. But there was a buzz in the hallway this morning. A new kid was starting today, four weeks into the school year. The collective excitement and curiosity of the school hadn't peaked to this level since M started at the beginning of the year.

"It's a guy, that's all I know," some kid with long hair admitted to his friends as M walked by.

"I heard he got kicked out of Turnington Prep," said another. The walls were talking, and M couldn't help but listen to every scrap that floated by.

"Do you guys know about this new kid?" she asked her friends. But when she turned, she noticed that they weren't by her side anymore. They had fallen back into a huddle behind M, speaking in hushed whispers.

No one said anything about this.

Relax, it's probably a test.

This is what we've been training for. It's finally here. They've come to take . . .

"Guys?" M asked, catching small pieces of what they were saying. "What are you talking about?"

"Sorry!" Jenny snapped around, cutting the girls' private powwow short. "No idea about Mr. X. But why would we? It's not like we're on the lookout for newbs." Jenny wore a nervous smile and M couldn't figure out why. Chloe and Emma were behind her, nodding in agreement like bobbleheads on springs, bouncing up and down, up and down.

"Hey, don't we have that, um, thing?" Emma asked the others.

"You're right!" Chloe burst out in agreement. "For Harch's class. We needed to get that thing from the library."

"A book?" guessed M.

"Yeah, a book on flint history or something. It's not important," said Jenny. "M, why don't you go ahead to class and we'll meet you there."

The group left in unison and disappeared around the corner, leaving M alone. She shook her head, confused at the strange interaction and her friends' sudden need to all go to the library at the same time, but she'd noticed that about them before. They were the kind of girls who did everything together. Come to think of it, M wondered, had she ever hung out one-on-one with any of them? To her surprise, she hadn't.

Hearing the first bell drone out, M wheeled around to go to first period — and bumped right into a boy carrying a load of books.

"Whoa!" he exclaimed as everything was knocked out of his hands. The books landed open-faced, with a series of thuds, on the ground. He froze for a moment with his arms open and chuckled with indifference. "Look out," he said flatly once it was over and done.

M knelt down to help with the mess. "Sorry, sorry, sorry, I didn't see you and . . ."

He smiled nervously at M's horrified rambling and stooped down next to her. "It's cool," he said. "I wasn't really looking where I was going, either. Um, I'm Evel. Otherwise known as the new kid."

"Yeah, I thought you didn't look familiar," said M as she flipped the splayed books closed and stacked them carefully.

The boy laughed again. "You're funny."

With things gathered, M and Evel stood back up. He was tall. Taller than her. He was also tan and Asian, dressed in a black hoodie as dark as his long hair. When he tucked the stack of books under his chin for support, M noticed a slight scar that ran under his jawline. He definitely looked older than M. Actually, he looked older than all the kids at Fort Harmon.

"Are you sure you're in middle school?" asked M.

"Wow, and you're not shy, either," Evel noted. "Um, let's just say I haven't been the best student in the past. But I'm trying to change that. Would you like to help me?"

"Me? How can I help? Besides suggest where you can get a backpack."

Evel motioned his head toward the hallway as the other kids moved around them. "You can help me find my first class before I'm late, for starters."

"Oh," replied M. "Sure. What class are you looking for?"

Evel readjusted the pile of books in his arms and pulled a crumpled piece of paper out from his pocket and handed it to M. "Here's my schedule. I think it's . , ."

"Math," she answered. "It's this way. Room 108."

As they walked, Evel kept talking. "Man, this place is big. How many kids go here, anyway?"

"I don't know, like a thousand, maybe?" said M as she led the way.

"How long does it take before you learn your way around?" he asked.

"It wasn't hard for me and I just started here this year," admitted M. "Give it a week, I guess. So, you're not from Harmon. You're too tan."

She let the statement hang in the air without asking a question.

"What can I say? I'm blessed with good genes," said Evel. "I've been all around. Born in Japan, moved to France, then to LA for a while. Now I'm here."

"But you've been in Harmon," said M. "Rumor has it you were at Turnington before FH."

"Rumor has it right," confirmed Evel. "They didn't care for my anti-backpack stance."

"You know what I say about that?" asked M.

"What?"

"Get a locker." M stopped in front of the door to room 108. "You have arrived safely at your destination."

"Thanks for the company. It was great bumping into you," joked Evel. "Maybe I'll see you around."

"Definitely," agreed M as she held up his schedule and tucked it back under his chin. "Today at two fifteen, in fact. We're in Art Appreciation together. Just a head's-up, there's going to be a test. Rough day to be a new kid."

Before Evel could get a last word in, M turned on her heel and hustled away to class.

Her heart beat a new rhythm in her chest. Evel was a different kind of disturbance. One that she hadn't been prepared for. It was a good disturbance this time, like seeing a shooting star and making a wish. Suddenly the flat routine of Harmon didn't seem so dull and predictable.

As she made for her class, a door whipped open and tagged the side of her elbow with a whump. "Hey! Ouch!" she cried out.

The man on the other side of the door slowly turned toward her. His head was shaved bald and he sported a white goatee that jutted out like a sharp extension of his chin. But what M noticed most was the man's size. Not his height, because he was short. What jumped out more was his sheer muscle mass. This wasn't a teacher. He was a steroid-abusing weightlifter by day and a back-alley brawler by night.

"Outta the way, girlie," he said with a Cockney accent. "I gots pupils that need schoolin'."

He shuffled off and left M gripping her arm and late to class. This was turning into the strangest day of her life.

CHAPTER 2
ACCEPT NO SUBSTITUTES

Jenny and the others spent the day chasing leads on the new kid. M observed them as if she were watching a movie that she already knew the ending to. The girls were working all their connections at the other tables in the lunchroom. Finally they joined her at their table, seemingly empty-handed.

"You know, for the life of me, I don't know why you are so interested in this new kid," M said. "He's probably just like us."

"He's not like us, M," Chloe corrected her. "He's a mystery. And, I mean, this isn't the nicest way to put it, but *this is Harmon*. Nothing ever happens here. No one moves here, no one leaves here. Our parents all went to school here, our parents all stayed here."

"I moved here," said M. "Does that make me a mystery, too?"

"Yeah, but you were, like, the one-in-a-million new kid," said Emma. "And you're not a mystery anymore. You're M. Trust me, this town isn't a two-in-a-million new kid kind of place."

"What are you guys, like the city inspectors?" asked M.

Chloe ignored the question. "Maybe he's in trouble with the law, or an undercover special agent, or a vampire."

"He's not a vampire," giggled Emma. "But he could be a werewolf. Werewolves can be outside during the day and they look just like you and me."

M stood up from the table with an audible sigh. "I'm done. Good luck on the fact-finding mission, you monster hunters."

The class before Art Appreciation was slow. Of course it was slow. It was math. Filled with piles of numbers and equations. But it shouldn't have been slow for M. She loved playing with math problems. She saw each one as an unfinished, secret code that needed to be cracked. It sounded nerdy when she thought that in her head, but her attitude had kept her in straight A's so far. Math was slow today because M was looking forward to her next class and seeing Evel.

When she got to art class, Evel was waiting for her in the hall outside.

"Did you know that someone punched a Monet painting once in Ireland?" asked Evel.

"No way that's true," argued M. It hurt her to think that someone could be so careless with priceless art. "What did that painting ever do to him?"

"Totally true," said Evel. "He strolled up to it and punched a hole right through it. He split the canvas and all. But want to hear the weird part?"

"Wait, there's a weirder part than someone knocking out a masterpiece?" asked M.

"Believe it or not, there is," said Evel. "It wasn't the first time a Monet painting was punched!"

"And you think that's going to be on the test?" M asked.

"No, but it caught my eye," admitted Evel. "And it made me excited to not be a Monet painting."

As they entered the classroom, Ms. Ohlmsted wasn't sitting at the front desk. Instead, the same monstrous bald guy from earlier that morning sat leaning back with his feet perched and crossed, watching each of the students as they entered the room.

Their eyes met and the stranger's stare followed her all the way to her seat. Other students filed in after M, but the man ignored them all and kept his gaze trained on her. Evel took the desk behind M, so she turned around to face him instead.

"Don't look now, but you've got a fan," Evel whispered. "Did you do something to his Monet?"

"I don't know who that is," M said. "But he nearly took my arm off this morning slamming open a door."

As if on cue, the man rose up from behind the desk. The suit he wore was so tight it barely contained him. The class quieted down immediately in his presence. Stepping toward the front of the room, the man cracked his knuckles and rolled his neck around, which let out a resounding pop that made the students cringe.

"Ms. Alls-Ham is under the weather today," he announced in his heavy British accent.

"That's weird. I saw her this morning and she seemed fine," said a girl in the front row. "Hmm, I can see her car in the teachers' parking lot. And, not to correct you, sir, but her name is Ms. Ohlmsted."

The giant whirled his head around to face the girl. "It is a pity," he said slowly. "See, unfortunately Ms. Alls-Ham came down with a case of too many questions and needed to see the school nurse. The nurse then hopped her right in a red-light cruiser to the hospital so's they can figure out what's up, doc. Ergo, I'll be your substitute today. Are we all understanding now? Or is there anyone else who needs a visit to the nurse?"

The class all shook their heads silently. No one wanted to ask this guy anything.

"Excellent, then," he said. "My name is Mr. Dartsey and today we will begin with a roll call. Now, as I say your names, please raise your hand. Gotta tick this off for the jolly ole prince-i-pal."

Dartsey pulled a list from the desk and began reading the names aloud. As he went through them in alphabetical order, hands went up and hands went down.

"Meredith Foreman," Dartsey called out.

M raised her hand. This piqued Dartsey's interest.

"Now, Meredith," said Dartsey with relish in his voice, "I see a note here that states you never use Meredith but that, in fact, you go by the letter M. That true?"

"Yes, sir," answered M.

"Well, ain't that a kick in the head," said Dartsey. "I used to know another M, from another time, but this M, he was a gentleman type. I thought he'd be the only M I ever met. And now, in the middle of nowhere, I meet you. Another M! Hah, life's funny that way, I s'pose."

He paused and nodded carefully at M again, but she didn't have anything more to add. After a few moments, Dartsey continued with the other names until he finally reached the last one. "Hold on now. Is there someone in this class named Evil?"

Evel raised his hand. "It's pronounced Evel, like *level,* actually."

"Of course it is," said Dartsey. "My mistake. Say, yours doesn't seem to be a popular last name, but it's one I've seen in my past. Tell me, do you have a sister?"

"No, sir," said Evel, who squirmed to sit up straight in his seat.

"Well, I s'pose that's another interesting circumstance," Dartsey said with a smile that turned into a sneer. "Okay, students. That ends the ticks, so let's get to the tocks. Most of yous came in expecting a test, but there'll be no Monet today. I'm afraid I'm not the biggest fan of Monet's blurry studies of our wondrous surroundings on Earth, and I'd rather you made your own informed opinions about his work. Woe be to me if I were to transfigure your take on something as intensely personal as personal taste. So's instead, we're going to take a look at *key-ara-skewr-ya.*"

Dartsey went over to the whiteboard and wrote down the word *chiaroscuro*. He underlined it with a quick, surgeon-like slash of the marker that made the entire class shake in their seats.

"Chiaroscuro is a brilliant little painting technique perfected by the Masters back in the sixteen hundreds . . . though it has a conceptual lineage that reaches back to the fourteen hundreds."

The class all looked confused.

"Which is to say," continued Dartsey in a huff, "that although other artists in the fourteen hundreds were using chiaroscuro, it didn't become an official technique, which is just a fancy word for 'way of painting,' until much later, when an artist named Rembrandt came along."

M's eyes grew wider at the name Rembrandt. She gripped her pencil tightly as she wrote the name and the term in her notebook. Another disturbance was taking hold.

"The word *chiaroscuro* itself is Italian for 'light-dark,'" said Dartsey. "In this painting style, artists use a mixture of light and darkness in their scenes to highlight the important moments in their artwork."

He turned on the overheard projector and an image appeared on the whiteboard. It was a painting of a man holding a candle and reading a book. The only light in the painting came from the candle in the man's hand, and it faded into gloomy shadows in the background.

"As you may or may not know, people's eyes will naturally

always go to the light and ignore the darkness, which is exactly what the artist wants to happen. In this particular piece, you're meant to look into the light, because the artist wants you to notice only what's in the light."

M studied the painting. Within the light cast by the candle were several objects that artists from Rembrandt's time were obsessed with: an hourglass, a globe, books, the candle itself, and a statue of an angel in the background. She put the pieces of the puzzle together. The hourglass signified the passing of time and life. The globe signified the world as we try to understand it. The open book represented the pursuit of knowledge. The candle, which wouldn't last forever, was another reference to time passing. But it was also a reference to man-made light, or fire, or creation. Then behind it all, barely seen in the shadows, was the statue of an angel, watching over the man like a celestial being.

"Most people think that the light is the spark for this painting," asserted Dartsey. "But most people'd be wrong. See, the light doesn't work without the darkness. That's where the art form comes in. It's how the two work together that matters."

The presentation switched from painting to painting as Dartsey continued his lesson. Each image showed a play between the light and dark choices of the artist. They created shadows that added drama, perspective, fear, and honest emotions in the artwork.

Then one painting flicked onto the screen that stirred a deep, dark feeling in M. Her chest expanded like a balloon was inflating inside of her. The painting was of a group of men dressed like Pilgrims huddled around a dead body. One of the men had dissected the arm of the body, revealing its interior veins, muscles, and bones. M knew its title without having any recognition of seeing it before.

"This," said Dartsey, "is *The Anatomy Lesson of Dr. Nicolaes Tulp*. Painted by Rembrandt in, oh, say, 1632, give or take, this work shows how the Master played with light and dark . . . and the in-between. Now, class, we are looking at an honest-to-life doctor giving his class a surgeon's peek under the skin of this corpse."

Dartsey let out a chuckle as some of the class squealed with whispered *ewww*s. "All right, all right, it's just a painting of a dead body, not a real dead body. Let's keep our heads on straight, then, shall we? And don't blame the doc for the gross scene. He's just doing his job. S'pose I'm doing the same thing with you, teaching and dissecting this picture for you, my eager minds."

He smiled with satisfaction at the connection he'd made. "No, if you blame anyone, you blame the Master for having this much talent to show life the way it really looks. Now, compare the corpse to the other men in the piece. I know it seems kooky, but notice how his face looks against the lively doctor and his students that are full of life. That's a technique that Rembrandt used to refine chiaroscuro and bend it to his will. It's not light or dark. It's just gray-ashen and used up. And that technique was called a —"

"Umbra mortis," M said in a quick inhale. Clips of her true past came rushing back in patches, like plunging her conscience into ice-cold water. Crash-landing at the Lawless School. The glass house at the Fulbright Academy. Joining the Masters. The black hole. Her real name. Her dead father. Her missing mother. Her *real* parents. The last night in her house when her friends, her *real* friends, had been captured and taken away from her. John Doe, the bloated, pasty leader of the Fulbrights with a mad plan to live forever. Jonathan Wild, the creator of the Lawless School and a mysterious person from ancient history who was reaching forward into her life somehow. The details were hazy around the edges and mysterious, hidden in her mucked-up memories like a song melody just out of reach. But she knew two things for sure. She didn't belong in Harmon . . .

And this Dartsey was bad news.

"Wha's that, Ms. Foreman?" the substitute asked with a diabolical grin. "Did you have something to share with the rest of us? Or shall I continue the lesson?"

Lesson. That's exactly what this was. A lesson. A lesson to M, so that she knew her place. She was the hunted, and Dartsey was the next thug in line to catch her.

"Rembrandt called that technique the *umbra mortis*, or 'shadow of death,'" she replied, showing no concern or fear. The other kids almost broke their necks turning to look at her. "You see, during Rembrandt's career, he worked for doctors in order to understand the human body, because to understand it meant he would be able to paint it better, in theory. Lots of artists did this. Leonardo Da Vinci was said to have performed autopsies himself, and he was one of the greatest artists of all time."

"Well, well, well, I'll be well," said Dartsey. "Ms. Foreman knows her stuff. Color me impressed."

"I could go on, if you'd like," bragged M.

"I'm sure you could, but..." Dartsey held up his monolithic finger and, eerily, the final bell of school rang. "We...are out...of time. Class, it's been a pleasure to serve you today. Do be balanced academics and read pages one hundred through one hundred ten in your textbookies for homework tonight. That was Ms. Alls-ham's request, not mine."

The class raced out of their seats and went to escape their behemoth substitute teacher. Already some of the kids were on their phones, posting about their insane class experience. M knew the news about Dartsey would be out soon, but she didn't know what that meant for her. But now she realized that Harmon was an unharmonious place. She was not supposed to be here.

"Oh, and one last bit," said Dartsey, and the students stood deathly still. "I needs to have a quick one-on-one with Ms. Foreman."

If there were allegiances in the classroom, they weren't with M. The rest of the class hightailed it out.

Except for Evel. "I can stay," he offered nervously.

"No," M said, steeling herself for what came next. "Wait for me outside. And whatever you do, whatever you hear, don't come back in here."

Evel, to her surprise, didn't blink twice at her order. He even left his books behind and was out the door.

"How did you find me?" she asked Dartsey once they were alone.

"Funny thing," he said, chortling. "I didn't come looking for you, I was looking for your pal Evel. See, he owes me a thing or three. Like two broken arms and a disjointed leg if my appendage-to-financial-debt ratio is spot-on. And believe me, it's always spot-on."

"If you came for him, then what do you want with me?" she asked.

"Well, when you break into a place with every intention of doing some vandalizing and you unexpectedly find a diamond," Dartsey reasoned as he cracked his knuckles again, "my dear, you always grab the diamond first."

"Careful there, jolly giant," said M. "Diamonds can do a lot of damage."

Dartsey slid a dagger out from his sleeve and hurled it at M. She flinched to the left and heard the blade whiff by her ear. He had been aiming for her head. This was a take-no-prisoners dustup, then. A second dagger flipped toward her, but M grabbed one of Evel's books and blocked the shot. The tip of the knife pierced the cover and stopped inches from her eye.

M ducked down and pulled the surrounding desks on top of herself for shelter. She opened her backpack and found nothing but books and a small mirror. More knives carved into the desktops above her. "No wonder they call you Dartsey," she yelled. "But you keep missing your marksy!"

"I ain't missing, dearie," he stressed. "I'm just playing pretend."

"Pretending you can win this fight?" M asked boldly.

"See's, I'm the cat and you're the mousey," said Dartsey. "And what you've failed to realize is that I've had your tail under my claw the whole time."

She listened to his boasting and rolled her eyes. Frantically, she loosened the straps to her backpack and wound them around several desk legs. *Don't fire until you see the soles of his feet*, she thought. Then Dartsey made his move and stepped closer. M saw his shiny, buckled shoes start to tread across the floor and she yanked on her backpack with all of her might. The desks around her flicked over with a brilliant crash and came down on his five-thousand-dollar patent leather shoes like a guillotine.

"GAH!" screamed Dartsey as he kicked the desks aside.

His eyes flew open in rage. He found M and lunged at her. But M grabbed Dartsey by his white goatee and pulled. Without the feeling in his toes to support him, the giant substitute fell hard against the ground and conked his head on the hardwood.

Dartsey rolled over. He was clearly stunned by the turn of

events. His eyes were unfocused, but slowly the situation came back to him as he stared up at M, who was holding a thick book over her head.

"I am the cat," she whispered to him before bringing the book smack down on him, knocking the thug out cold.

She flipped the Art Appreciation textbook over and smiled. "How's that for an art history lesson, scumbag?"

The room was torn to shreds, with small blades covering the desk like porcupine quills. Splinters of wood were all over her and scattered on the ground. She dusted them out of her hair and off her clothes before grabbing her backpack and heading toward the door.

She stopped to look at the attendance list on Ms. Ohlmsted's desk. The name on the paper read *Meredith Foreman*, but M realized that person had never existed. This Meredith Foreman character was no more.

M Freeman, for better or worse, had just come back from the dead.

CHAPTER 3
FAMILY LIES

Sneakers squeaked in the hallway as students left for the day. Laughter and teasing echoed outside the windows as parents waited in a patient row of cars to gather their children. Those kids probably had snacks waiting for them at home. They'd fool around online for a while, maybe play some after-school sport, then do their homework before dinner and eventually be off to bed. But not M. She had to make a move and make it fast.

She breathed heavily and steadied herself, trying to calm her adrenaline rush before racing home to face her fake parents. If she wasn't thinking straight, there was a real danger that she could disappear from herself again. And she didn't want to be lost anymore.

M's hands shook as she took the attendance sheet for a memento. A physical memory in case she forgot who she was again. Who knew what else was waiting for her beyond that door?

As she folded the paper in half, another name on the list jumped out at her. A name that didn't have any business coming back into her life. Zoso. Just the written name made M's skin crawl as she recalled her violent history with the venomous Devon Zoso. Devon Zoso, who stole the necklace her father gave her. Devon Zoso, who set off the black hole and destroyed the Lawless School. Devon Zoso, who was working with John Doe. But the Zoso name on the attendance sheet wasn't attached to the young phenom double agent.

It belonged to Evel. Evel Zoso. Suddenly Dartsey's question about him having a sister made sense. M had never heard of Devon having a brother! The hope she felt from Evel's arrival earlier had been knocked out as cold as the unconscious Dartsey on the floor behind her. M squeezed her fists tightly and crumpled the sheet of paper. She counted to three and then let go of all the pent-up negative energy inside her. If Evel had come to Harmon, he did it for a calculated reason and M had a pretty good idea what that reason was. To finish what his sister had started.

"M," came Evel's voice from the hallway. It was barely a whisper that shook with real anxiety. "Are you, um, are you okay in there?"

M slipped through the open door and locked it from the inside before she closed it. "We need to get out of here. Now."

"And Mr. Dartsey?" asked Evel with an audible gulp in his throat.

"He's done substituting for a while," M answered as she pulled Evel along with her. She wanted to get out of this school before any more surprises showed up. Walking briskly,

M continued talking to Evel while keeping an eye out for other attackers. "Listen, I don't know what you did and I don't care. Whatever is between you and dagger-throwing Dartsey stays between you and him. As far as I'm concerned, I was in the right place at the wrong time. I didn't save you, okay? I don't know you and I don't care about you one bit."

They reached the school entrance and stopped while M made sure the coast was clear.

"Back there, I don't think I . . ." mumbled Evel.

"Back there you left me alone in a room with a madman," said M. "I would think that being a Zoso, you'd at least have the guts to handle the task yourself."

Before Evel could answer her, M jerked him outside into the afternoon. The day was warm for this time of year. Kids were playing football on the lawn. The line of parents in cars had emptied and the school buses had all left for their routes. M stormed directly down the street and into her house.

"Mom! Dad! I'm home!" screamed M. "And I brought a new friend!"

The house was perfectly still and quiet. M shushed Evel by putting her finger up to her lips and signaled for him to stay put. There was no one downstairs. M stealthily motioned for Evel to move upstairs with her. She went through the entire house and no one was there. They were alone.

In her room, M dumped out the books from her backpack and started stuffing clothes in it.

"I think we got off on the wrong foot back there," Evel

offered, trying to break the tension. He took a step into her room. "I'm here to —"

"I know why you're here," interrupted M as she pulled more clothes from her closet. "And don't come into my room. You are not invited inside this door. Stay where I can see you."

She rummaged through her top drawer and found her life's savings in a jar. The change rattled inside as she flipped it into her backpack. There was probably only ninety dollars in there, all collected from her weekly allowance. M watched the jar sink into the mess of clothing and wondered where the money had *really* come from. Did it really belong to her fake parents? Or was someone else trying to make her think she had a normal life? She faced Evel again. "So, is there, like, a bounty on my head or something?"

"Well, yes, as a matter of fact," admitted Evel. "But . . ."

"But what? Oh, I know, I bet you'd be willing to look the other way and give me a five-minute head start since I handled your thug for you, is that it?" snarled M. She was ready for a battle, but Evel didn't seem to want one. He had walked into her life like a hostage, unarmed and unassuming. She'd seen the look on his face when he saw Dartsey. He was legit freaked.

"No, I . . ." Evel stood in the doorway, carefully considering what to say next. "I want to help."

M zipped up her overstuffed backpack. "You? Help? Me? Don't make me laugh. Especially because there's nothing funny about what's going on here."

She slumped down to pull another pair of shoes out from underneath her bed. Sitting back on her knees, M noticed the photographs hung around her mirror. Were her friends in on this secret, too? She reached over and pulled them down like pulling petals from a flower. *She knows me. She knows me not. She fooled me. She fooled me not.* Polaroid versions of her friends stared back at her. They were all smiling like they were in on a private joke, but what if that private joke was her?

"Maybe I'm just crazy," M whispered to herself. Here, in her room where she had felt so safe and comfortable this morning, M wished just slightly that she *was* crazy. That her parents would show up and take her somewhere to seek medical help. But she knew better.

"You're not," answered Evel. "Crazy, that is. You're not crazy. But we can't stay here. It's not safe."

"Yeah, no duh, Evel," said M. "Welcome to my life."

Below them on the first floor, a creak sounded out. They weren't alone in the house anymore.

Evel automatically backed into M's room and actually moved behind her. M gave him a look and realized that he was cowering. "Really, dude? You're going to use me as a human shield to whoever is downstairs?"

"I'm not cut out for this," he murmured nervously. "I shouldn't have come here. This was a bad idea. This was the worst idea."

"Calm down, Chicken Little," sighed M. Maybe he wasn't Devon Zoso's brother after all? "I want you to stay here," she said slowly. "I am going to see what's happening. If you hear anything violent erupting, for both of our safety, just stay here."

Evel nodded immediately with conviction. Then he squirreled away in the nook behind M's bed. She could hear him hold his breath. She almost told him that holding your breath never works if you want to avoid someone. It's almost impossible to avoid hearing people's deep inhalations between holding breaths. Slow and steady breathing wins hide-and-seek every time.

Slinging her backpack over one shoulder, with a second pair of shoes in her hands, M called out, "I'm coming downstairs."

As she rounded the corner prepared to face her mother and father impostors, M was met instead by her friends seated at the kitchen table. Chloe and Emma were on the sides and in the middle sat Jenny with a syringe as a centerpiece.

"We need to talk, M," said Jenny.

"I don't have anything to say," M replied as she walked carefully toward them.

"Things aren't working out here so I'm glad you packed," Jenny said, ignoring M's comment. "We're moving to the next safe house. You've been compromised."

M laughed. "Compromised? You mean I'm conscious. I'm aware. And I know what's in that shot — another memory serum. So here's how this is going to shake out. I'm leaving Harmon and you're not going with me, whoever you are.

Because if you try to stick me with that again, it will be over my dead body."

"Well, since Emma here is trained as an EMT, I think we'll be able to keep you from death's door," said Jenny with a self-satisfied smile that gleamed with silver braces. "But we can't protect you if you won't let us."

"I don't need protecting, in case you didn't see the thug I dropped back in Art Appreciation," bragged M.

"Talented, yes," admitted Jenny. "Lucky, too. The next Lawless brute won't be caught off guard. And good luck if the Fulbrights learn you're here."

Before M could reply, the side door opened and her fake parents walked into the kitchen from the garage carrying groceries.

"Oh, hello, *miette*," her fake mother said sweetly, nodding to her friends. "You know your friends are always welcome over for dinner, but please let me know ahead of time. I think we've got just enough kale and organic sausage to serve everyone . . ."

She trailed off as she spotted the syringe on the table. The captive daughter was out of the bag.

"What's wrong, darlin'?" her fake father asked his fake wife.

"She knows," her fake mom exhaled.

For a minute, the entire room seemed uncertain what would happen next. It was the moment after a bad accident, when no one is concerned about anyone else but themselves.

Feeling for any scrapes, cuts, bruises, broken or missing limbs, the fake lives in the room took stock of their roles in this game. M's fake family wasn't in control. Her friends were. And now her friends weren't in control, M was. And that's not a factor they were prepared for.

From the living room, there was suddenly a deep breath that caught everyone's attention. A piece of metal clunked against the kitchen floor and rolled under the table. M watched as her fake parents dropped their groceries and ran for the door. Jenny, Chloe, and Emma pushed back on their chairs, but the table was big and the eat-in space in the kitchen was small. The chairs knocked ungracefully against the walls and trapped the girls when the gas canister erupted in a plume of white smoke. Evel ran in from the living room with a wet towel wrapped around his head and an extra one for M, too. The smoke flooded the entire house in seconds. Her eyes stung, even under the cold, wet towel.

"This way!" he screamed, pulling her from the room.

They darted out the front door and into a limo that was waiting across the street. Once inside, the limo peeled out and drove away faster than she thought possible for a limousine. Evel pulled off his towel first. His eyes were swollen. Against her better judgment, M left hers on and laid back against the seat. She coughed and hacked up remnants of the viscous gas from her lungs. Her throat burned, but the feeling was familiar.

"Where did you find that tear gas?" she cackled with a rough-edged voice.

"Aarrggghhh!" strained Evel as he punched the empty seat next to him in pained frustration. "I found it in your house when you left me upstairs. Your parents had it in their room." He coughed again. "What kind of parents have tear gas in their room?"

"They're not my parents," said M. "And I thought I told you to stay put?"

"You did, but it seemed like the right thing to do," Evel argued. "Tear gas? That's what that was?"

"What did you think it was? A bomb?" asked M.

"I don't know, maybe?" Evel confessed. "I just thought it would cause a diversion long enough for us to escape."

"Escape to where, Evel?" M pushed as she jerked the towel from her face. Even in the tinted windows of the limo, the light felt like white-hot fire to her eyes. "And what kind of Fulbright doesn't know a can of tear gas when he holds it in his hands?"

"I'm not a Fulbright," he said solemnly.

"Well, you're not from Lawless, either," assured M. There was no way his cowardly antics were an act. "So what does that make you?"

"I'm a Ronin," he said in the quiet hush of the limo. "And we need your help."

CHAPTER 4
THE NO-MIND

Ronin. M had heard the term before. They were the leftover outcasts from the Lawless School and the Fulbright Academy. The failures. Underachievers. The poster children and storied examples of what students tried to avoid at all costs. To join their ranks meant that a student had been kicked out of one school or the other. And once cut, Ronin were kept under watch for the rest of their lives by the school that expelled them. But until this moment, the concept of Ronin had only been a threat to keep students in line. M stared blankly at Evel as if she were looking at Bigfoot.

"We?" she asked.

"Yes," said Evel gravely. "I'm afraid so."

"Wait, wait, wait," said M impatiently. "There's no way you're a Ronin if you're Devon Zoso's brother. She's the golden child. You can't come from the same family and not pick up at least a hint of those skills and smarts. How do I know you're not hijacking me right now? That Dartsey wasn't just a tactic to prove I'm really M Freeman?"

She couldn't tell if it was anger welling up in Evel's face or if the tear gas had irritated his skin to a bright red color. But then Evel shot her a devastating look that froze her in place.

"This may come as a surprise to someone like you, but people don't always become Ronin because they flunk out of school. I saw how the Fulbrights were training recruits. They were building an army and I didn't want any part of it. So I opted out."

"Well, good for you, I guess," said M.

"Hardly." Evel slunk back in his seat. "The fallout from my decision was way bigger than I expected. I was only twelve years old — how was I supposed to know what would happen? My parents lost friends, family, and their jobs. All their financial accounts were frozen because of me."

Evel choked out the last words. He must be fifteen now, but he wore the weight of his decision like this all happened yesterday.

"Well, this choice limo makes it look like you got over the money problems," noted M.

"At a price," said Evel. "There were ... concessions. My family had to 'make things right' after I dropped out. My parents kicked me out of the house. They tell people I'm dead now, if they mention me at all. And poor Devon, she became 'spoken for' — drafted by the Fulbrights way too young. My parents pushed her insanely hard to do whatever they asked of her."

"Well, they got their money's worth with Devon," said M. "How do I know you're not trying to get her out of her indentured service by kidnapping me?"

"I haven't seen her since she was nine years old, M," said Evel. "I am not working with her. I doubt she'd even speak to me now."

"And you get some sort of hush-money salary to stay out of the way," said M. She picked at the leather seats and pulled her legs in close.

"I've lost more than I will ever get back, if that's what you're trying to imply," snapped Evel. "But this isn't a trap. What you were in back there, before I showed up, *that* was a trap."

"You told me you were here to help me," said M. "And now you're asking me to help you. What's going on?"

Evel pulled off his jacket and revealed an arm covered with needle scars.

"What are those?" asked M as she recoiled slightly.

"As part of the Ronin rules, we are tagged on a monthly basis with a tracker, like endangered animals," said Evel. "Then one month nobody showed up. Rumors started spreading. We heard that something bad had happened to the Lawless School. That the war was over."

She had been at the Lawless School's deathblow. Truly speaking, M played a major role in its destruction. But so had Evel's sister, Devon.

At Evel's pause, M asked, "You keep saying *we*. I thought Ronin weren't allowed to interact with one another."

Evel wrung his hands together nervously. "We're not. But that didn't stop a group of us from finding one another. We'd meet online, through backdoor channels on social sites. Like I said, it's not that we are bad at our jobs. A lot of us just didn't want to work for the company, if you catch my drift."

The Fulbright life had given her pause from the very beginning, too. She wished that the Lawless School had raised the same flags or warning signs with her. It should have, from the very moment she crashed the plane. But back then she had thought that this was what her father had wanted for her. That wasn't the case after all. He had wanted much more from her.

Evel continued, "Another month passed and no one showed up to check on us. Without the trackers, we scrounged enough courage to meet one another in person for the first time. There were nine of us that had grown close over the years."

"Were?" asked M. Hearing the past tense verb triggered an awful feeling in her gut.

"We met a few times before a new person showed up at our doorsteps," Evel began. "The first wave of attacks captured three of my friends. It was the Lawless graduates. They wanted revenge and the Ronin were easy targets. At first, we thought they wanted to send a message to the Fulbrights that whatever truce had been in place to keep Ronin safe was over. The war had finally risen to the surface. Then we heard about you."

The sky went dark outside and the stars lit dimly along the highway. The car drove south. Abandoned businesses stretched along either side of the interstate, with empty parking lots. In the distance, shadowy mountains lifted into the sky. It was a side of America M had never seen before.

"Where are we?" asked M.

"Wow, do you remember anything?" asked Evel.

"I remember a lot of things," said M in a hush. "But there are admittedly some . . . gaps."

"Well, you're in West Virginia now," said Evel. "Coal country. And home to your oddball town of Harmon. We were lucky to find you."

"But how did you find me?" asked M.

"A virus," admitted Evel.

"Excuse me?" said M.

"A computer virus. Coded specifically to ping into the secure Ronin back channels we'd created that no one was supposed to know about," explained Evel. "We were wrong. About our communications being untraceable, we were dead wrong. Someone had been watching us all along. But the virus didn't attack. It was wrapped in a riddle of numbers, like a combination lock. A combination lock with a timer, and the only way to disarm the virus was to answer the riddle."

"You cracked it," acknowledged M. "You're a crimer, aren't you?"

"Crimer?" said Evel. "I'm a techie, if that's what you mean. And yeah, I cracked it after weeks of studying the code."

"And what was the message?" asked M.

"It's better if I show you," said Evel. The limo pulled off the highway and into a closed shipping facility.

Oversize garage door ports were shuttered as far as the eye could see. There were no windows, either. Streetlights above them lit the shadows of the barren lot as the limo drove in and out of the darkness.

"This place used to be a postal hub," Evel told M. "Closed down a few years ago, a casualty of the digital age. People don't write letters anymore. The building suited my needs, so I moved in last month."

The location wasn't far from Harmon. They'd only been driving for forty minutes or so. Still, M felt hundreds of miles away from her fake life. The limo turned the corner to the far side of the building so that they were completely hidden from the view of interstate traffic. As they approached another loading dock, a ramp rose out of the ground and the large white garage door rolled open to allow the limo inside.

M stepped out first. The room was smaller than she expected. Grease stains covered the concrete ground. There were tools on the wall kept in immaculate order. The screwdrivers, wrenches, and hammers were all positioned from smallest to largest. M looked down again and noticed that the limo was parked on a car lift with a mechanic's bay underneath.

Evel joined M and led her by the front seat of the limo. It was empty.

"Evel, who was driving?" asked M.

"Oh, it's automated," he said carelessly. Then he looked up to no one and said, "I'm back, Alfred. And please let the others know we have company."

"A success, then, sir," echoed a disembodied voice from all around them.

"Automated?" puzzled M. "Alfred? Who are you? Batman?"

"Nah." Evel laughed. "I am a fan, though."

He opened the door and a set of lights illuminated, revealing a mile-long open-floor warehouse that expanded for over a city block. High-end computer equipment was set up from wall to wall. M felt like she'd entered a submarine, but then she saw beyond the computers to other unbelievable vehicles parked in the distance: a helicopter, a jet, a boat, and even a tank.

"Do you really need a tank?" M said. "It seems a little much."

"Haven't needed it yet," said Evel. "But the day is young."

"How much money *do* your parents have?" she asked, suddenly frightened by the sticker shock of this outcast's lair.

"I don't know how much *they* have, but I have a lot." Evel reached a panel of computers and sat down in a chair. A hundred-inch screen flickered on in front of him with a series of numbers streaming across it. He diligently typed without looking at his keyboard once. When he was done several faces came on the screen.

One was a redheaded girl with a mangled ear. Under her vid-feed was the name Kinja. Another was a blond-haired boy known as Scott. He seemed to have a winking problem, some sort of tic, but then M realized that it wasn't a tic. His left eyelid was missing. A third girl joined the chat under the name Nell. But it was the fourth face to sign in that M recalled right away.

"Derrick Hollows?" M blurted out. Derrick Hollows had been a first-year at Lawless with M. She remembered how he had fallen prey to an Idents grift where they stole his identity and shared it with everyone across campus. "You're a Ronin?"

"Wait. Is that M Freeman? What does she have to do with all this?" complained Derrick.

"So you're the one who blew up the Lawless School," acknowledged Kinja. "Well done."

"Yeah, great job, Freeman," Derrick said angrily. "I could have been there, you know. You could have killed me!"

"Chill out, Hollows," Evel intervened. "You were kicked out *way* before she brought the place down. And now she may be our only hope of surviving."

"I don't like it," said Scott as he leaned back to squirt drops into his left eye. When he looked at the camera again, the drops dripped down his cheek like tears. "How are we supposed to trust a Lawless brat? They're the ones trying to kill us."

"Kill you?" asked M. "Wait, I need an update. I've only been myself for a few hours now and I don't even know what day it is."

"It's Tuesday," Scott replied. "October ninth."

October? She couldn't have been out for that long.

Suddenly another memory returned: her fight with the Fulbright in her father's secret room when she'd been stabbed with that serum. *Oh no*, thought M. *Jones*. M closed her eyes and remembered her friend lying on the ground, silent and not breathing. That was way back in February. Had she really been living her fictitious life in Harmon for almost eight months?

"You need to tell me about this message." M focused. She needed to push through the flashbacks and concentrate on her next move. The screen of mostly new faces watched her, waiting for someone to begin the conversation. "Because it could be a trap."

"We thought so, too," said Evel, taking the lead. "When you are in our position, everything could be a trap. We cracked the code. Three vital pieces of information were hidden in the background noise of the virus. They were hard to decipher and extract. Someone went to a lot of trouble to hide this intel. But we don't know why or who."

"We think you can shed some light on this for us," Kinja spoke up.

"Why me?" asked M. She glanced again from the faces on the screen to Evel and back. Derrick Hollows stared daggers into his camera. His lips pursed and his jaw clenched at M's question.

"Because the first concrete info we pulled was a GPS coordinate, or coordinates," said Evel. "It was hard to figure out what they meant because they kept changing second by second. They moved, you see. Constantly, except for seven hours each night. That's how we realized that we were after a living thing: It was sleeping at night."

M reached down and felt her wrist. The tracker from the Fulbrights was still stuck in her arm, a coarse bump bubbling up just beneath her skin. "You were following me."

"The second intel was this peculiar blueprint," continued Evel as he motioned toward another screen. A diagram of a full-body suit was set against a graph background. Schematic formulas were written in the margins and pointed to the different sections of the suit. A suit M had seen before. One she had worn before, in fact.

"This is a specialized uniform created by a kid named Keyshawn Noles," said M. "He must have made this virus in case . . . in case he didn't make it. When did you receive it?"

"Last week," confirmed Scott. "It slipped through a heavily guarded firewall and found its way to about sixty Ronins. Which is shocking, to say the least. Because this virus also coincided with the start of our friends' abductions."

"You really are part of this, aren't you, Freeman?" said Derrick with a hint of resentment in his voice.

"I am now," said M firmly. "You said there was a third message in the virus?"

"*The no-mind not-thinks no-thoughts about no-things*," quoted Evel. "Does that phrase mean anything to you?"

"It's a Buddhist saying, right?" M posed. She retreated to a time with her real father, M Freeman. He'd been teaching her to ride a bike. *Don't think of the street, don't think of the bike —*

in fact, don't think about anything. Let your body take over and the mind will follow. In times like these, your thoughts can be your worst enemy. The no-mind not-thinks no-thoughts about no-things!

Suddenly M found herself at the core of the biggest mystery of her life and she knew exactly how to make sense of it all. "It's me. I have something and Keyshawn is trying to remind me."

"Can we talk to this Keyshawn character?" interrupted Scott. "If he's the one who sent this to us, then maybe . . ."

"No, he's gone," said M suddenly. She had no idea how or why she knew this, but the high security and urgency of his virus spoke volumes.

"Like your other turncoat friends?" Derrick accused with venom in his tone. "You, you disgust me, Freeman. You have the gall to walk in here and pretend like you're so innocent. I think *you're* the trap."

"Take it easy," Scott tried to interject, but Derrick continued his rant.

"We know you joined the Fulbrights and we know you escaped from them, too. So who's been harboring you for all this time? Why did we have to pinpoint you and pull you away from your perfect little life?"

"That's enough!" Kinja yelled.

"No," said Derrick. "It's not enough . . . but it will be."

Everyone looked puzzled as a sly smile crept across Derrick's face.

Suddenly, on Scott's end of the line there was an explosion that blanked his screen for a moment. The blond boy looked left, stunned. Then he was shoved out of the frame noiselessly until M heard his body thump against something hard and far from his computer's microphone.

"Scott!" hollered Evel. "Scott, are you there — what's happening?! Are you all seeing this?"

Kinja's feed was next. It blurred, bending her image into a warped picture and then straightening out with a dark shadow behind her. "Kinja!" screamed Evel, but he was too late. Her face was crashed into the computer's camera with a jolt. Muffled movements meant a struggle was surfacing on her end, but M and Evel were powerless to help.

"Look upon my face, M Freeman!" bellowed Derrick Hollows maniacally. "I want to be the last face you see before you're taken away forever!"

"You!" hissed Evel. "Hollows! What have you done?"

"Nothing a good Lawless graduate wouldn't have done in the first place," he bragged. "You Fulbright suckers. I've been playing you from the get-go. You went to make your move today, so I gave my Lawless connection an anonymous tip on where you losers were hiding out. I'm surprised you survived Dartsey, Evel, but then again, I hadn't planned on you actually finding Freeman."

"But you're a Ronin!" argued Evel.

"Not in my heart," Derrick said with a demented smile. The sound of struggles still echoed over Kinja's and Scott's feeds.

"You don't have a heart," challenged Evel. "Because whether you realized it or not, we were the only friends you had left in the world."

"Well, then, friend to friend, I'd advise you to start running for your lives," Derrick suggested snidely.

Over Kinja's and Scott's cameras a heavy breathing came closer. Black smoke dissipated and a lone figure came into view in each feed. A masked figure with glowing green wires pulsating with life stared back at them. It turned its head slowly, looking confused, as if it had no idea how to use a computer camera. A gloved hand reached up and tapped the camera once, letting out an extremely loud *whumph* when it connected. The sound made M flinch and her stomach dropped into her feet.

"*Get out of there, Derrick*," M warned. "You can't trust the Lawless School. It's the Fulbrights! They're coming for you!"

Something moved in Derrick's feed that grabbed his attention. M and Evel watched as the fear in Derrick's face exploded like a rocket in the night. Sharp, intense, and shocking. "No, no, no, what are you?" he screamed as he cowered back from the screen. Then, without warning, he was lifted straight off the ground and thrown against the rear wall. To the untrained eye, an argument could be made that Hollows had been the victim of a ghostly attack by a poltergeist. But M knew better. Only a magblast could cause that kind of damage.

"What's going on?" hollered Evel nervously. He backed

away from his large monitor, surveying the horror. His friends were gone. Replaced by a crew of masked Fulbright creeps.

"We want what you've got, Zoso," a voice echoed through the screen. "You have to the count of five to give Freeman over."

"Or else what?" interjected M.

"One."

"They're bluffing," Evel explained to M, but it sounded more like he was trying to convince himself. "There's no way they could find us."

"Two."

"I rerouted all the feeds; this place is untraceable," stammered Evel.

"Three."

"They found us already," said M in a whisper.

"Four."

"No!" Evel asserted to the Fulbrights before him. "So go on and count to five. I won't be the one who gave you Freeman. That's not going to happen."

Silence.

Evel turned to M, exhaled, and smiled. "See. I told you. Nothing. They were bluffing." He hit the escape button on the keyboard to close out of the conversation, but the masks on the screen did not go away. Three giant Fulbrights stared curiously straight ahead. Their eyes were blank and empty, void of any emotion or any signal as to what they were planning. "Alfred. Get these traitors out of my sight."

"I am afraid I cannot do that, sir," the computer answered coldly.

"Alfred? What's wrong?" he asked.

"I have a message for you, sir," the computer continued. "What is four plus one?"

"Five?" Evel whispered and immediately all the computers in the room began to spark and short-circuit. Blasts of tiny pops erupted like the crackle effect from fireworks, as Evel's own personal assistant, Alfred, reduced itself to a melted motherboard.

But Evel's broken tech wasn't what caught M's attention. That was only a sleight of hand compared to what the Fulbrights had in mind. It was the shaking dirt on the ground, the slight rattle of the tin roof overhead followed by the high-pitched whine that perked M's attention. She shot up and grabbed Evel, pulling him with her as she darted across the room and back toward the garage where they had parked the limo.

"What," he asked as he ran beside her, "are we running from?"

"Missiles," M shouted, but her voice was blotted out by a crush of hot air that lifted them off the ground.

CHAPTER 5
SCORCHED

It was not like a black hole. There was a brightness that lit up the room before there was any sound. A light shined from behind M as she ran, casting an angry glow across the computers that lined the room. It felt like a giant had turned on bright lights she had never known existed and its purpose was to scare the life out of anything in its path. M watched as the walls and ceiling around her loosened and rippled like they were made of water, bending in and threatening to lose their structure and support. The sight threw her off balance, like she was on a ride at an amusement park. But she had not been prepared for this ride.

Then the light became brighter and the air around them hotter, stinging like an atmosphere of wild bees. Suddenly the air was pushing them forward, moving them faster toward the garage door at the end of the large open room. They were almost there when M finally heard the boom.

And it wasn't just one explosion — there were multiple explosions set off like a massive domino effect, with each domino blowing the other one up instead of knocking it down.

Boom. The jet. *Boom.* The helicopter. *Boom.* The boat. *Boom.* The tank. *Boom.* The supercomputer. *Boom.* Them.

Only M and Evel didn't go *boom.* The last heated blast had tossed them into the garage and M was able to slide them both under the limo and into the mechanic's bunker, about five feet beneath the concrete floor. They both watched a ripple of fiery air sweep above them as they cringed to the lowest point in the bunker. The metal tools around them shook and jangled menacingly, while the small room filled with the smell of melting tires from above.

And then it was over. The furious dragon's breath that had surrounded them and cleared its devastating path through Evel's apparently not-so-secret, converted-post-office headquarters was gone. The room didn't breathe anymore.

"What in the world . . ." said Evel as he finally exhaled. He sucked in a huge gasp of air, like someone who had previously been drowning underwater.

"More like *where* in the world can we go to escape the Fulbrights," whispered M. Not because she thought someone might hear her, but because she thought any loud sound could potentially set off an avalanche of brick, mortar, and rubble. And she did not want to be buried alive.

There was a steady thrum of ringing in her ears from the blast. It pulsed with her own pulse, so in a way she was thankful for the noise. The noise meant she was alive. That *they* were alive.

"Evel, is there any other way out of here?" she said softly, but M's new friend had checked out. His eyes were glassy; his neck barely held up his bobbing head. "Evel!" M insisted in a stern but hushed tone. She grasped him by the cheeks gently and held his head still, facing her. "Another . . . way . . . out?"

Evel was covered in white dust, like a ghost trembling in her hands. M imagined that she must look the same way to him, so she spit in the palm of her hand and wiped the debris off her face. A lone bulb swung above them, flickering on and off with electric life. "Please, Evel, they're coming back."

His eyes widened as he realized that she was right. Evel blurted out, "The rails. There's an underground track that leads to the other side of the mountain. They . . . they used to deliver mail to the next town over. It was a different zip code, but they didn't have their own post office. So their mail came here."

"Lead the way to that track, Evel, or we're cooked," said M as she pulled him up to his feet.

"We're . . ." He paused for a breath. "We're in it now."

Evel leaned toward what looked like a dead end in the small mechanic's chamber and pushed the wall open. A cold wind blew in from the darkness, seeming to pull both of their tired bodies inside. The tunnel was blindingly black and smelled like wet earth mixed with damp air. The cooling sensation felt amazing against her slightly burned skin.

M continued walking in and kicked one of the rails with her foot. "We walk," she said.

"No," said Evel. "We ride. It's faster."

M followed his voice and could barely make out the shadow of an old manual handcar with a seesaw-style bar attached at the middle. "How long has it been since this thing was used?"

"Seventy years, maybe?" confessed Evel. "I didn't think I'd ever need to make a getaway. It's not like I planned to be firebombed."

"Then do you know if this track still leads somewhere?"

"I know it leads away from here and that seems like the best plan right now," said Evel.

"It's the only plan right now," admitted M as flecks of dirt fell lightly from above them. The Fulbrights were making another move.

M jumped on the handcar with Evel and they both tried to pump the bar, but the metal was rusted tight.

"We should run!" cried Evel. "This thing isn't going anywhere."

"No, we need wheels if we want to survive the next blast," strained M as the bar inched under her. "We'll never make it on foot. We'll be buried alive."

Evel nodded and pulled up with all his might while M pushed her entire weight down on the other end. Then they reversed tactics in a coordinated effort until the bar slowly loosened and the handcar broke free of the dilapidated hold that the years had suspended it in.

Once the bar gave way, they pumped it up and down frantically, creaking to higher speeds as the track dipped farther down into the dark earth. Wind picked up around them as the crackling sound of fire faded away and was replaced by the empty, cool hush of the tunnel.

"It's working!" Evel smiled. Or at least M imagined Evel was smiling as he said this. It was impossible to see anything down there.

Turns in the track came quickly and without any more warning than a sharp jolt that swung their bodies in different directions. It was like riding a bull while wearing a blindfold. There was no way to anticipate which way the track would throw them next, so M and Evel held on to the bar and continued pumping for dear life.

The next boom from above was muffled, like thunder clapping far off in the distance, but everything around them shook like they were clenched in an angry fist. The handcar bucked off the track, sending the kids flying forward. They landed hard on their shoulders and slid in the wet dirt, luckily landing outside of each metal rail. M looked over at Evel and was surprised that she could dimly see his face. There was light coming from somewhere.

"Did we make it to the other side?" asked Evel.

M stared forward into the darkness. Then she looked backward at the buzzing shadows coming toward them. "That's not the light at the end of the tunnel I was hoping for!" she screamed.

A ball of fire was pushing toward them from the second missile blast above ground. It was ripping through the tunnel like smoke drifting up a chimney. They were trapped in an exhaust path and for a second time today, there was no escape.

As the light grew brighter and the air grew hotter, M grabbed Evel again. The handcar had flipped over during the blast and now stood jammed and arched in between the dirt wall and the left-side rail. Its wheels were still spinning uselessly as the backside of the car stood in the air. Pulling Evel with her, M quickly crouched behind the handcar, using it to shield them from the oncoming blaze. It flared around them with an intense heat that felt like being inside of the sun. Her eyes were clinched shut, but M could hear the handcar sizzle behind them as the demonically hot air whooshed past them and continued on its way.

With the immediate threat gone, M thrust her hands into the cold, wet soil of the wall protected by the car, and shoveled it over her hands and face to cool the burning. Then she did the same to Evel, who was wheezing in short, fast breaths.

Together, they sat still and listened as the fireball died out ahead of them with a sizzling *whoompfh* that echoed back through the tunnel.

"Don't touch the handcar," M warned. "It's toast." She could smell the acrid scent of burning metal and seared sulfur in the air as well as see the car's glowing red outline. She felt the gravel crumbling between her fingers as she brushed her hands together. "Come on. No need to wait for another attack."

"But what if they release another bomb?" asked Evel. "We were lucky to have that handcar here."

"Yeah, but we're not lucky enough for them to fire another round of missiles," cautioned M. "If I know the Fulbrights, their next move will be to make sure there are no survivors. They'll be on the ground any minute now."

With that, the two kids ran away from the now defunct and destroyed shipping station. They held their hands against the dirt walls to guide them through the darkness until they reached another door some twenty minutes later. The metal frame had been blown off its hinges and lay crushed against the back wall of an empty warehouse.

"We made it," whispered Evel.

"We made it this far," corrected M. "But now where do we go?"

"Sercy," said Evel. "If we can find a car, then I can get us to Sercy's. He'll know what to do next."

"Sercy?" asked M. "Who's that? And how do I know this guy won't turn us over like your old pal Derrick did?"

"He won't," said Evel, who peered through a window, searching for a ride.

"Well, excuse me if I don't trust your judgment on who you are allies with," said M. "What we need are my friends back. Merlyn and Jules may be the only people I trust now."

"Then we need to get to Sercy," repeated Evel. "He's the magic man in the Ronin world and he's not far from here. If you want to find your friends, he can do it."

M weighed her options and didn't like any of them. She paced quietly, thinking of her best next step when Evel spoke up again.

"Look, there's no reason for you to trust me, I get that. But I know how you feel right now. You're confused, abandoned, hunted, unwanted, lonely, angry, and like ninety other types of dwarves that didn't make the cut in *Snow White*. You're a Ronin now, whether you like it or not."

It was true. M had a million different alarms going off in her head and she wasn't sure which one to act on.

"Here's what I've learned," continued Evel. "You having all those feelings is exactly what the Fulbrights and Lawless want. Distrust, uncertainty, and, most of all, doubt that anyone can ever help you again. They want to shake you up so bad that you can't do anything to hurt them. Because if you feel powerless, then they will own you for the rest of your life.

"But what I realized . . . what a lot of Ronins finally realized, is that we're not powerless. We're not alone. And we're not cowering in some corner of the world trying to hide from them." Evel paused and looked around. "Well, at least not normally. Sure, we hide, but —"

"Okay, I get the picture," M interrupted. "You could have stopped at *We're not alone* and it would have done wonders for your speech."

"Yeah, well, I don't make a lot of speeches." Evel attempted a smile but his face looked too tired.

"So, we need a ride to reach this Sercy fellow?" asked M as she walked toward one of the closed garage ports in the warehouse.

"Yeah, he's not far, but too far to reach on foot," called Evel from across the room. "And it's probably too conspicuous for us to walk through the streets if we tried."

"Then we should travel inconspicuously," said M as she pulled a dust cloth off of an old mail truck parked in the port. "Now, check the locker box over there and I'm sure we'll find the keys."

CHAPTER 6
COLLECTIBLE

The truck was not the smoothest ride M had ever been in, but it carried them from point A to point B without raising any red flags. Of course, it helped that the Fulbrights were probably still searching for them on the other side of the mountain. Reports from the radio claimed that there had been a gas leak in the small town and that the fire was under control by the time the volunteer fire department arrived. However, those reports were from the FM side of the dial. Once they switched to the AM chatterboxes and conspiracy enthusiasts, the story changed into an unexplained mystery where the local fire departments were turned away by a government agency. This was certainly closer to the truth. The speakers buzzed with monologues and rants.

If you ask me, my fellow outraged listeners, this is the problem with the world today! Shadow operations, deceptions, and unchecked power are all at work right in our own backyards! And what are they trying to cover up? There are no major gas lines near that blaze; anyone who lives here knows that. So what are these men in black trying to hide? We've heard the reports and we know the truth! Fire from the sky, soldiers in specialized gear, a building reduced to ash and rubble . . . this was no gas leak. I say we've had a bona fide extraterrestrial visit. And they did not come in peace.

Evel switched off the radio and let the rattle of the empty cargo bed fill the van. "Idiots. Either they get one hundred percent wrong or forty percent right."

"That's not the radio's fault," said M. "The Fulbrights are A-plus geniuses when it comes to cover-ups. How far are we from your connection?"

"Well," started Evel nervously, "we're close, but I have to confess something."

"I don't like the sound of this," said M as she glanced over.

"I wouldn't say Sercy is my *connection*," squeaked Evel. "So much as he's a person I've met online."

The truck hit a bump in the road, cutting off Evel, who shifted uncomfortably in his seat before recovering. "But he's going to help. He built the lines of communication for the Ronins. He brought us together and without him I wouldn't have found you. You'll see. This guy is like the Wizard of Oz."

"The wizard was a sham, remember?" M reminded him. She shrugged. "But I'll try anything once."

"Good, then you should turn here." He pointed to their right.

"This place?" asked M. "Sercy lives in the suburbs?"

"Guess so," said Evel, who had been reading off a small piece of paper he'd kept in his wallet. M couldn't help glancing at the hastily written directions and noticing that the top read: "emergency only."

As they pulled onto a freshly paved road, they passed a sign that read WELCOME TO BRIAR'S LANDING. But as they drove through the wooded entryway, what lay on the other side was much different. At first the subdivision looked to be filled with new construction set back from the road in nice-sized lots. But the deeper they drove, the more M realized that this was a neighborhood graveyard filled with ghosts of half-finished houses and cleared land. The plots were sectioned off into decent-sized yards, but many of them were empty. Those that weren't had skeleton frames, abandoned foundations, or fully constructed houses without any residents in sight.

"He's just ahead," said Evel. "House number 666."

"That's just plain childish," said M as she rolled her eyes. "What kind of gumball uses that address in real life and not just as their online handle?"

They rolled up and stopped at the last house in the neighborhood, which was probably the first one built. It sat at the top of a small hill, and as M got out of the truck, she realized that she could see the entire subdivision and road up to the house from this vantage point. Perhaps Sercy wasn't so childish after all? He'd found a perfect hideout deep within the forgotten properties of Briar's Landing.

The house itself was nothing outlandish or extravagant. It was a redbrick colonial with most of its color washed away by rain and weather some time ago. Fallen leaves covered the front yard as the trees shook them off with the wind. The porch creaked with every step, as Evel reached forward with a shrug and pressed the doorbell.

Instead of the standard *ding-dong*, a familiar video game theme song rang through the house.

"Is that Super Mario Brothers?" asked Evel.

"I'm not the right person to answer that," M admitted. "What kind of guy is Sercy supposed to be?"

"He's . . ." Evel paused to find the right word. "Eccentric."

"You can say that again," agreed M.

After the music from the doorbell ended, there was a buzz and a click as the front door opened by itself. M entered first, followed by Evel. The door closed shut behind them. She looked around for cameras but couldn't find any. Still, she was sure they were being watched.

The hallway was filled with framed old comic book covers. Every superhero she could imagine was suspended behind glass — all first issues, too. The hallway led them to a larger room where the collection grew even larger. Wallpapered with a floral pattern fit for a grandma's house, there were also three full-size Iron Man uniforms that gleamed and several hideous goblins or giant orcs positioned around the perimeter of the room as if they were standing guard. Their faces were twisted into horrible sneers, but M recognized them as film costumes. Aside from the lifelike figurines that were taller than both M and Evel, the room was completely empty. No furniture, no pictures, no TV, just the quaint wallpaper serving as a backdrop to the creepy-looking characters looming and frozen in place.

"What do you humans want?" a voice snarled. It came from the ash-gray orc closest to them. M noticed the hair on the orc lift gently in a breeze that seemed to come from the ground beneath them.

"Sercy, it's me, Evel Zoso," M's guide spoke. "We need your help."

"Evel, who is this unassuming person you have brought into my realm?" the orc said, twisting its head slowly and evenly to gaze in M's direction. The orc was a robot.

"You already know who I am," asserted M. "Or else you wouldn't have let us into your funhouse. Now I need to find my friends, if they're still alive. That's where you come in."

"Aww," the voice complained, suddenly sounding deflated and let down. "You're a real killjoy, aren't you? I was hoping for a more theatrical introduction. First impressions count, you know? But we'll dispense with the games. Step into the middle of the room."

M and Evel looked at each other before moving to the room's center. The quiet was replaced by the sound of hydraulic motors sighing as the floor beneath them started to sink. M watched the ceiling as it grew farther and farther away from them. The room was an elevator, and they were going down.

"Yeah, *more* theatrical than this," M mumbled.

The wallpaper finally ended, replaced by a glass wall. M's heart skipped a beat as she remembered her time in the Glass House at the Fulbright Academy. She unconsciously ran her hands over her wrists, perhaps making sure that she wasn't wearing glass shackles, either. Beyond the glass was a light that shone from underneath, casting eerie shadows on a rock cave wall that surrounded them. They were inside the mountain now. After a few slow minutes watching the stalactites inch toward the stalagmites, the elevator reached its destination. Floodlights were positioned on either side of the exit, shining high up into the air.

The bottom of the cavern was large — at least fifteen times the size of the house. Spreading in every direction were rows and rows of server computers. They created a grid of blue lights that looked like a miniature, sprawling city in the underground gloom.

"You knew the rules, Evel," a young woman with unkempt brown hair said as she walked toward them. "No meet-ups. Never in real life."

Sercy was Evel's age, M guessed. She wore a loud red Hawaiian shirt with a floral print and faded light blue jeans that were worn almost white.

Evel stammered, "You, you're a —"

"A girl, yeah, I know," said Sercy. "It's one of the reasons I hate meeting people in real life. They all have that same look, like women don't exist in digital life outside of those glamour-avatars in video games. Get over it and tell me why you broke protocol."

"This is an emergency," pleaded Evel, who was clearly still shaken by the surprise revelation. "They attacked the others, captured everyone. We barely got away with our lives. Missiles, Sercy. They shot missiles at us."

"And you thought it would be a good idea to come here?" snapped Sercy. "They've got *more* missiles, you know."

"We weren't followed," said M confidently. She looked this computer genius over and then focused in on the servers around her. "You'd know if we were."

"You're right, I would know . . . but that doesn't excuse Evel here for taking the chance," Sercy argued.

"Then it's my fault if you need to blame somebody," said M. "End of the drama. Evel says you can help me. You've proven yourself to be a very capable, if theatrical, person."

"You bet I am," said Sercy calmly. "But why would I want to help you?"

"Because I need to stop the end of the world."

Sercy laughed. "Ha! You and every other Greenpeace nut out there. I'm just trying to stay alive down here and make an honest name for myself. What makes you think I want to save the world?"

"Call it a hunch," insisted M. "But if you don't want to save the world, maybe you'd be interested in beating Lawless and the Fulbright Academy at their own game."

Sercy's eyes widened and she smiled. "Now you have my attention. What do you need?"

"Help me find my friends," said M. "That's if they're still . . ."

The cave echoed M's silence as she paused. She didn't have the heart to imagine what John Doe did to her friends after she escaped. No, not after she escaped . . . after she left them behind.

Sercy stared back at M, then she waved the newcomers deeper into her lair and they followed. Hidden among the servers was a lone folding chair in front of five different computer screens. Sercy stretched, cracked her knuckles, and gave M an energetic smile. "You gonna give me a name or do I have to guess?"

M held her breath. She had no idea what truths lay in Sercy's computer. But those truths were probably going to be ugly.

"Juliandra Byrd."

CHAPTER 7
SHOWSTOPPER

The mail truck rumbled slowly up the steep mountain road. Cars passed by it, hurried and angry, whipping into oncoming traffic and blaring their horns.

"Can this thing go any faster?" asked M.

"This old rust-bucket?" said Evel as he checked his side-view mirrors and watched another car blast past them. He rolled his eyes helplessly. "Sure it could go faster, but I *really* love sparking road rage in other drivers on mysterious back-country passes that I've never driven through before."

"A simple no would have been enough," said M, glaring at him from behind a foldout map.

They were both tired and agitated at their situation, but they'd had no time to rest. Sercy had found both Jules and Merlyn after a few hours of super computer skills, but while Merlyn was staying in one place, Jules had hit the road. According to Sercy, she moved from city to city on a weekly basis and rarely visited the same place twice.

"Are we there yet?" asked Evel.

"Admit it, you've been waiting to say that for the entire trip," said M. She traced the line Sercy had drawn on the map leading from West Virginia into Kentucky. "Looks like it's twelve more miles or so once we reach the other side of the mountain."

"So who is this Byrd person?" asked Evel.

"Jules is one of my best friends from the Lawless School," said M. "If we have any chance of stopping whatever is on the horizon, we'll need her on our side."

"You're lucky she was so close to us," said Evel.

"If it's luck you're looking for, you're driving up the wrong mountain with the wrong passenger," M cautioned.

"You think we're driving into a trap." Evel fidgeted with the radio dial. Static fuzzed across every station, but he kept trying. He'd joked earlier that the thought of driving over the Appalachians without sleep or music was a punishment that probably fell outside of the Geneva conventions.

"It's a trap," M agreed. "But maybe we can get there before it gets sprung."

The top of the road evened off, giving M and Evel a glorious view of Kentucky's famous hollows. The rolling hills were covered in forests and dipped down into valleys that nestled into the shadows as if they were purposely hidden.

"I do believe I've acquired our target," said Evel as he motioned toward the front window.

At the foot of the mountain, there was a tent. And it wasn't a camping tent. It was a two-pitched, yellow-and-red big top tent that could probably be seen from space it was so bright against the green background.

"Don't tell me she ran away to join the circus," muttered M.

"It's not the worst idea," said Evel. "I mean, you don't stay in one place too long. You keep everyone you know close and make sure they all travel with you. And if the radio stations are missing here, you can bet that there's no cell phone tower around to ping any incriminating information about you. She's probably safe and sound there. Are you sure you want to pull her out?"

M was quiet. The wind whistled around them as the truck coasted downhill and finally started to pick up speed. "I can't leave her here. It's too dangerous."

"M, what if you're the one bringing the danger to her?" asked Evel. "I mean, I've known you for, like, barely two days and look at me now."

"Evel. Shut up," M said flatly. "We're all in danger now. And the only way we can stop it is if we work together. So whether Jules wants to see me or not, I need her. Because without her, we're all . . ." She drifted off. The truck rattled noisily along as the empty cargo bay behind them echoed the wobbling walls like shuddering thunder.

Suddenly the radio sizzled to life with an ominous jolt of guitar solos from a classic power ballad. "Well, then!" cried Evel. "It looks like we've reached some form of civilization. Just in time to get out of the car and risk our lives . . . again."

They let the radio fill the silence between them as their drive continued down the mountain. Several songs later the radio eased back into a static-fuzz as the road leveled out. They'd made it over the pass, but whatever radio connection they'd briefly had was out of reach once more.

"Pull over here," M said, pointing to a nook in the forest.

Evel gently turned into the trees and the slick ride of the road switched over to the choppy bumps and snapping under-brush of untouched earth. He drove carefully between the tree trunks until the road behind them was out of sight. He found a set of woods with a thick canopy overhead and parked. "This should hide the truck well enough. We'll walk from here and hope we don't have to get back in a hurry."

M nodded and jumped out of the front seat. She led the way toward the circus tent as Evel trailed behind her. Music echoed through the hollow, booming bass that sent a low-end *BUMPH* bouncing around their heads. When they finally reached their destination, they were met with humongous speakers set up on stilts in a circle around the perimeter and aimed outward.

"Are they trying to ward off evil spirits or turn the forest creatures into party animals?" yelled Evel over the blasting music.

They moved forward, under the speakers and toward the back of the large tent. Once they were beyond the speakers, the music strangely quieted.

"Hmmm, directional speakers," noted Evel. "You don't see that at many traveling carnivals in the middle of nowhere."

"What's a directional speaker?" asked M.

"It channels the sound in one area only," explained Evel. "Listen. We're out of the speakers' path, so the sound stays out there."

M and Evel continued on to the edge of the woods, where they discovered a caravan of trailers and trucks parked beside the giant yellow-and-red tent that stretched into the sky. M nodded toward the makeshift town. "This must be what they call the backyard. It's where the circus acts live and get ready for the show."

As they talked, a man walked out from behind an eighteen-wheeler truck that probably carried the tent when it was broken down. He laid eyes on the two kids immediately and waved, very friendly-like. "Afternoon, ma'am. Sir," he said. "If you're looking for the entrance to the show, it's 'round the other side. This here's the behind-the-scenes area. VIPs only, I'm afraid."

That voice — M had heard it before, and it made her turn as white as a ghost.

Evel could tell that something was wrong with her so he spoke up first. "Thanks, mister. That sure explains a lot. My sister was looking for the elephants, only I told her that circuses don't do the elephant thing anymore on account of it's just so downright cruel. Let's go, sis. Mom is probably going out of her mind looking for us."

Evel waved a *thanks, we're okay now* wave and started

walking away, but M remained frozen in place. He turned and pulled her toward the front of the tent. When they were far enough from the backyard area, Evel steadied M. "All right, are you going to tell me what that was all about?"

"That was Terry," said M, stunned.

"Oh," said Evel sarcastically. "That explains everything."

"He was my limo driver." She paused. "Well, not *my* limo driver, but he drove me in a limo when I interviewed for the Lawless School. He works for Lawless. But he usually drives large rigs from town to town."

"Like an oversize tent. Well, that's great," Evel grumbled. "So much for the element of surprise."

"He didn't recognize me," said M, regaining her composure. "I think we're okay."

"Let's get inside, anyway," said Evel. "We don't need you running into anyone else from your past. Except Jules."

The entrance of the tent had a giant dirt parking lot in front of it filled with what must have been every car that had blown by M and Evel while they had been inching up the mountain in their mail truck.

"Good thing we didn't bring the truck," joked Evel. "Then we'd be in real trouble."

M fell in with a line of people waiting to buy their tickets. The circus tent had no billboard. There was no grand announcement of what this place was or what acts were likely to be found inside. A single booth stood between the outside world and the tent's beckoning interior.

"Two, please," M told the man in the booth. He looked half asleep as he took Evel's money and handed over two red-pink ticket stubs torn in half.

"Enjoy the show," the man said dully.

"World's worst carnival barker, if you ask me," said Evel as they walked inside.

The tent was bathed in an otherworldly glow due to the evening Kentucky sun casting through the red-and-yellow fabric. Two giant tent poles held the roof aloft, which created three separate rings on the ground where the performers would act, while the audience sat around them, coliseum style.

M scanned the crowd. It was mostly made up of families out for an adventure. Children with bags of popcorn and parents with bags under their eyes, but everyone was smiling. "This," she marveled. "This is real."

"Wait, is this your first circus?" asked Evel.

"Yep," admitted M. "And probably my last. Let's keep watching for Jules."

The area was lined with ushers waiting at every aisle to guide people into the seats. One helped them find a pair near the lip of the center ring just as the master of ceremonies stepped onto his sandy stage. The ringleader wore a tall top hat with a blue suit jacket and tails that added to his grandeur.

"You didn't come to hear me yackity-yack, did you?" he screamed to the audience through a megaphone. The audience replied with a hearty "NO!"

"Then feast your eyes upon the aerialists above you," the ringleader called out while looking up. The audience followed his gaze and there were a set of trapeze artists already swinging toward each other. "And remember, if they fall, we couldn't afford a net. So do your best to catch them if they tumble your way!"

Evel studied the room. "Hey, there really isn't a net!"

The aerialists floated effortlessly to and from each other on the trapeze, coming together and apart with a clap of white chalk every time. M strained to see their faces, but the artists wore masks over their eyes to add an air of mystery. She watched their body movements, how they gripped the bar and how they flung their bodies out into the void.

"Wires," she concluded. "There's no net because they're wearing safety wires. That's not Jules. Safety wires aren't her style."

"No way they're wearing wires," complained Evel as he squinted upward.

"They're loose. Attached to the belt of each performer," confirmed M. "Hard to see, but they're there."

Then each of the aerialists seemed to make a mistake. They both flipped at the same time, passing each other in the air. However, instead of catching the trapeze in front of them, they each missed their targets and fell gracefully toward the audience. The crowd screamed and gasped in shock, but their fear turned to applause as the wires caught and both artists soared majestically like angels just inches from the packed house.

"Told ya," said M.

"You're the kind of person that ruins magic tricks, aren't you?" said Evel.

"There's no such thing as magic." M noticed the ushers had all left through the front entrance. "It's all science, smoke, and mirrors. And this place is full of smoke and mirrors." She tugged on Evel and pointed to the front entry. "I want to show you what happens while the locals ooh and aah over the trapeze artists' shtick."

Every usher in the tent was slipping out of the entrance and into the parking lot.

"Where are they going?" whispered Evel.

"Casing the cars in the parking lot, I'm guessing," said M. "Looking for cell phones, maybe. Credit cards. Anything the drivers won't notice is missing until later, and will think they just misplaced."

The ringleader walked back into the center court. "Ah, my friends, what better way to laugh together than with a car full of clowns!"

A teeny-tiny car drove through the left ring while honking a horn that blared *how-WOO-ga, how-WOO-ga*. It pulled over and the small side door opened. Then the clowns poured out of it, one after another after another until twenty-five of them had emerged wearing rainbow wigs, painted faces, and oversize hobo clothes.

They fell to the floor, stumbled over one another, and tossed handfuls of glitter around.

Evel shivered. "I hate clowns. How can so many creepy things fit into one tiny car?"

As the fools performed, the ringleader called out again, "And now, the Byrds will fly sky high on a wire so thin, you'll swear they are walking on air!"

The clowns stopped clowning around and everyone in the audience looked to the top of the tent once more. Three people were poised above the audience in white leotards. M couldn't make out their faces since they wore masks like the previous aerialists. Then the smallest of the three darted across the wire, showing no hesitation or fear. The performer flipped, bounced, and twirled through the air, landing each time on the tightrope as steadily as if she were walking up a set of steps.

"Is that her?" asked Evel.

"If that's not her, I'll eat my hat," answered M.

"But you're not wearing a hat," he pointed out.

"Then I'll eat that clown's hat," said M as she watched the tightrope walker dance fifty feet above them. The room went quiet. It was as if the entire audience was holding their breath seeing Jules skip through the air with the greatest of ease. A smile warmed across M's face. She'd done it. She'd found Jules, and Jules was alive.

"You've got a visitor," said Evel as a clown eased in next to M and put his arm around her. M smiled politely at the painted-faced fool with a giant red nose, but she tried to ignore the situation. The last thing she wanted to do was draw unnecessary attention to herself by being the butt of a joke. But the clown wouldn't move.

While Jules performed more feats, M's eyes cast over the circus floor. She counted twenty-five clowns out on the floor. That was a problem. Because the clown sitting next to her made twenty-six.

The impostor grabbed M's wrist tightly and whispered in her ear, "On my go, head for the clown car before this big top gets blown down by the big bad wolves."

M nodded and faked a laugh. From somewhere far away, M could hear the telltale signs of helicopter blades beating through the sky. Then an explosion of wind rushed through and the walls of the tent flipped up, exposing an army of Fulbrights waiting to charge.

Evel slapped M's shoulder and pointed toward them. Then someone in the audience gasped loudly as the unexpected gusts shifted the tightrope violently. M looked up to see Jules falling limply to the ground. She made to jump forward and help her friend, just as Jules had helped her in the Box when they first met. But the clown's grip squeezed her wrist powerfully.

"Freeman, I said on my go!" he snapped. Except that he wasn't a he. The clown was a she. A she named Zara Smith — M's former roommate and sometime rival from the Lawless School. "You were never very good at taking orders."

An invisible wire snapped to life and held to the tightrope walker, who bounced in midair like a caught fish. The mask fell off to reveal a person M had never seen in her life.

"But where's Jules?" M asked herself.

"GO!" screamed Zara.

M whipped around in time to see a steady stream of magblast waves ripping through the air. The Fulbrights were firing their specialized weapons that used magnetic pulses to attack their enemies. And it looked like the Fulbrights hated clowns, too. 'Cause they were taking out every last one.

On Zara's cue, M took hold of Evel's arm and ran for the clown car. Wind bursts crushed around them. M knew enough to dodge the blasts, but there were so many she felt like she was being pummeled by a tsunami. Her legs slipped out from under her and Evel floated off the ground. The world suddenly flipped over forcefully and the dirt floor became the sky. Luckily Zara was next to M and caught her wrist. When the swirling blast calmed, she fell to the ground with a thud, Evel landing on top of her in a heap.

"Human kite time is over, M," Zara called out. "Get in that car now, before —"

A long, deep cracking sound moaned and M realized why Zara wanted inside that clown car so badly. The big top was going to come crashing down. M scrambled with Evel toward the car. A set of clowns battled with the Fulbrights with handkerchief whips that lashed at the intruders. Bright flashes and bangs erupted where there was once only a ringleader and a room full of suspense. The audience was running for the exits now, too. It was mass chaos and the car was surrounded by people scrambling in every direction.

"Where are we going?" yelled Evel.

M jerked him down to his knees as she dropped down, too. "Make yourself small and get to the clown car."

They crawled through the crowd unnoticed. The magblasts had stopped for the time being, which meant the Fulbrights had moved on to hand-to-hand combat with the clowns. When M and Evel finally reached the car, they climbed inside. The entire interior was gutted down to the metal frame. There were no seats, just a milk crate placed strategically behind the steering wheel. And every window was painted except for a slit over the driver's-side windshield.

"So that's how they fit so many people in here," guffawed Evel.

"No jokes. You know how to drive this thing, right?" M insisted.

"Sure?" Evel said unevenly as he sat on the crate, started the engine, and peered through the small, unpainted opening in the window. "I mean, I can't see anything, but let's hope for the best, I guess."

The driver's-side door swung open and two clowns stood staring at M and Evel. One of whom was Zara.

"Oh, no way you're driving, Ronin," snapped Zara as she pushed Evel into the open trunk space. He fell backward with a clunk. Then she tossed the other clown in and climbed onto the crate, revving the car to life. "Hold on to something solid, everybody. It's gonna be a bumpy ride!"

With the crowd out of the way, the clown car tore through the remaining fighters and aimed for the back of the tent. Fulbrights fired magblasts at the car, but Zara somehow played each blast against the other, bouncing from one attack and using the second attack to balance the car. But each hit rattled the clown car's frame and sent the passengers careening into each other. Finally, the car ripped through the tent and into a field of trailers. Zara went to turn on the headlights, but there were none.

"I can't see anything, Freeman," yelled Zara. "You know what to do."

Without thinking twice, M kicked out the front windshield just as she had done in London when they were chasing Ms. Watts. "I don't like déjà vu, Zara," said M.

"Me either," said Zara as she shifted gears. "But I can deal with it if it means we get to live another day. Now get down so we're not so conspicuous."

M started to say, "It's a clown car!" but Zara zipped away just as the main tent pole finally split apart behind them and fell in on itself. Weaving around the trailers, the car dodged the spotlights that shone down from the helicopters overhead. Finally, the car broke through the backyard and headed for the woods.

"Plug your ears, everyone!" screamed Zara as the dark

forest came closer and closer. The wind howled through the open windshield as they rushed to the other side of the directional speakers. Suddenly a low tone pulsed through M's body that made her want to vomit. She clutched her hands against her ears, trying to block out the horrid sound. Evel turned green and folded over with dry heaves. Meanwhile the other clown, who up until now M had disregarded, leaned his head against the painted window.

Kentucky trees were shadows in the night, lit only by the roving helicopter lights, but Zara drove on like a sonically guided bat. Even she didn't look so well, though. The giant speakers were powerful, far reaching, and far retching. Evel was the first to upchuck. M was a close second.

"Ugh!" coughed Zara next. "The things I do to save the world."

Some distance into the woods, when the sickening rumble of the speakers was out of earshot, the car pulled over. It was hissing steam from under the hood and smelled awful inside. Zara helped the other clown out and sat on the wet ground. M and Evel slouched out of the car, too, and took deep breaths of fresh mountain air.

"How?" asked M as she regained her composure. "How did you find us?"

"I never lost you." The moonlight cast over Zara's face and M could see where the paint was smudged from her sweat. Zara pulled off the ridiculous red nose she'd worn the entire time and began wiping off what was left of the paint with her oversize tie. "You ran away."

"Fort Harmon. My fake parents. My fake friends. That was you?" asked M as she clenched her fists and gritted her teeth.

"Well, me and, like, twenty other people," corrected Zara. "And it would have worked if it weren't for this pesky kid."

Evel smiled. "Isn't that the kettle calling the pot pesky?"

"Don't be witty," snapped Zara. "That's my thing. You stick to getting sick in the back of clown cars. I think that's more your speed."

"Why did you turn me into a prisoner?" M broke in.

"Listen, Harmon wasn't my idea. I was following orders." Zara leaned over to check on the other clown. "And before you go all twenty-questions on me, maybe you should wait until you can talk to the real ringleader."

M stood up and started walking back toward the circus tent. "No, thanks."

"Come on, don't be a sore Freeman," begged Zara. "Where are you going? If the Fulbrights don't get you, the Lawless crew will."

"I'm going back to find Jules," confessed M. "She's back there . . . back at that circus freakshow. She could be trapped by the Fulbrights, or stuffed into Terry's Lawless van by now! I have to find her."

"Freeman, you can be the most inspirational *and* ignorant person in the world sometimes," said Zara. "And FYI, you're heading in the wrong direction. Byrd's been with us the whole time."

The second clown sat up, took off her wig, and wiped her face. "Long time no see, M."

CHAPTER 8
OUT IN THE OPEN

The clouds above them passed, letting the moon peek through and cast its glow over the forest floor. Juliandra Byrd was sitting next to Zara, dressed in a costume with juggling balls for buttons and shoes twelve sizes too big. M's heart stopped for a moment as their eyes met.

"Jules," M whispered. She had been so pumped full of adrenaline, so ready to storm the circus and save her friend, that now, suddenly without a mission to complete, M was lost. Lost for words, lost for actions, and lost in the woods. She walked slowly over to Jules, who stood as M came closer. This wasn't a phony or an apparition or a memory. Jules was here and she was alive.

The corners of M's mouth pulled up into an uneven smile. She put her arms around Jules and squeezed her tight. M held her friend like a life preserver in an endless ocean. But Jules did not hug her back. Instead she remained as still as stone.

"Jules?" M asked again. She pulled away to face her friend. "Are you okay? Are you hurt?"

SLAP!

Jules smacked M across her cheek, hard. Hard enough to snap M's head to the side and leave a mark from the clown paint she'd gotten on her hands.

M slowly turned her head back. Jules was breathing rigidly, as if every breath conjured dark thoughts — dark thoughts about M.

"You don't get to ask," Jules started, "if I'm okay. Or if I'm hurt. You don't get to ask me anything anymore."

"But the tent . . ." M's cheek stung viciously. "The Fulbrights, Lawless, I . . . we . . . saved you."

SLAP!

M was briefly thankful that this time Jules had struck her other cheek.

"You didn't save me at *all*, don't you understand that? That 'circus freakshow,' as you so childishly put it, is where I come from. It's where I belong. It was the only safe place in the world I had after you left me — after you left *all of us for dead* months ago. And then just when I think I'm finally done, when I've finally come to terms with everything that happened, you came back. You came back to *save* me. But who do you think those soldiers were really here for?"

Suddenly the world melted away. M couldn't feel anything, not even the ground underneath her feet. This shame wasn't a new feeling. Over the last year she'd endangered everyone she'd considered a friend. She'd failed everyone who'd depended on her. M had left a wake of death and destruction behind her, sacrificing too much in the name of a mission she didn't even fully understand.

Jules had barely gotten out alive. And now M had pulled her right back into the fight.

The two girls stood facing each other in the night. Jules's shoulders were flexed, her fists clenched and ready to battle. M, on the other hand, hung like a ghost, like the slightest wind could sweep her away into the sky.

"While I hate to interrupt this overjoyous reunion of BFFs," said Zara as she waved an arm between them. "And believe me, I really *do* hate to interrupt your special moment, but we've got Lawless *and* the Fulbrights on our trail now. Our clown car is toast, so it's on to our next option: running for our lives. Sound good to everyone?"

"There's a train," Jules said without taking her eyes off of M. "Back near the tent. We always made sure we had several escape routes in case . . . in case of emergencies."

"Well, this certainly qualifies as an emergency," admitted Zara. "It seems like our spirits are broken, but does your point-ing finger still work, Byrd? Which way to the train tracks?"

Jules cut her stare and focused on Zara, who actually stepped back. "It should be west of here. Follow me."

Jules headed away from the others without looking back.

"Um, Jules," said M. "You're heading south."

Jules abruptly stopped. Her whole body tightened and strained. Then she turned right and waved everyone on. They walked carefully into the forest. Evel and M kept to the rear.

"I thought you said she was your best friend?" Evel asked M.

"She is," answered M.

"Are sure you understand the definition?" Evel stepped on a stick and it snapped loudly. The entire crew froze and held their breath. The crack was exactly the kind of slight sound that could be picked up by the Fulbrights from a mile away.

A minute passed, and Zara signaled that it was okay to continue. "Watch your step next time, Bigfoot. And let's all keep quiet. It's not a great time to chat."

They hiked in darkness for another hour before reaching a small clearing that cut across the forest like a tunnel through the trees. The dirt ground became a mound of small rocks surrounding train tracks. Zara held up her fist as she checked the path to the left and right of them. It was clear.

"Now we wait until a train comes," she whispered to the others. "Byrd, don't suppose you know the schedule?"

"Nope. Left it back at my burning home." Jules went to sit down on the ground and lost her balance. She landed hard on her rear end.

"Whoa, are you okay?" asked Evel.

"I'm fine!" snapped Jules. "Just worry about your own back. I've got mine covered."

But M wasn't so sure about that. Why hadn't Jules been swinging through the air on the flying trapeze or death-defying on the high-wire act? Sure, it took skills to be a clown, maybe, but that wasn't the role she'd expected her friend to play. Not after everything she'd seen Jules do. Something was wrong.

After they had been waiting for a while, Evel broke the silence. "How do we, um, get on the train?"

"We give the conductor our tickets and then find our seats in first class," said Zara carelessly. "Where did you find this jokester, M?"

"Ignore her," M told Evel. "We're going to hop the train."

"But don't trains travel at, like, a hundred miles per hour?" Evel pointed out.

"Not this train." Jules's voice was low and distant. "It's a freight train, so the top speed is around sixty miles per hour."

"That's still faster than I can run," said Evel.

"There's a series of curves in this pass," Jules continued. "The train has to slow down. We'll probably be looking at a ten- to twenty-mile-an-hour hop."

Evel's face went white as the ground around them started to shake slightly. M leapt to her feet, ready to fight for her life, but she quickly realized that the disturbance didn't mean they were under attack. It was their ticket to freedom.

A lone light floated in the sky, moving toward them with great speed. The train was moving fast. Really fast. Maybe too fast for them to jump aboard.

"Okay, kids, don't try this at home." Zara smiled with a wicked excitement. "M's new weirdo pal, I want you to go first.

I'm not sure what you're capable of, so it's going to be Freeman's duty to make sure you get on that train."

"What do I do?" Evel asked M. He was suddenly covered in sweat.

"It's easy, just follow my lead. Let's start running now." M pulled Evel along, darting down the path just beside the tree line. With a tremendous noise, the train burst forth through the night and appeared alongside them. The wind pushed at their backs and seemed to increase their speed, but the train was still much faster. As soon as the lead car pulled ahead of them, M reached up and grabbed hold of an empty flatbed. She was tugged off the ground immediately and felt her legs fly into the air. She used her momentum to whip herself up onto the car and leaned over the edge, reaching out for Evel. He grasped at her hand a few times before she was finally able to get a grip. Unfortunately, his feet didn't clear the ground in the same way. They dragged, kicking up a maelstrom of rocks and dust. M's arms felt like they were being pulled out of their sockets, but she held tight as Evel's eyes grew wide and frightened.

"PUSH OFF THE GROUND!" she screamed.

Clumsily, Evel skipped into the air, barely clearing the ground. M rolled backward and flung him around as hard she could. It was enough to get him on board with a thud.

Zara was next, and she slid on board like a snake moving across the desert: effortlessly. Jules, on the other hand, was struggling. The train had quickly outpaced her and she was falling behind. M leapt into action, hopping from train car to train car, chasing Jules until they were even with each other, close to the rear of the train.

"Now, Jules! It's now or never!" M called.

Jules finally took hold of a hanging ladder, but her strength had been wiped out from the run. She dangled dangerously close to the powerful wheels that drove unrelentingly against the tracks, her legs flapping lifelessly as the train made its turn and began to speed up again.

M clasped Jules's wrists.

"It's no good," shouted Jules. "I can't feel my arms. Let me go, M. Let me go!"

Jules was barely holding on by her fingertips, and her grip was slipping. M could feel her friend being pulled back down to the rolling earth by gravity, sliding from her grip, but she couldn't let go.

"No!" she yelled back. "Hold! On! That's the first thing you ever told me in the Box. So hold on, you idiot. We'll make it through this together."

She reached down in a jolt and grabbed a fistful of Jules's clown costume. Then she pulled on the oversize suspenders just as the train hit a bump that bounced Jules and M into the air. M lost her balance and began to fall forward, but Zara snatched her from behind and pulled both girls to safety.

"No one's dying on my watch," Zara said in a huff.

Jules lay facedown in the boxcar, wheezing. She couldn't catch her breath. M scurried back, the horrible truth dawning on her at last. The Jules who used to scale walls and leap off of Siberian trains in the Box was gone.

"It worked," M gasped. "Doe's machine worked on you. It . . . it ate you alive."

"No," wheezed Jules. "It didn't eat all of me, just the best of me. Just what made me special. And it left behind everything else. I'm . . . I'm just a kid now. A regular, ordinary, uncoordinated kid. And I have you to thank for it."

With that, Jules turned her head in the other direction and curled into a ball.

Evel finally reached the boxcar. He was also breathing heavily, and leaned against a stack of crates. "Wow, what did I miss?"

"Just M realizing that she's ruined her best friend's life," said Zara. "Oh, and it looks like we landed in the sweet motherland of Honeycrisp apples." She muscled open one of the crates to reveal scores of the fruit. "Eat up." Zara took a hefty bite of one apple and tossed another to M. "An apple today means that we got away."

CHAPTER 9
STOP, DROP, AND ROLL

By the time morning light beamed through the small holes in the boxcar's rusted walls, everyone was sick of Honeycrisp apples.

A set of dull thuds jolted M into sentry mode. "Everyone down — they found us!"

"Relax, it's just Jules," said Zara lazily as the train clacked along the rails.

Jules bent over and picked up the two apples that were rolling across the floor. They were beaten and bruised just as badly as the kids on the train.

"What did those apples ever do to you?" asked M.

Jules ignored her and tried to juggle the apples again. And again the apples plunked onto the floor.

"She's been doing that all night," said Evel with a yawn. "The apples go up, the apples fall down."

Jules was sweating with concentration as she tossed another apple into the air. "I can get it back. That part of me that was taken, I can get it back. I am going to get it back."

Still the apples fell.

There had been little conversation after they'd boarded the train, and if anyone claimed to be sleeping, they were liars. The travelers were tired, sore, and angry, but most of all they were ready to get off this train. Zara lifted the latch and slid open the door. A blur of trees flew by and the clacking of the train that had rattled their nerves all night suddenly became louder. M hadn't even thought that was possible given the echo factor inside the boxcar.

"Evel, you ever practice jumping off a moving train at the academy?" asked Zara.

"No." Evel gulped and turned to M. "How about at Lawless?"

M, Jules, and Zara all nodded without looking at one another, because yes, as a matter of fact, they had. "More times than I'd like to remember."

Jules cut in. "First, we'll wait for a turn, sometime when the train has to slow down. Jumping from a speeding train is a bad idea."

"But jumping from a speeding train that has slowed down slightly is a good idea?" asked Evel.

"No one wants to jump from a train, dummy," said Zara. "It's *always* a bad idea. But when the only options you have are bad ideas, you go with the least horrible choice."

"When you jump," Jules continued, "jump forward, along-side the train, but also away from it. Then roll over one shoulder and pull yourself into a ball. Let yourself keep rolling until you come to a natural stop, and then stay still until you catch your breath. Get up slowly afterward, too. You don't want to jump up and stand on a broken leg."

Evel stared at Jules. "Aren't you the one who's just a kid now?"

"A kid who paid attention in school," said Jules. "The Fulbrights stole my soul, not my brain."

"Turn's coming," announced Zara.

M felt the train lurch to the right, which shifted everyone toward the open door on the left side of the car. A field of wildflowers opened up as the edge of the forest moved away from the train tracks. They couldn't ask for a nicer landing spot.

"New kids go first," said Zara as she grabbed Evel and pulled him over to the door. "Oh, and don't bite your tongue off."

"What?!" But before Evel could finish his thought, Zara shoved him out of the train. M watched as he landed awkwardly and disappeared into the waist-high weeds.

"Jules, go!" directed Zara.

Jules at least jumped with determination, but her body sprawled unnaturally in the air. She looked like a free-falling octopus, limbs flopping around bonelessly.

M turned back to see Zara smiling. "Just like the good old days . . . or the bad old days, aye, M? I'll see you on steady ground." And with that, Zara leapt and rolled into the tall grass.

The train began to straighten out of its turn and was picking up speed. The wind strengthened suddenly and M felt her legs give just the slightest bit of pause. She knew she'd missed the best window of opportunity to jump, but that wasn't going to stop her. She pushed out of the boxcar and tossed herself toward the field. The crush of her full body weight landed on top of her left side as she started rolling. The quickness of the train had acted like a slingshot, throwing M faster and harder than the others. Uncontrollably, she flipped side over side, crunching against the rocky ground over and over. She was rolling downhill, but downhill toward what? She knew that if she tried to straighten out her arms, she risked breaking them, so she stayed tucked into a ball. She bounced once, bounced twice, and bounced a third and fourth time. Each landing knocked the wind out of her and sent jolts of pain rippling through her body. This was how tenderized meat must feel. Or maybe how nails feel as they were hammered into the wall. Or cars in a multi-car pileup. The aching list went on and on through M's mind until the rolling was replaced by another sensation: falling.

M had reached the edge of her destination — a steep cliff at the end of the field — and kept going.

She quickly unrolled herself and reached out, grabbing blindly for anything within grasp. Luckily she seized hold of some stray roots growing out of the dirt of the overhang. Her legs dangled beneath her. She whipped around to see the train they'd been riding continue on safely across a bridge. Then she looked down to see a mile-long drop straight down, with nothing to catch her if she fell. M clung to the roots, but these roots weren't strong. They were frayed, brittle, and exposed. Slowly, with soft pops of dirt, the roots tore out of the earth, dropping her an inch lower at a time.

"M?" she heard in the distance. "Come out, come out wherever you are!"

She tried to scream, but her voice had been pounded down into a whisper. "Here! Over the cliff!" She coughed a hollow cough and attempted again to scream, but there wasn't enough air in her lungs.

So M started kicking the side of the drop-off. She kicked dirt clods away from the earth and sent up dirt clouds like smoke signals, hoping that someone would see her SOS. The dust floated all around her and slipped its way into her nose, her mouth, and her eyes. It felt like she was being buried alive, but she kept kicking up the dirt.

Then she felt a hand grab her wrist. Instantly she grabbed the arm back, releasing the roots to lock on with both hands.

"Steady yourself and use your legs to walk up the side of the cliff," the voice strained above her. It was Jules.

For a fleeting moment M thought about the fumbled apples from the train. Would Jules drop her, too? But M did as she was told, bracing her feet and legs against the cliff and crawling upward, one small step at a time. Finally Jules pulled her over the edge and back onto level ground. Well, not only Jules. It had been Jules who'd grabbed M, but Zara had held Jules and Evel had held Zara, linked in a desperate human chain. Breathless, everyone relaxed, sprawled out in the grass. The two old friends were next to each other and shared a smile before looking back up at the morning sky.

"Looks like you owe me again," said Jules.

"I've always got your back," M wheezed as best she could.

Only a beat passed before M heard another noise — the unmistakable sound of car tires rolling across gravel. M held on to the earth as if the world were going to try to shake her off it again. "What now?" she whispered.

"Let's hope it's the cavalry," said Zara. "'Cause if it's the police, then we've got a lot of explaining to do."

"And if it's the Fulbrights?" asked Evel.

"Then M had the right idea," said Zara. "We'd have to jump over that cliff and pray for the best."

The crew stayed low and hidden in the grass as a black van rolled out of the forest. The windows were tinted and the vehicle looked sharp and dangerous in the sunlight, like a nightmare reaching into the daytime. The van parked, and nothing happened for what felt like forever to M.

Suddenly, on the other side of the canyon, there was an explosion. M flipped onto her stomach to find the source of the sound. Her eyes followed the train tracks across the bridge, and there in the distance a plume of black smoke grew into the sky. Someone had blown up the train.

"Fulbrights," accused M. She'd know their scorched-earth tactics anywhere. Fulbrights were rarely subtle. But did that mean the van was Lawless, coming to make her pay for what she'd done to their school?

The side door of the van finally jolted open and a boy came running out. He wore a black shirt and black pants, and his blond hair flopped as he raced toward them with tremendous speed and urgency. "Zara! We've gotta go!"

Zara's head popped up from the grass and she started waving her hands at the others. "Go! Go! Go! Everyone in the van!"

The boy helped Evel up first and pushed him toward the van, then he grabbed Jules, but when he saw M, he paused. "You?"

"You?" echoed M.

He seemed surprised, but then again, M was surprised, too. She knew him, but she'd been sure the worst had happened to him. His name was Foley, and he'd been with Lawless until he'd fallen in battle with the Fulbrights. The last she'd seen him, he'd been in a medically induced coma and strapped into Doe's student-eating machine.

M heard another sound in the distance. Helicopters. The whirring buzzed like a swarm of high-pitched mosquitoes. She turned and saw their small shapes circling the explosion. They were searching for something more. They were searching for survivors. They were searching for M.

"Hey, lookie-loos, less staring death in the face and more running for your life!" shouted Zara as she waved M and Foley on.

"We've got a half hour before they sort through that wreckage," Foley stated with an eerie certainty. "After that, they'll head this way. Best not be here when that happens."

M looked at the van across the field as Evel and Jules climbed inside the belly of the autobeast. "You were . . ."

"Yeah," Foley agreed with M's unsaid statement, because whatever she thought had happened to him had definitely happened to him. She didn't need to list the tragedies he'd suffered; he'd lived through them all. "I was, and now I'm not. Now I have a chance to help a larger cause and so do you. Come with us if you want to make a difference."

Another explosion rocked the countryside. It was probably one of the tankers on the train, but M didn't turn around to see the new flames licking the sky. She headed toward the black van and jumped in, too.

There was no driver inside and neither Foley nor Zara made a move to take the wheel. Then the van revved up and took off as soon as the side door closed behind them. The steering wheel turned and navigated itself.

"Of course it's remote controlled," M complained as she reached for her seat belt and buckled it.

The inside of the van was just as dark and mysterious as the outside. Evel had a wild look on his face, as if he needed a minute to catch up to what was happening. She couldn't imagine what was going through his mind, but when their eyes locked, she tried her best to calm him down. She whispered, "It's okay," and nodded calmly. That seemed to work on him. But Jules was frozen, staring fearfully at Foley as if she were looking at a ghost.

Bouncing in their seats, the crew reached for anything they could hold to steady them as the van stumbled over the uneven forest floor. Zara and Foley sat on the bench seat in the front and were deep in quiet conversation. M had seen them in this position before, in the limousine right after she'd first discovered that she was going to the Lawless School, when Foley and his recruit Merlyn had been attacked by Fulbrights. Foley was the only person she'd ever seen Zara be human around, and back then, that had been enough to make M trust him. But the M in the back of that limo wasn't the same M in the back of this van.

"Answers," demanded M sternly. "Spill it now."

Zara cut her eyes at M and started to say something, but M stopped her short. "I don't want to hear from you. I want to hear Foley's story."

The van went silent. It was the kind of silence that fills the space in between when the principal walks into a classroom and when they call out someone's name. It was the silence of every student waiting to hear whether they were in trouble or not.

"I don't have the answers," Foley said apologetically.

"Let's start with how you got here," directed M.

"Do you want the short story? One minute I was fighting Fulbrights in Germany alongside you, the next I was at home in LA and my parents were freaking out because I'd been 'missing and presumed dead' for almost a year. I mean, after the black hole struck the Lawless School, they thought I was lost forever."

"You really don't remember anything else?" asked Jules.

"I mean, not at first. But then my parents sent me to a therapist, some kind of hypnotherapy doctor. He dragged a lot of bad things out of my memory, things I didn't remember at first. Things I'd rather forget."

"The coma?" asked M.

Foley nodded slowly . . . nervously. "The coma, the Fulbrights, the pressure chamber, having the — what's the right word . . . *essence* of me taken or, like, separated from my body. Do you remember that feeling, Jules?"

Jules's face went sour. She clutched at her stomach and nodded.

M watched Foley as he reached over and placed his hand on Jules's shoulder. He comforted her. He comforted Zara. But still, he seemed off to M — trapped somehow, as if he'd never escaped the Fulbrights. Like a burning building filled with smoke, he had the same shape on the outside, but something mercurial was twisting inside of him.

"Hey, I'm Evel by the way," Evel said, interrupting the

moment. "Nice to meet you and thanks for saving my life. But let me get up to speed. The Fulbrights kidnapped all of you, then John Doe stole pieces of you, then let you go home to your parents?"

"He didn't take me," said Zara.

"Or me," said M. "But he tried."

"Doesn't that seem weird to you guys?" said Evel.

"He's right," Jules spoke up. "What did John Doe want? Why did he steal the best parts of us and send us back home? Why are we still alive?"

"Like I said, I don't know," Foley repeated. "But it started something. A secret war that's spilling over into a not-so-secret war now. There have been attacks on Lawless graduates. Large scale attacks. My parents . . . the Fulbrights found us. I barely escaped."

He stopped talking and breathed heavily. Zara wrapped her arm around him, almost in an embrace. M could hear the audible clicks in his throat where he was choking sadness back. And she knew exactly what he was talking about. The coordinated strike on Evel and the other Ronins that she had witnessed was cold, calculated, and ruthless. The Fulbrights hadn't cared at all who saw their attacks or who was in the way, even innocent bystanders. No one was safe.

"Foley reached out to me." Zara finished his story and connected the final dot that led to them working together. "He wasn't part of the original plan, but we need people on our side now more than ever."

"What side? What plan?" M questioned sharply. "I'm not going to be part of some Lawless plot again."

"You don't have a choice," said Zara. "See, as far as we know, you *are* the plot. My job was to watch you, remember? I watched you at the Lawless School. I tried my hardest to keep you away from that psycho, Ms. Watts."

"Then why didn't you *warn me* about her?" snapped M. "Maybe that would have saved us all some time and kept more than a few people alive."

"Oh please, you couldn't know about the plan. A magician never tells the volunteer from the audience how the magic trick works," said Zara. "The last thing we needed was you giving us away to Watts. She didn't know what we were planning."

"We? Like you and my mom?" spat M. "Or we, like you and my fake parents in Fort Harmon? Or we, like you and Devon Zoso? Did you plan for me to meet Evel, too?"

"Wait, I've never met these people before," promised Evel. "And my sister has a crazy mind of her own."

"Look, Freeman, this is delicate," reasoned Zara. "Believe it or not, there are parts of the plan that I don't know about yet or that I can't even understand. What's happening is bigger than you and me and everyone in this van. But Devon Zoso, she worked by herself, though she still played a part in the big picture. How was I supposed to know that she was a double agent? I had my hands full saving your hide all over the globe from Watts."

"So you delivered me, Jules, and Merlyn to the Fulbrights wrapped up in a bow?" suggested M.

"Well, in handcuffs at least," said Zara. "According to your mother, you needed to join the Fulbrights. You learned something there, something important, just like your father did. But what it was, we don't know. When you chased me down in New York, you weren't supposed to catch me. I have to give you credit there . . . you're more capable than you look. So we tried to tip you off in the subway. Personally, now that we're getting everything out into the open, I wanted to bring you with us, I did. But that wasn't my mission. It wasn't your mission, either. You needed to be captured again."

"Your mission was getting the moon rocks," realized Jules. "You weren't after M that night, were you?"

"Bingo, Byrd. Imagine my surprise when your goody-two-shoes crew showed up. So I let you do the sleuthing, then took what I needed. But Freeman couldn't lose one little battle, even if it meant winning the whole war. We had to throw her back to the 'good guys.'"

Zara paused. She looked directly at M, almost in the same way she looked at Foley, with emotion. "Then, hours later, we found you wandering the forest miles from your house, M. You didn't recognize me. You didn't recognize your mother. You'd been scrubbed clean like a computer. Whatever you had, it was worse than amnesia. Our doctors told us the old M was gone. So we placed you somewhere you'd be safe. Or at least somewhere we thought you'd be safe. But you escaped dream-ville. Then my job was to find you. As you can see, I'm good at my job."

There's the old Zara, thought M as she sat still in her seat. Emotional and honest Zara was more than a little unsettling. "Well, I've got a new job for you," she told Zara. "I want to meet your *we*."

CHAPTER 10
FULL CONFESSION

It was the kind of house people drove past every day, tucked under a set of trees just far enough from the one-lane highway. Most travelers wouldn't even give it a second glance. If they did, they'd see only a home with a decrepit quality. The windows were grimy, the siding was rotten in all the right places, and the shutters were a washed-out shade of green. It was all cultivated and expertly planned. M realized it as soon as they turned off the road. This kind of quiet design took just as much effort as prepping the White House lawn or painting a stage set for a TV show. It was made to look like what people saw . . . and that's what made it an excellent safe house.

Three cars were parked in the front yard, scattered as if they'd pulled in from every direction. The placement of the vehicles gave an impression of carelessness, recklessness, but M knew better. She quickly saw that each of the cars was in the perfect position for a clean getaway.

The others were asleep in the van. They'd driven all day through four different states and didn't stop for gas once. The rest of their ride hadn't been rainbows and lollipops, nor had it been the homecoming M had expected. Foley was mysteriously back. Jules was safe and unsound. Evel was basically along for the ride, and good old Zara was her same bad old self.

M couldn't sleep. She gazed blankly out the window as they rolled along wooded back roads, trying to think of exactly the right words she wanted to say to her mother.

Now the van pulled silently behind the house and into a shabby barn that wasn't visible from the street. The barn doors opened to let them in and closed after they'd parked. Or when someone parked. M hated not knowing who was driving the car. She also hated not knowing who was driving this new organization that dragged her along as a passenger. But when the no-driver turned off the van, M knew that her questions would be answered soon.

"We're here," said Zara.

"Where's here?" Evel mumbled as he woke from his deep sleep and wiped the drool from the corner of his mouth.

"Close to my house, if I'm not mistaken." M had mapped their path every mile marker along the way.

"A few towns away," Foley replied, then caught himself and looked at Zara, who shook her head disapprovingly.

"So I was right. Thanks for confirming, Foley," said M. "But how do you know where I live?"

"I . . ." Foley sat up quickly but forgot to remove his seat belt. It locked him in place and threw him back against his seat awkwardly. "I wasn't supposed to say that. Forget I said that, everyone. I guess I'm still the new guy."

"It doesn't matter," said Zara as she unlatched his seat belt. The sound of the strap zipping back cut through the silence in the van. It sounded like a threat. "Freeman figured it out before you let the cat out of the bag. Let's just get in the house already."

The interior of the barn was actually in good shape. From the outside M had expected to find peeling paint, rotten wooden beams, and critter nests in every corner, but that was far from the case. The walls were reinforced with steel sheets that gleamed in the bright industrial light fixture that shone from above. Still, there were no gadgets here, no computer server surprises like she had found at Evel's warehouse, Sercy's lair, or even at the Fulbright Academy.

"What's with the urban design?" asked Jules. She tried to gracefully jump from the van but slipped, catching herself clumsily against the wall with her hands. Instantly her eyes showed panic and she jerked her hands away as if the wall had been scorching hot or shocking to the touch. "Whoa."

Interested in Jules's reaction, M followed her lead and put her hand out. The walls weren't warm or electrified. They were vibrating. Small pulses flashed silently through her fingers. "What does this do?"

"It destabilizes radio waves." An old man shuffled around the side of the van. He leaned heavily on a cane and spoke in almost whispered breaths. His arms were thin and frail, while his cheeks were gaunt. The whites of his eyes matched the white of his hair, and his face had dark sunspots that stood out against his light mocha skin. He pushed himself forward carefully. "Meaning no GPS or other guidance system can find this place unless we want it to."

"Which is very helpful when your enemies have missiles," added Zara.

The older gentleman smiled and M caught a glimpse of something familiar in his expression. "Do I know you?"

"I don't think so," he answered mysteriously. "But we're glad you've arrived. There's someone inside who has been waiting for you."

Zara led the way as the group walked from the barn to the back door of the rickety house. There was a sun-washed back porch with wooden planks that bent and bounced softly under every step M took. She watched the cracked paint flakes blow away in the wind.

The screen door yawned open and flapped shut with a slap. The furniture was well worn within an inch of the fabric's life. The smell of mothballs and scented candles mingled in the air. Jules and Evel fell into a coughing fit as soon as they walked inside.

"You get used to it," Foley whispered to them.

"It's aggressively grandma-smelling," mumbled Jules as she pulled the neck of her clown shirt up to cover her mouth and nose.

M stepped forward and heard a faint sound coming from one of two chairs that faced away from them. Someone was humming a song, and the melody transported M years back to her childhood. It was the same song her mother used to hum at night whenever M couldn't sleep. Instantly, she felt calm and nervous at the same time. With both feelings fluttering against each other, her insides vibrated like the walls in the barn.

"I found you, Mom," announced M in a parched voice.

The humming stopped. "Ahhh, poor *miette*, I am not your mother, but I am your friend." An ancient hand motioned for M to come around to the other side of the room. A woman in a headscarf rested there, dwarfed against the high-back chair. She was methodically working two giant knitting needles as she smiled. Her yellow teeth flashed from under her lips and her watery eyes sparkled in the small sunlight that filtered through the curtains.

"Madame Voleur?" M was shaken. "What are you doing here? How do you know that song?"

"Zee song, it is an old song that I used to teach my students. Zee melody is calming, no? So ve vould use it venever ve vere anxious. I see your mother used it visely. A baby is zee most anxious-making zing on zis planet." Her needles clicked and clacked as she spoke. Her hands moved automatically. The older woman didn't bother looking down at her creation, which looked like a mile-long scarf. It lay in piles at her feet like a clothed snake. "Ah, you are vondering about my craft. I remember you running true zee stages of Zee School of Seven

Bells back at my home in France to calm yourself. Vell, zis vorks zee same vay for me."

"What do you have to be anxious about?" asked Jules from under her collar. "Besides the smell in here?"

"Zee better question, Ms. Byrd, vould be vat do *ve* have to be vorried about." Voleur's face turned sad and serious. "Zere is much danger now. Ms. Freeman, I owe you a full explanation. Now is zee time for questions. I vill answer as much as I know."

"Where is my mother?" M asked first.

"Hidden, protecting the last of zee moon rocks."

"Are you crazy?!" gasped M. "You haven't destroyed the moon rocks yet? What about the meteorite? Where's the meteorite that I stole from John Doe?"

"Now zat, ve destroyed. Zat vas an unnatural element and has been banished from zis earth. Ve are not fools, Ms. Freeman."

M couldn't believe her ears. "Who are you people?"

"Ve are zee ones who vill save zis vorld from Lawless and zee Fulbrights. Neither side can be trusted. You know zis, yes?"

She did know this. M knew this with all of her heart. "How can I help?"

"You are already helping, *miette*. Zis is vhy ve hid you away. I am sorry for the extremes of our actions, but placing you in a tiny town vas all ve could do."

"Excuse me, ma'am," said Evel. "But what did you think would happen to her there? What if she never returned to herself?"

"Ve had no choice, Mr. Zoso." The old lady shot him a sideways smile. "Yes, I know who you are. You are an interesting fellow. Vord vas you vere deceased . . . but ve are lucky to have you vith us, even if you did allow zee others to find Ms. Freeman. There vas no vay of knowing vat vould happen to Freeman. We hoped zat zee serum vould vear off."

"And it did," said M.

"Ms. Freeman, your father sent you on a journey zrough two very secret schools for a reason. Vat it is, ve do not know."

"I can connect the two worlds of the Fulbright Academy and the Lawless School," M started. "I have proof."

"Baloney," interrupted Foley. He stayed seated on the beat-up leather sofa, but his voice was fast and a little panicked. He brushed the sandy hair out of his eyes, but his focus was solely on M. The gaze spooked her a little.

M stared back. "I can prove it."

"How?" asked Foley.

"By going back to where this all started." M steeled herself for what was coming next. "I need to go home again."

CHAPTER 11

FRIEND OR FOE

Madame Voleur's crew prepared for their mission like bees buzzing around the ramshackle house. M watched as Zara and Foley flitted around, gliding through doorways and packing gear quickly and methodically. It was as if they'd been planning this all along, but M could tell that they were nervous. For one thing, Zara was humming while she worked. Zara never, ever hummed. The effect was unsettling to M. It played like a warbled record in a horror movie. At any minute the music could stop and something unspeakable would be at their throats. And stranger than the humming, Zara kept sneaking glances at Foley as they passed each other. Foley also tried to play it cool, but his eyes kept shifting from person to person, watching them, all of them, as if they were suspects in a crime and he was the detective trying to solve everything. M even caught Foley stopping to check himself in the mirror a few times, like he wasn't expecting to see his own face there. Nerves make people do the weirdest things.

Even the mysterious old guy was hustling, packing up futuristic-looking gizmos that did who knew what.

Jules was in the corner, carefully tossing a red ball of yarn from one hand to the other. She held it like it was a live bomb instead of loosely wound strings. Sweat glistened along her hairline as she strained to keep focus on catching the ball again and again.

Madame Voleur watched her. "Keep trying, *miette*. Don't give up."

The red ball thumped softly on the ground and unraveled as it rolled away. Jules let her head fall backward and uttered a frustrated sigh.

"Do you think we'll really need all this?" M asked, motioning to the collection of gear.

The older woman clicked her knitting needles together calmly and spoke. "Vere you are going is dangerous. Especially if vat you say is true and you have proof."

M moved closer to the old woman. "It's just a house."

"Not anymore. Zat place has changed for all who lived zere, both you and your mother. For your mother it has become a great sadness. She lost her husband vile she lived zere. She almost lost you zere, too." Madame Voleur let the needles rest in her lap. "But for you, it is even more complicated. Vat zey are packing now, it is for zee real-world danger. Zee Fulbrights or Lawless soldiers who may be zere. But *you* must pack more powerful weapons for your journey."

"More powerful?" asked M. "Like lasers? Freeze rays? Bombs?"

"Like patience. Understanding. Serenity," said Madame

Voleur. "Zee war waiting for you at your home vill be fought in your mind. You will feel many conflicting emotions: darkness, happiness, uneasiness, anger, fear. But vat you take vith you after you go home, zat depends on you. I vould suggest zat you try to focus on hope. Zat is vat zee vorld needs right now. Not zose other weapons. Because where zere is hope, zere vill always be life."

A warmth radiated through M as Madame Voleur made her point. And whether or not it was because the afternoon sun was beaming through the window and striking her on the back, it didn't matter. She relaxed. She was going home.

Madame Voleur reached over and patted her leg gently, reassuringly. "Now zee vorld is in your court, *miette*. And remember. It is the only one ve have."

"All packed," declared Foley, interrupting the moment. "Let's head out, Freeman."

But before M could answer, Madame Voleur flicked one of her knitting needles like a dagger, end over end, until it struck the floor by Foley's shoe. He stepped back cautiously.

"Ah, ah, ah," ticked the old lady. "You, Mr. Foley, vill stay here vith me."

"And do what?" asked Foley. There was a challenging tone in his voice. While his words had formed a question, it came out sounding more like *How dare you!*

"Plenty, plenty." Madame Voleur cocked her head toward him and gave Foley a yellow-toothed smile. "For starters, I need a new red ball of yarn. And zere's no reason vhy ve should send everyone to zee Freeman estate. You are zee backup, how does zat sound? Oh, and of course, you can protect little old me. Now be a lamb, and can you please fetch my needle from beside you?"

Foley grinded his teeth and steadied himself before pulling the long needle out from the floor. He handed it back to Madame Voleur and said, "Anything you need, boss."

The others held still, not sure what they had just witnessed. It was M who broke the silence. "Like Foley said. Let's head out while we still have the light."

The black van navigated its way through the low mountain turns. M was sitting next to Zara while Evel and Jules sat in the far back. The older man rode shotgun in the front seat. M imagined how strange it would look if the police pulled them over right now. No one driving, but a car full of passengers.

She watched the older man in the front seat. He was quiet and seemed content to keep to himself, but M had caught him sneaking glances at her and Jules a few times. It was like he knew them and was scared of them at the same time. M searched through her memory bank, but she still couldn't place his face.

She leaned in to Zara and whispered, "What's his story?"

"You mean, you don't know?" she asked, surprised. "I thought he was with you."

"What? What are you talking about?" snapped M, suddenly worried that danger was riding in the front seat. "I've never seen him in my life."

Zara shrugged casually as if M had asked her what she wanted to eat for dinner. "You must have met him. He's the only way we found you."

"Found me?" echoed M. "Like, at the circus?"

"Yeppers," said Zara. "Dude contacts Madame V, tells her he knows where you are — or at least, where you'll be — and then I'm sent out on yet another mission to save your hide. You sure you don't know him? I mean, we don't even know his name. He made that part of the agreement. No names, no questions. Said it was for your own good."

"And you trusted him?" M's eyes widened at Zara's lack of concern.

"Madame V trusted him," reassured Zara. "And I trust Madame V. Besides, he's been right so far. You're here, you're safe, and now you're going home. You're a regular queen of the world thanks to him, but this guy still has you freaked. Whose house do you think we were just at? All that tech stuff? That's not Madame V's deal. She's old school."

M couldn't believe what she was hearing. A stranger shows up from out of nowhere and knows exactly how to find her . . . but not until after she'd survived a Lawless and Fulbright attack. If she looked up the word *suspicious* in the dictionary,

116

there'd be a picture of this guy next to it. She was tired of all these mysteries. It was time for answers.

"Hey, mister," M burst out. "Old man know-it-all in the front. What's your name?"

"Part of the deal," he answered while still facing forward. "No names."

"Okay, then," allowed M. "Don't tell me your name, but you need to tell me how you knew where I was after I escaped Madame Voleur's make-believe world."

The old man sat for a minute, thinking. His thumb tapped against his fingers one at a time, as if he were calculating a math problem in his head. "No," he said calmly. "If I tell you, it would change things too much. I'm not the important part of this equation. You are."

"People keep telling me that and I'm not buying it anymore." M leaned forward over the center console and grabbed his wrist so that his fingers stopped their rhythmic counting. "I think everyone in this van is important. In fact, I think everyone I've come across in my life is important. Good people that aren't here anymore." She paused a moment, thinking of her missing friends and family. "Listen. I'm nobody without everyone else in my life. And now that includes you. So tell me, or Madame V will knit you a straitjacket as soon as we get back to your place."

The old man's head swung low as his chin touched his chest. M could see the gray hair thinning and bald spots where his brown skin shone through. Then he let out a sigh that ended in a high-pitched wheeze. "Your tracker," he admitted. "I told you there was a reason you needed that tracker. That it might save your life one day."

"No," M said softly, almost under her breath. "No, no, no, you couldn't be . . ." The finger tapping, the high-tech gear, the tracker. "Keyshawn?"

The old man turned and, for the first time, M could see the resemblance between the Keyshawn she knew and the Keyshawn who sat before her now. His face had been washed away by time. Worn down like statues in the park over the years. But he still had the same spark of determination in his eyes. A swell of feelings consumed M. Keyshawn had been a friend, but he had also been an accomplice in the very scheme that stole Jules's abilities and fed them to that awful monster, John Doe. Was he here to make things right, or to make things worse?

"No way," gasped Jules from the backseat. "Keyshawn? You were so . . . young. And now you're so . . . old. What happened?"

"I . . ." He searched for the gentlest words to discuss such a sore subject. "I've asked myself that same question over and over again. The most logical explanation I can come up with is that I was not part of Doe's original plan. You see, M was half right when she said Doe wanted to use you as a secret army to do his dirty work. That was true. And it was work he didn't want anyone else to know about, apparently. Except for those closest to him. But there was always a second half to the plan."

"He stole us right out from our own skin," said Jules.

"Yes." Keyshawn nodded. "He stole your strength and agility, Jules."

"Merlyn," murmured M. "Doe stole his computer skills, didn't he?"

"I would imagine, yes," agreed Keyshawn. "But from me, maybe he didn't need anything? So he stole what suited him most. My youth."

The mood in the car turned sour. They weren't just fighting a mental case with an army anymore. They were fighting a diabolical supervillain.

"There is," Keyshawn continued, "a good side to all this."

"I'm finding it really hard to see the positives," said Jules.

"Doe didn't have M or Cal." Keyshawn let out a weak grin. "And without your skill sets, I'm not sure everything went according to plan."

"But wait," said M. "What about Foley? He was there, too, in one of those chambers. What could Doe have wanted with him?"

Keyshawn shook his head and turned back around to look out of the front windshield. "I've been asking myself that same question. I don't have an answer yet."

"I can get it back, right, Keyshawn?" asked Jules. "My strength, my agility, I can earn it back. If I try hard enough, will it return to me?"

"I don't know," he repeated softly.

The van fell quiet again save for the sound of the tires

coasting over the road below. As they moved closer to their destination, M never felt so far away. Far away from her mother, her father, even her friends in the car. She hoped there was some clue at her house that could make that feeling disappear.

"Home again, M," said Zara as she waved her hands like a magician's assistant toward the turn into the Freeman estate.

CHAPTER 12
NO PLACE LIKE HOME

The front entrance was the first sign that a long time had passed since M had been back home. And from the looks of the once-strong wrought-iron gates hanging off their hinges, it wasn't only time that had passed through her house, but something destructive and powerful. The gates were splayed open like wings on an ancient insect about to take flight. The rest of the fence hadn't fared well, either. The length of metal security was now laid flat and buried into the earth instead of standing guard around the perimeter. There was nothing left to protect the Freeman residence.

"What happened here?" asked Jules.

"You're asking the wrong person," M said quietly as she surveyed the damage. "I only lived here."

"Looks like a twister carrying a giant came through and stomped on everything in sight," said Zara. "I hope you can still find what you're looking for, Freeman. John Doe did a number on this place."

"Yes, he did." M looked down at her fingernails. They'd been polished, painted, and manicured just a few days before, but now they were ragged, chipped, and worn. She remembered striking John Doe's cheek on that night and could still feel his crumbling skin beneath her nails. Suddenly, she found herself digging underneath each nail, trying to clean out whatever might be stuck.

"Good. That means we're on the right track." Zara smirked and gave M a wink. "So are you having fun yet or what?"

"Your friends need new hobbies," said Evel as the black van drove down the driveway.

The turrets were missing against the deep blue sky. They had always peeked over the long, hilly driveway and were usually the first thing M saw of the old Victorian house when she came home. But now there was nothing there except sparse white clouds that hung in the sky like the magician's smoke that lingered after a sleight-of-hand disappearance. It would make a terrific *TA-DA!* moment for an audience expecting to see a magic show, but in the van, M couldn't believe her eyes. The house was gone, plain and simple.

The driveway ended abruptly at the edge of a deep pit. Surrounding the hole in the ground were pieces of wood as thin as toothpicks scattered recklessly across the yard. M's home had been smashed to smithereens.

The van rolled to a stop and the passenger doors opened smoothly. M was the first one out. The debris of her past life crunched underfoot with every step forward.

"Wow," Zara said as she walked to the edge of where the home used to be. "There must have been something super important in there, Freeman."

"That hole must be sixty feet wide and sixteen feet deep," reckoned Keyshawn. "It was a big mansion, huh?"

"You were there," Jules reminded him. "We both were. Don't you remember?"

"Oh yes." Keyshawn laughed and shook his head. His eyes were clouded and distant. "I *was* there, wasn't I? I can't for the life of me remember a thing about that night. My mind's not what it used to be."

"Sixteen feet? That's deep," said Evel. "Like two floors deep. What were they digging for? Did you have a basement or something?"

"A basement *and* something else." M scooted to the edge, sat, and threw her legs over. She surveyed the dugout area. "I don't suppose we have a rope, do we?"

Zara jogged back to the van and jerked a hook attached to a winch on the front bumper. The wire cable trailed her and let out a *zizz*ing sound that echoed in the silent evening. It sounded like the world was being unzipped. "Hold on to this and I'll lower you down."

The winch heaved slowly as M eased into the pit. At the bottom her shoes sank an inch into the wet mud. She slipped, but then waved to the others to let them know that she was okay. Once she steadied herself, M closed her eyes, clipped the winch hook to her belt loop, and stepped forward. She retraced her path from the maze at the Fulbright Academy, the same path from her basement that her father had mapped out to lead M to his secret safe room.

She paced carefully in the open space until she found herself where the basement should have ended. But instead of a wall, there was another open space. It was where her father's safe room had been. Doe had dug it out, but had he found what he was looking for?

She stared into the space and felt a chill deep in her bones. Standing there, M was carried back in time. She remembered Jones crumpling to the ground in front of her. She knelt down and placed her hand in the mud where his body had lain, but like the house, there was nothing there now. She sat back on her legs, which pushed her knees deeper into the mud. They were losing the light, which was exactly what Madame V had warned them against. M closed her eyes again and tried to remember the room only, not what had happened in the room. She deleted Jones, removed the Fulbright and his twisted fingers lying on the floor. She even removed herself, and then M remembered the secret doorway that led to an escape route.

"There," she whispered. M stood up and stumbled her way to the far wall. She traced the muddy sludge from the earth, feeling for an opening. "I know you're in there."

"M!" shouted Jules. "There's a fire! In the distance, look! Smoke!"

M twirled around and looked up into the sky. A thin line of black smoke twisted into the air like a signal. She knew that they should investigate, but she was so close to finding what they had come here for — the Lawless School yearbook.

"M!" It was Zara this time . . . and Zara hardly ever used her first name. "Time to go before something bad happens."

M ignored her and kept digging into the wall. The smoke grew deeper and covered more of the sky, but it didn't matter as much as finding the entrance that had swallowed her whole just a few months before. If she found the entrance, she could find the escape pod. That's where she last remembered holding the yearbook.

"Not yet!" M yelled, but at the same time a loud *pop* erupted in the distance. It sounded like a clap of thunder in a storm that was miles away. She wouldn't have given the sound a second thought if it hadn't been for the rippling ground around her. It was a small tremor, but it felt so unnatural that M stepped back from the door. When the tiny quake ended, another sound took its place. A gush of wind rushed from some channel beneath her. Hot wind that made the mud around her rise in temperature in a matter of seconds. "Not now," M said to herself. "I'm so close!"

But before M could try to find the secret passage again, she was ripped backward and dragged through the mud. One breath later, the space M had been standing in was engulfed in flames that shot through the escape-route door. The door itself exploded into fiery pieces of molten steel mixed with mud, followed by a sea of blue blazes that roiled and filled the pit like a swimming pool of fire. And M was going to drown in it.

The winch hook carried her across the crater and slammed her against the wall closest to where the rest of the team stood. M felt the air burst out of her lungs as she was jerked up the muddy bank like someone possessed. Next thing she knew, M had flipped onto grassy land and felt the whip of weeds against her ears and cheeks, followed by the thud of her back against the van's front bumper as the winch finished its winding journey. She saw stars in her eyes and could barely breathe.

"M! Are you okay?" Jules rushed to her side and unlatched the hook from her belt loop.

M nodded frantically and strained to catch her breath, but the air had been knocked clean out of her system. Slowly she felt a warm sensation in her feet. M centered herself and focused on her legs. Her shoes were scalded and smoking from the blast, so she kicked them against the dirt to cool them off. "Where?" She coughed. "Where did the explosion come from?"

"Where there's smoke," said Zara, "there's fire. Get in the van, everyone. We're going to play forest ranger on whoever set off that smokestack."

Evel and Jules helped M into the backseat. Then Zara took the wheel and drove the van off the driveway directly into the forest. The bumps throttled the passengers, but Zara kept her eyes trained on the smoke in the sky.

"There, on the ground," pointed out Keyshawn. "The explosion came through this way underground."

Outside of the front window M could see a ripple in the forest floor that laced from her house to some other location deep in the woods. The solid ground had exploded open and made a path . . . a path that ran toward the mysterious, rising smoke.

"M, was there an underground escape route from your house?" asked Zara without taking her eyes from the cluster of trees that surrounded them.

"Yes," she answered weakly. "I was almost at the entrance when the blast blew me back."

"Zara pulled you back, M," said Jules. "Not the explosion. She saved your life with the winch hook. If she hadn't reacted so quickly, you'd be . . ."

"Well done," said M, with a wheezing laugh.

"I don't see how you can laugh at all this," said Evel. "How many explosions can one person walk away from, M? I'm pretty sure you've hit your limit just in the time I've known you."

"She's tougher than she looks," Zara stated flatly as she careened through the woods. "Now let's see who set off our homecoming present."

The van pummeled into an open glade and Zara slammed on the brakes, bringing them to a skidding stop right in front of a bonfire. Shreds of ash scattered in a cloud as the flames stretched upward and licked the darkening sky with bright orange tendrils. A trio of shadows loomed by the fire's edge, as if they were waiting for trouble to show up . . . wishing it would, even.

Keyshawn opened his door first, stepping out and walking around the front of the car to face the fire. Even from inside the van, M could feel the intense heat from the burning world outside. Zara joined Keyshawn, while Jules and Evel stayed rooted to their seats. The air around them warped and shimmered in a dangerous way that felt like they were already deep in the heart of the inferno.

"I'm going, too," said M as she struggled out of the side door.

Zara called out to the shadows, "You know, you need a permit to burn on this property. I assume you've cleared this with the proper authorities, followed safety precautions, and all that."

"Zara Smith," came a voice from the swirling dust. "Well, I expected a lot of people, but Lawless didn't mention your name on the list of creeps we would have to fix."

"I didn't know I was broken," Zara said.

"People rarely do," said the shadow as it moved forward into the bright light to reveal Adam Worth, the leader of the Masters. And by his side were his ever-so-indestructible henchmen, Angel Villon and Rex Sykes. "Did you miss us?"

"You?" Keyshawn was holding a handkerchief up to his mouth and nose to keep from breathing in the smoke, but he dropped it as he spoke. "We left you in Prague with Devon, waiting for the Fulbrights."

"I remember the situation, but I don't remember you being there, old man," said Worth. "Let's just say that we aren't ones to stay in one place for too long. But here we are in real time, right? Why dredge up the past when we can talk roasted turkey? You're here looking for something and we came here looking for something, too. The difference is we got here first."

M stayed hidden behind the van, sitting and listening to the ghosts she thought she'd banished and left behind.

"But you don't know what you're looking for," said Zara. "So you set as much as you could on fire."

"You know what I say, Smith. If you can't beat 'em, burn 'em."

M could hear Worth's smug smile in his every word.

"See, no one could find your old roommate, Freeman," explained Worth. "Which gave me and the boys a grand idea. Why not pull her house apart, bit by bit? It was like torture, you know, good for the evil soul. We started in her room, peeled everything away layer by layer. Posters, walls, carpet, floor, subfloor, and so on until we left a hole where her home used to be."

"Did you find what you wanted?" asked Zara.

"Nah," spat Worth. "It felt great, but tearing down the house was a waste of time. Then, today, we get a surprise call from Dr. Lawless. He tells us that, lo and behold, we've been looking in the wrong place all this time. Suggests that we should look in the woods around the house. Sure enough, we found the strangest thing. It seemed so important that we had to destroy it. Thus the bonfire to end all bonfires."

Hidden from view, M stared at the long shadows cast from

the blaze. The more massive shadow slowly inched closer to the others. It had to be Rex Sykes, and there was no mistaking his intentions. Rex wanted to smash.

She took a deep breath and stepped out from her hiding spot. "I feel bad. You went to all this trouble and I didn't even bring marshmallows."

Adam's eyes went wide in the dancing light. "Freeman?" He sounded impressed. "I heard you crawled out from under some rock in nowheresville, but I didn't think you would scatter back here."

"Yeah, you can't go home again, Freeman," cooed Angel. "Didn't anybody ever tell you that?"

"Gentlemen, ladies," started Keyshawn. He looked back and forth between the Lawless thugs and M and Zara. "You've obviously destroyed what you were looking for and we're obviously not going to find what we came for, so perhaps —"

But Rex interrupted him. "You came here looking for a fight."

"No, that was not our intention," denied Keyshawn as he stepped between M and the others.

"Well, old man, you've found one." Rex had a crazed look in his eyes and M could already tell that this situation wasn't going to end well for either side.

Angel leapt first, tackling Zara. They wrestled into the darkness.

Then Rex stomped forward and took a wide swing that connected strongly with Keyshawn's jaw. M could hear

Keyshawn's teeth clack together. He crumbled to his knees immediately like a building being demolished. Keyshawn's shoulders slumped and his head stayed down. Rex prepared to pummel him a second time when Keyshawn suddenly hit Rex's thigh, lower back, and spine in a quick succession that looked like a secret ninja strike. The giant let out a sick-sounding gurgle and hung in the same position as Keyshawn caught his breath.

"You need to stand still and learn some manners." Keyshawn's arms trembled against the ground and barely held his slight frame upright. "Always respect your elders." With that, Keyshawn passed out.

Before M could call to see if he was okay, Adam Worth was facing her. First he swiped the legs out from under her, and M crashed to the forest floor with a thud. Her head hit a stick and snapped it in two. She heard the wood crack and thought for a moment that it was her own neck. Adam leaned over her with his fist locked and loaded, ready to strike. M tried to scramble out from under him, running her hands through the dirt, looking for a weapon but came up empty.

"Should have stayed hidden, Freeman," he said with a miserable smile etched across his face. "This is going to hurt you more than it hurts me."

Thwack!

Zara emerged from the darkness and clocked Adam on the back of the head. M crawled away from the fight toward the car, but Keyshawn's freezing strike was wearing off on Rex. The behemoth kid stuttered forward. He grabbed M's ankles, swung her around like a rolled-up carpet, and tossed her next to the fire. The flames were inches from her face and the heat melted the air around her. As she looked through the fire, M could make out what was burning inside: the escape pod that had once carried her to safety. She rolled over and could see behind the fire for the first time. A train path led out of the blaze and into a tunnel that must have been where she'd ended up during her escape from the Fulbrights months ago.

The sounds of more struggling came from behind her, so M turned to see Rex wrestling with Jules and Evel. It was less of an actual fight and more like Rex playing with two squirming puppies. Her friends only succeeded in slowing him down, but they were never going to defeat him. Seconds later, Rex flicked them both against the van like he was tossing dirty clothes into his hamper.

M stood up slowly to face him, when a strange sensation overtook her. They were being watched. Someone else was there, waiting to attack. Then, within the actual fire, M saw a new shadow rise up like a ghost. Spewing from the fire like a giant spark, a fourth person leapt at M. She cringed away from the flame-covered body, but the stranger was too fast. Suddenly a bright fire consumed her as the attacker's arms wrapped around her. M cried out in pain. Flames licked the back of her neck, stinging her every inch as the smell of her own singed hair filled her nostrils. This is what it felt like to be a thing on fire. Finally emergency measures kicked in and M stopped, dropped, and rolled, but she still couldn't shake this new threat. She wore it like a fiery suit, clinging to her wrists and ankles.

Then all at once the raging heat that was swallowing her ceased. It was replaced with a cooling sensation, like drifting in a lake. As quickly as the battle had started, it was over. Her attacker was gone and everyone else around her, good and evil, were staring back at her instead of fighting each other. Their eyes were wide, as if they, too, didn't know what they'd just witnessed. M was about to stand up when she felt a familiar fabric close in around her from the top of her neck all the way down to her feet.

"My suit?" She studied her arms and her body. Her plain clothes were gone, replaced by a sleek, tight-fitting garb that was almost pitch-black. Then, slowly, a red glow emanated from the suit as lines of circuitry came back to life. M could feel a new energy surging through her. It *was* her Fulbright suit! It had somehow been stashed in the burning escape pod, and sensed her tracker once she was close enough.

"Oh, you guys are in trouble now," Zara warned Adam, Angel, and Rex. "I'd say you should run, but I really want to watch M take you down a peg."

Rex screamed and charged M, but M lifted her magblast and fired a shock wave that connected with Rex and swept him off the ground. The giant was thrust back into a tree that shattered into splinters, knocking him out immediately.

Then she turned to Adam and conjured up a whirlwind of smoke that she held in her hand as if she were a powerful wizard. "Now that I have your attention, tell us what you were looking for, before someone really gets hurt."

"A book," admitted Adam. His face was calm. Too relaxed for someone who had just seen her take out his muscle with a flick of her wrist. "The *Mutus Liber.*"

The mysterious book that Cal had stolen from the British Library (and then stole from them) had come back into M's life in a violent way. "It's not here," said M. "We've got it somewhere safe. Somewhere you'll never find it."

Then, out of the darkness, Angel Villon appeared and flashed a ghostly white burst of light in M's eyes. The brightness blinded her, but she still fired the magblast shot at Adam. She heard the force connect with the forest in a crash of leaves and branches.

"Look out, M!" she heard Jules scream, but it was too late. She felt something wet splash over her magblast hand, followed by a swift kick to her midsection. M clutched her stomach with her left hand and lifted up her right. Fresh paint fumes hit her and she instinctually reeled back from the smell. *Paint beats the magblast,* M remembered from when she locked horns with Zara on the construction scaffolding in New York. *How could Angel and Adam have known that would work?*

M heard more scuffling around her, probably Zara, Jules, and Evel taking on the Lawless kids. Quickly she flipped up the mask that hung behind her like a hooded sweatshirt. It seamlessly clicked into place and the goggles tightened around her eyes and adjusted her vision. A paint can was on the ground with a stream of drops leading back toward the van. She followed the tracks with her eyes only to find Jules and Evel under siege from Angel. M flipped her left wrist so that her suit sleeve stretched out into a black whip and coiled around Angel's leg. He looked down, surprised, as she jerked him away from her friends and dragged him back to her.

Angel pulled a hidden pair of shogun blades out of his backpack and swiped clean through M's whip. The suit snapped back into place around M's left hand, which stung like she'd been slapped by a humongous rubber band. M clutched her hand as Angel jumped to his feet and twirled the blades in a threatening way. "What else do you have in that adorable Fulbright suit?"

Keeping her eyes fixed on him, M flexed her right hand and a sword was constructed out of the suit's programmable matter. The blade looked deathly black against the fire's backdrop. Slowly they paced around each other, foot over foot in the dirt. Keeping their distance, the opponents were searching for the best striking point. Then a tingling sensation flashed from the nape of M's neck and spiked through her entire body. She darted left automatically as Rex lunged from behind her with a sneak attack. Angel also stabbed forward with his knives, but M fought them off with one swing of her sword. Then she formed a battering ram with her left hand and walloped Rex. Still the giant only shrugged off the blow. He was a monster. Knocking him around just seemed to make this kid stronger.

M turned and ran. This wasn't the right time to fight these losers. Keyshawn had been right. They'd beaten M and Zara to the escape pod fair and square, but they'd never known about the yearbook. The fools had probably blown it up when they were playing with matches. Her proof was gone and so was her home. Now all she could save was her friends. M scooped up Keyshawn and threw him over her shoulder thanks to the added strength of her suit. Pacing backward toward the van, she called out, "Jules, Evel, start the car, we're getting out of here."

In front of her, Angel and Rex stalked with their knives and fists drawn. M realized too late that they had formed two points of a triangle around her. She turned to find Adam Worth at the third point, cutting her off from the others. She eased Keyshawn back to the ground.

"Leaving so soon?" Adam held Zara in one fist like a trash bag. She was slumped over but breathing. To Zara's credit, Adam looked pretty roughed up, too. Bruises and welts covered his face. "Dr. Lawless wants to meet with you."

"I'm a little busy right now," said M. The others crept closer and closer.

"But you can make time for old friends, right?" said Adam as he dropped Zara. "Why are you always in such a rush when we're hanging out? If I didn't know any better, I'd think you were trying to ditch us."

"Well, I wouldn't want to be rude," M said, stalling for time. "Maybe if we let the others go, then you and I can go catch up by ourselves, Adam. What do you say?"

"Nah." Adam gave Zara a gentle nudge with his foot and flipped her over onto her back. "We fought hard to catch these little fishies fair and square. It would be a shame to throw them back into the ocean. I'm not a catch-and-release kind of guy. You should know that. What I want, I get. Now you can come willingly or kicking and scream —"

Adam's threats were cut short by a nearly silent *thift*. A surge of blue-white voltage traveled over Adam as he froze with more than fear. He had just been shot by the deep freeze. M whipped around to hear two more blasts connect with their targets, Angel and Rex, who became rooted in place.

"Remember those, M?" asked Foley as he stepped out of the forest. "I know I'll never forget the deep freeze you put me in."

M breathed in the strange smoke of burning metal and forest mulch. "What are you doing here?"

Foley lingered in place and tucked his blond bangs behind his ear. "Madame V was worried. You were taking too long."

"I had things under control," said M as if she had something to prove to the older boy.

Foley surveyed the damage that surrounded M. Zara was

out like a light, and so was Keyshawn, while Jules and Evel were still struggling to start the automatic van. "Sure. You had them eating out of the palm of your hand, didn't you? Tell me, was having them trap you and pound your buddies into submission part of your genius plan?"

M retracted her sword and bent down to check on Keyshawn. "Maybe."

"Devious," joked Foley as he walked to the van and opened the trunk. He pulled out a fire extinguisher and headed to the bonfire. "Nice suit, by the way. Where'd you get it?"

"Keyshawn made it for me at the academy," she answered. As she tested Keyshawn's pulse, she remembered that Foley had been at the academy, too. "You really don't remember anything from your time there?" she asked.

"I really don't," said Foley as he stepped past Rex and Angel. Both of them followed him with their eyes, but they were powerless to move. "Now let's find out what proof you're hiding in your backyard."

Foley pulled out a tiny contraption that looked like an airhorn. "Stay where you are if you like breathing. The chemical used in this extinguisher puts out fires by erasing the oxygen in the air."

An explosion of foam calmed the flames in no time. The smoke cleared to reveal M's escape pod. Foley went to open the latch but stopped short. "Hmmm, this metal is going to be awfully hot. M, would you do the honors? Assuming your supersuit can handle the heat."

Setting Keyshawn's head down again, M walked over and pulled the latch. The door cracked open an inch, but then she pushed it open the rest of the way. The window panel was smashed where the suit had broken through and the rubber seams had turned to an ooey-gooey black liquid inside the lip of the hatch door. Inside, slightly singed and resting on the seat, was a book with a familiar insignia on it. A skull with keys for its mouth stared back at M.

"What do we have here?" asked Foley as he peered over the edge of the charred vehicle, careful not to burn himself.

"A yearbook," whispered M.

"All this for a stroll down memory lane?" asked Foley. "I expected secret plans to the end of the world, not a list of student signatures that say *Have a great summer, dude, see you next year* like ninety different ways."

"It's not that kind of yearbook," said M. "This is special. It's the first yearbook ever for the Lawless School."

"Sounds dated, not dangerous." Foley laughed nervously as he inched closer to the pod. Suddenly there was a sizzle sound and he pulled away, shaking his hand in the air and howling. "AHHHHHH!!!!"

"Are you okay?" asked M.

Foley bounced around and blew air on his hand like he was the big bad wolf. "Yeah, yeah, yeah. I'm fine. Just feel dumb. Now grab your precious book and let's get out of here before anything else goes bloody wrong."

Carrying his hand against his chest, Foley went over to

check on Zara. She slowly came to and hugged him. "Foley? What are you doing here?"

As if on cue, a clapping *kaboom* shook the night. "Oh no," said M as she held the book. "Get in the van now! That came from Madame V's direction!"

CHAPTER 13

THE ANSWER

"You left her *alone*?" yelled Zara as the van careened down the twisting mountain road, threatening to flip over and tumble into the forest at every turn. M gripped the handlebar above the rear-passenger window with one hand and held the Lawless yearbook close with the other as Foley veered around each curve.

"She *told* me to go find —"

"You know better than to leave her alone," Zara interrupted. "What's going on with you, Foley? You left your assignment. That's always when a plan falls apart. You're the one who taught me that!"

Foley only shook his head as he raced on. He had no excuse other than he was following orders. But that wasn't good enough for Zara. She sat battered and beaten in the front seat, but the thought of Foley abandoning his post was evidently what hurt her the most. She refused to look at Foley for the rest of the drive.

"How's Keyshawn doing?" M asked.

He was lying in the last row of seats with his head in Jules's lap. "Okay, I think. His breathing is steady, but he's still unconscious. Rex really knocked him into next week."

"*Uuhhhhhhuuuhhhhh*," came a moan from the trunk of the van.

"Shut up, Rex," said M to the deep-freezed Masters crew who were stacked on top of each other in the back like life-size cardboard cutouts. "We'll see if you have anything smart to say after we make sure that Madame V is safe."

Foley pulled off the road just before coming to the house. The flickering lights of giant red flames danced through the trees.

"It doesn't look good," he admitted.

"Dude, we got Star Wars-ed," said Evel from the backseat. "Like Luke on Tatooine, when he goes to save R2-D2 and the Empire sets fire to his uncle's moisture farm. We're lucky to be alive."

"I don't like being lucky," said M. "I'm going in."

"No!" interjected Foley. "Don't be crazy. There's nothing left in that old house worth risking your life for."

"Madame V is." It was Zara. "I'm coming with you, M. Give us ten minutes and if we're not back, get out of here and don't look back."

The two girls left the van and snuck through the forest to the house.

"That suit lets you see in the dark, right?" asked Zara. "So take a look at the perimeter. Anyone there?"

M flipped on her mask and searched the woods. No one was there. No other heat source except for the burning house. She switched signals to pick up movement, but everything was still. "Clear. I'm going in to find Madame V. The suit will protect me, but you won't be able to follow."

"I'll keep watch," said Zara as the house burned in front of them. The getaway cars were still in place, untouched. Zara paused and swallowed hard before adding, "Be fast and stay safe. And if she's in there, please save her, M. She's all I have left."

M nodded and hit the ground running faster than she'd ever run in her life. She felt the suit carry on even faster, throwing her legs back and forth. Every step felt lighter and lighter as if she were racing through air instead of over the grassy lawn. She braced her arms over her face and smashed through the front door. The sound of the fire enveloped her. It was a symphony of crackling wood and vampire hisses.

Then she saw the place for what it had become. Where there once had been a quaint cabin, now there was only a melted cove of ramshackle rooms bleeding into one another. The floor was warped so she carefully tread on the most sturdy-looking areas, lest she drop through the molten ground into the basement below. The two chairs were charred like elder trees in a forest fire. M remembered how sturdy they had looked just a few hours before, and now how frail they seemed, burned to a crisp.

"Madame V!" she screamed over the roar of the inferno. "Madame Voleur! Where are you?!"

M searched through the house room by room. The bathtub was empty and the bathroom mirror beaded into reflective tears. The kitchen was blazing out of control, while the stove was a blackness that made M's stomach turn. Then she started down what was left of the staircase to the basement. The first step crumbled beneath her, the ground itself disappeared, and M crashed to the basement's concrete floor. Above her the ceiling dazzled like an angry heaven preparing to rain down fire. And there in the corner was a singed body surrounded by the markings of an outward blast. M gagged at the sight. She sat, defeated, and clutched the end of a long scarf, once colorful, now as gray as used charcoal. It turned to ash in her hands and led back to the body. They were too late.

M shimmied out a basement window, crawled a safe distance, and lay on the ground looking up at the stars. Those same uncaring, unaware stars that had watched so much go wrong in her life. Beautiful, but forever distant. "Stay where you are," M whispered to the sky above. "Sometimes I feel like you are the only thing that's certain in my life."

Then she rolled over and saw someone darting away in the shadowy forest. M sprang into action, crossing the field like a lion running down its prey. She caught up easily, tackling the fleeing figure, who dropped a small metal case. The case tumbled away and M's adversary lunged for it, but M snagged the case first.

The person jumped into a battle stance. It was Zara.

"What are you doing?" asked M.

"Protocol," said Zara. "Now give me the box."

"No." M examined the case. It was alloy lined, built to last, and covered with dirt. "You were hiding this. Why?"

"Because it's worth hiding and we're lucky it was still there," Zara answered. "Now give it back."

The two girls stood in opposition to each other as the faint sound of sirens carried over the trees in the distance. Lifting the case, M tried to see through the steel frame, but it wouldn't give up its secret. "Tell me this isn't what I think it is."

Zara pursed her lips.

"Madame Voleur said she destroyed every piece of the death comet!" M squeezed the case and the edges of it cracked but did not break.

Zara jumped forward and screamed, "No! Don't! It's not the comet!"

"I'm going to smash this case into pixie dust no matter what's inside." M pulled back her hood. "Tell me what's in here that's worth saving or it's gone."

"It's something your pal Keyshawn developed. And it's important. So important he didn't tell anyone else about it. Not Madame V, not your mother, only me." Zara eyed the red and blue lights fast approaching through the trees. "He kept telling me that it was the answer."

"The answer to what?" asked M.

"The answer to stopping another black hole," she said. "He knew that the meteorite could fall into the wrong hands again. He's been working on this for a long time."

"And why would he trust you with this and not the others?" Something still didn't feel right to M.

"I don't know," Zara said honestly. "He just said that he knew me and that at the right time I would do the right thing. So here I am. At the right time. Doing the right thing. And you're trying to stop me."

"Is this why you sent me into the house?" asked M.

"No." It was a simple one-word answer, but M could hear the hope in it. Zara held her hand out and M gave her back the case. "Did you find her?"

The scene of charred remains flashed back to M and the truth caught in her throat. A good criminal and a good friend understand that there are times for honesty . . . and there are times when hope needs to win against all odds. And Zara needed a win. "I couldn't find her."

Zara smiled and seemed satisfied with that answer. "See, Freeman? Madame V's too tough to go out like that. Let's get back before we have to talk to those guys."

A fire truck pulled onto the lawn and its passengers leapt into action. M watched the firefighters through the trees, and thought how different her life was from theirs. They were here to put out fires. M was here to start one.

"Come on," said Zara as she slid the case into her back-pack. "We need to get back to the van. And listen, we can't tell anyone about this box. Anyone."

"What box?" M smiled.

"Attagirl, M."

CHAPTER 14

NOWHERE TO RUN

Although the van was off, the engine still rattled out tired pops and metallic ticks as M and Zara returned. They slid open the door as carefully as possible. They didn't want to draw any attention to themselves, especially with the police cars cruising around the scene of the fire.

In the far backseat, Keyshawn was still passed out. His chest rose and fell with every breath, which M took as a good sign, a modest victory in a day filled with defeat.

Foley was in the driver's seat, looking as pale as a ghost. His hands clutched the steering wheel, but he flinched at the click and slide of the side door. "And?"

"The safe house isn't safe anymore," said Zara. "But we're lucky. Madame V got away."

M expected Foley to relax at this good news the same way Zara had, but he didn't. He smiled, but the muscles in his arms stayed tense. "That's good. Where is she?"

"We don't know. Gone," said Zara. "Foley, what orders did she give you after we left?"

"She wanted me to follow you," Foley answered without hesitation. "She didn't trust the old geezer."

"And where'd you get the deep-freeze devices?" asked M. "That's a Lawless weapon."

"The old guy had them at his place," said Foley. "You should grill him about it."

"He's passed out, so you're the best chance we've got of figuring out what happened back at the cabin," said Zara.

"I don't know what happened," he said defensively. "She told me to stay, I stayed. Then she told me to go, so I went. I was following orders. I didn't stop to ask her why!"

"Hey!" Evel cut in. "Can we pick a better place to argue? Preferably far from the police and not next to the scene of a crime while holding three people against their will in our trunk?"

Jules nodded. "I'm with Evel. What's our next move?"

"We wait," said Zara. "Madame V will find us and let us know what to do."

"No!" The franticness in M's voice startled the others, but she couldn't reveal what had really happened to Zara's mentor. "I mean, what if . . . if . . . Madame V were captured? I don't think hiding out and waiting for a communication is our best option. Whoever did this, they want to put a scare in us. They want us to stick our heads in the ground like ostriches so we miss what they're planning. There's got to be others in your group, Zara. Let's reach out to them."

Zara looked back toward where the cabin used to be. A wet smell of mud, rotten wood, and campfires hung in the air. "We're it."

"Wait, excuse me?" said Jules. "I thought you and Madame V were part of some super agency, like Lawless or the Fulbrights? Without anyone else, we're sitting ducks."

Zara shook her head. "M's mother is all we have left. We were spread thin when we had to hide M. After you escaped, word spread. Lawless *and* the Fulbrights found us. Most of the team was captured . . . or worse."

The truth sank in. They were outnumbered and alone. Six kids against the two most secret and powerful societies in the world. In other words, they were toast.

Then M spoke up. "Listen. We're not sitting ducks. And we're not waiting on some trumpet-blaring hero to come save us, because we're the heroes. Foley, we need to find Merlyn."

"Merlyn. Of course." Foley sounded confused hearing the name. "Does . . . he live around here?"

"Yeah, don't you remember?" asked Zara. "You picked him up for the reckoning. You were his guardian. Then you had a run-in with the Fulbrights and we had to pick you up on the way to the drop zone."

Worry lines squirmed across Foley's forehead. He made a sucking sound through his front teeth. "I'm going to be straight with you: The name's not ringing any bells."

"What did they do to you at the academy?" asked Zara.

M leaned over the middle console and tapped something into the van's GPS system. "Here. I did some light reading on Merlyn while I was at Sercy's. That's his address. Now let's go before whoever set that fire puts two and two together and figures out our next move."

"But first we need some fall guys for this fire," said Foley. "And I know who would be the perfect trio to send a message to Fox Lawless. He needs to know that we're not scared of him." Foley pointed to the trunk of the van.

They pulled out Adam, Angel, and Rex, still stiff and immobile from the deep freeze. "Don't get too cozy, boys," she said. "We're going to call in a helpful tip to the cops in fifteen minutes. Good luck."

Then the crew jumped back into the van. Zara hit enter on the GPS and the van started by itself, reversing gently while Foley nursed his burnt hand in the driver's seat without touching the steering wheel. The navigator luckily took them in the opposite direction of the destroyed cabin. M didn't want the others to see how demolished the place had been. Plus she didn't want to give the police any reason to stop them while they drove past. Still, everywhere M looked, guilt was lurking. She felt guilty for not being able to save Madame Voleur. Guilty for lying to Zara. Guilty for dragging Jules, Keyshawn, and Evel into this twisted trap. Outside, the trees lined the unlit street like roadside gawkers watching their getaway van with disapproving eyes.

She leaned back in her seat and ran her fingers through her hair. Everything around her smelled like smoke. She wore the scent like a whisper of disaster. On the seat next to her was the Lawless yearbook. To M, it was less of a book and more of a tombstone. It marked the end of her home. The end of her father. The end of Jones. The end of her time at Lawless and the end of her time at the Fulbright Academy. But it wasn't the end of her mission, because now she had proof that both schools were connected. If this information got out, the Fulbrights and the Lawless grads would revolt against Doe and whatever he was planning.

M picked it up. The fire had done its work. The cover was brown at the edges and pages were stuck together, melted and molded by the sheer destructive temperatures from inside the escape pod. The yellow pages that did survive now curled at the margins and warped into odd folds that bent the kids' faces into strange shapes, so they were barely human-looking. Not that it mattered anymore. This book was so old, none of these people were alive now. She was chasing a ghost through these distorted pages, but she didn't even believe in ghosts.

"Find anything?" asked Foley from the front seat.

"Not yet," admitted M. She watched Foley's eyes in the rearview mirror. He shifted back and forth between watching the road and watching her.

She flipped through the crusted pages looking for the incriminating picture of Jonathan Wild, but she missed it on her first pass. M returned to the front of the book and began again, this time smoothing out the curled edges of each page, looking at the page numbers.

Losing patience, M flipped the book upside down, then held the front and back cover out like a bird's wings and shook them. The inner pages flapped and rustled like they were trying to fly. She cracked the spine, too, and peered into the binding where the pages were glued together.

"Um, Freeman's gone crazy," said Foley.

"I'm looking for any tears or rips, places where someone might have torn a page out," said M. She found a slivered strip of carefully shorn paper. "Zara, you said I was found walking through the woods, right? Who found me?"

"Your mom," said Zara, whipping around in her seat. "She didn't mention an old yearbook, though. Why?"

M slammed the book shut. "I think she might have stolen the only thing that proves John Doe is behind everything."

"But your mom's good, right?" asked Jules from the back. "She's on our side, yeah? I mean, she's your mom."

Her mom had taken on many roles during M's life. Mother. Stranger. Bully. Art historian. Artist. Copy artist. Thief. Criminal. Prisoner. Savior. Betrayer. Liar. Defender. But would she have stolen from her own daughter? "Zara, do you swear you didn't know about this?"

"I swear." Zara's mouth dropped open in a show of shock and concern. It hadn't dawned on her that M's mom might have double-crossed her and Madame V.

"It's okay, Zara," comforted M. "My mom can sneak up on you like that."

An uncomfortable quiet took over the van. Everyone was deep in thought when the GPS navigator broke the silence. "You have arrived at your destination."

The van turned into a driveway that ran up a small hill to a modern-looking house. The roof was flat and jutted out over a row of wall-sized windows that showcased every room in the front of the home. It was like looking into a dollhouse, with the den, dining room, and a library exposed for the world to see. *The best way to pretend you have nothing to hide is to show that you have nothing to hide,* thought M.

"So, how do we play this?" asked Jules. "I mean, these are Lawless parents we're dealing with. They'll probably want M's head on a platter."

"Look at that house," said M. "If we have any chance of winning the Eaves over, then we need to be honest and upfront with them. Let me go first, by myself. I owe Merlyn's parents a long explanation. Maybe after they hear what I have to say, they'll help us."

"And if they don't?" asked Foley.

"Let's burn that bridge when we get to it," said M as she made to step outside.

"Wait," said Zara. "You can't go up there in your suit. You'll scare the dickens out of them."

"You're right," M admitted. The glowing red wires in the suit did add a demonic flare. She slipped the suit off and left it behind, except for her glove, which she stashed in her pocket.

"Should we have a signal, in case things get out of control?" asked Jules.

"I've got my magblast glove, so if I need you, the message will be loud and clear." M left the van and walked up the manicured path to the glass front door. Even gazing directly through the windows, she still had no idea what was waiting for her on the other side.

CHAPTER 15

LEMON SQUARES, TRUTH, AND DARES

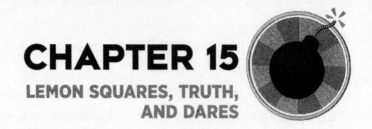

A low-toned bell rang once from inside the house when M pressed the illuminated button by the front door. The sound echoed peacefully and calmed her down. She didn't have much experience meeting her friends' parents. The exception was Calvin Fence — who she supposed was more of an enemy now, actually. Either way, it hadn't gone well. Cal's mom, Ms. Watts, had tried to kill her. His dad, Mr. Fence, had been abducted while on a mission with M. Not the best batting average for meeting friends' families.

But this was a dire situation. Keyshawn needed medical attention, both Lawless and the Fulbrights were after her, and Merlyn was one of the few people on the planet she could trust.

In the window, M could see her disheveled reflection. Her clothes were wrinkled and looked slept in, though still probably a better choice than her battle suit. She tried to tame her hair, but each time she patted it down it sprang back like an umbrella popping open automatically. There were soot smudges on the side of her neck that wouldn't rub off and a nice-size goose egg above her left eye, probably where Adam or Rex had connected during their fight. But she put on a smile and placed her hands behind her in the most unassuming pose she could muster.

From behind the library shelves, a woman emerged wearing a black dress with three-quarter sleeves. Her blond hair bounced airily with each step and her bright red high-heeled shoes clicked as she approached the door. She looked through the glass and gave M a sideways, curious smile before turning the knob.

"Hello?" Her eyes met with M's and then moved past her to the black van parked in her driveway.

"Hello, ma'am, I'm friends with your son, Merlyn. Is he home?" M felt silly asking the question. It was an act of courtesy and social politeness, but gosh-darn-it if she didn't sound like a blast from the past goody-two-shoes.

"He is," confirmed the woman as she stepped aside and invited M inside with a lithe hand gesture. Everything about her was graceful, as if she were completely unbothered by a strange-looking kid showing up on her doorstep unannounced at nine o'clock at night. "I'm Merlyn's mother, Mrs. Eaves. May I have your name?"

"Freeman. M Freeman."

"Of course." The woman showed a polite flash of white teeth that read as both relaxed and threatening. "We've heard so much about you. It's wonderful to finally meet in person. Will your friends be joining us?"

"Respectfully, ma'am, only if it's okay with Merlyn, yourself, and Mr. Eaves," said M.

"Then let's go ask Merlyn, shall we?" Mrs. Eaves eased the door closed and led M deeper into the house. There was a long zipper running down the back of her dress that made M reimagine the woman as a robot, how the metal teeth flowed along her spine and stood out so drastically against the black fabric. The situation felt suddenly dangerous, but M followed along.

Behind the library shelves the home opened up into one large, open room divided only by furniture into a kitchen, a den, and a dining area. A large TV beamed bright colors as two cars raced in a video game across the giant screen. One car swerved sloppily out of control, careening against the walled edges of the racetrack. It held the position of *Last Place* according to the blinking text above its roof.

A low-end rumble shook the floorboards under M's feet. She looked down and was again taken by Mrs. Eaves's red shoes. They clasped tightly around her ankles and had thin heels that were more like weapons than fashion. A *screech* erupted from another set of speakers to M's left, which made her flinch. But then Mrs. Eaves made another smooth hand gesture like a concert conductor quieting an orchestra and miraculously the television volume lowered.

"Mom," complained a shaggy-haired boy who sat cross-legged on a couch with his back to M, "it's not as real with the sound turned down so low."

"Merlyn, you have a guest." His mother nodded in M's direction in a way that at first made M feel like the video game was more important than her. The introduction was more of an apology for ruining her son's night. But when M saw Merlyn's eyes light up, she realized that Mrs. Eaves was being careful and cautious, handling M like an unstable weapon that could do even more damage to her son if not handled delicately.

"M, you're alive!" Merlyn bolted up and gave her a crushing hug. "I knew you must be alive. See, Mom and Dad, I told you."

"You did, son," agreed Mrs. Eaves. "And it looks like you were right, thank heavens."

"Geez, where are my manners? Can I get you anything?" asked Merlyn as he pulled back and held M's shoulders as if to study her and make sure he wasn't dreaming. "We've got water, juice, tea, fruit —"

"I'm fine," M interrupted. "No, thank you, that is."

"Well, Ms. Freeman, to what do we owe this late-night honor?" Merlyn's father rose out of his chair and set his video game remote down on the glass coffee table. He was thin, like Merlyn, with a thick set of glasses, and he wore a T-shirt that read *Have you metadata?* That made M laugh a little. The app didn't fall far from the operating system.

"Sorry about dropping by unannounced, Mr. Eaves," said M. "My friends and I were passing through town and thought it would be rude to not stop and say hello."

"Oh, you should definitely invite them in, dear," pled

Merlyn's mother. "I insist. And you know, I have the perfect treat. Lemon squares. Freshly baked."

In the pristine kitchen, a lone tray stacked with lemon squares sat on the white marble island. Mrs. Eaves walked over and lifted the lid up and pretended to smell the air around them. "I do so love the smell of fresh lemons. And we made more than enough for you and your friends." Then she clamped the lid shut again.

"Mom, lemon squares are great, but this is M here!" said Merlyn. "We've been through . . . well, a lot together. Can you give us a minute to catch up?"

"Sure, honey." His mother's voice trailed down at the end, like her feelings were hurt, but his parents left the room. "We'll be upstairs if you need anything."

"How are you?" asked M once they were alone. "Like after that night." She was introducing a darkness into the room, but she didn't have time to tread lightly.

Merlyn shuddered, just slightly, at her question. "I'm good, you know? I mean, I'm not super into computers anymore. Guess I lost my taste for it. Still like video games, though, even if I'm horrible at them."

"Who doesn't? So . . . what are you doing for school . . ." M began, but Merlyn spoke over her.

"This is a bad idea, coming here, M. Who's in the car?"

"Old friends," M said. "What's going on, Merlyn? Why was coming here a bad idea?"

"Who. Is. In. The. Car. M?" Merlyn's voice was suddenly concerned. He spoke slowly and emphasized every single word.

M took a deep breath. "Keyshawn, for starters, and he's hurt. Zara, of course. Jules. Foley, who's being really weird. And Evel Zoso, Devon's older brother."

"Foley's with you?" Merlyn looked perplexed. "And Keyshawn, didn't he serve us up on a platter to John Doe?"

"It's not over, Merlyn," M insisted. "There's something bigger coming, something world-ending, and we are the only ones who can stop it. If you're in, then we need you. We need you even if you're not in, but I'd rather you join us willingly."

"You need to leave," he said. "I'm not joining you. I'm worthless out in the real world now."

"You're not worthless to me." M paused and saw Merlyn's trembling eyes. There was more than fear in them. There was shame.

"I know that, M," he confessed. "That's why my parents used me in this trap."

"Trap?" M looked around the house again, this time in a different light. It wasn't as much an open living space as it was a room with nowhere to hide. Windows surrounded her, peering out into the black night outside, which meant that anyone outside had a perfect view of her in the well-lit home.

Merlyn shook his head. "I'm sorry, M. My parents and Dr. Lawless, they set this trap for you as soon as I was returned. You walked right into it, and I can't help you now."

"He's right, Ms. Freeman." The sly voice snuck into the room like a foul odor, catching her by surprise. Dr. Lawless stepped down the floating staircase dramatically, which M assumed was the only way he knew how to enter a room. His long red hair was pulled back into a ponytail that wrapped around the shoulder of his black business suit like a snake. He was leaning on a cane in his left hand, though M wasn't certain whether he needed it, or if the cane was another fashion statement . . . or another weapon.

"See, you might have learned a thing or two at my school, but we were studying *you*, too. We've learned your weaknesses . . . like caring about your friends. A gullible trait you apparently share with your late father. Very regrettable, if you ask me. And now here you are to save Merlyn Eaves just as we planned. There's no more running, my dear."

"I'm not running," stated M as she slid her hands into her pockets. "I'm visiting my friend to make sure he's okay."

Dr. Lawless gave a low chuckle. "We both know that's not true. Tell Mr. Eaves about how you've collected the people in the van. Tell him about saving Jules first, about visiting your own house first. Or rather, the hole in the ground where you used to live."

M stared at him coldly but remained silent.

"We're even now, you lousy brat," Lawless continued. "You destroyed my home and I've destroyed yours." He stepped directly in front of M, so close she could hear his leather glove scrunch as he gripped his cane tighter with anger and anticipation. "The only thing Mr. Eaves will be joining this evening is the long list of individuals disappointed in you."

Merlyn paced the floor and held his head with his hands. "You can't just barge in here and ask me to leave with you, M. You can't just ask me to leave my parents, either. They love me, you know."

"They used you as bait to get me here," M reminded him with shock in her voice. "And I'm not asking you to leave your parents. Invite them along. Let them know that I'm out to take down John Doe and everything he stands for. I would think that Lawless here would give that mission a gold star."

The red-haired Fox Lawless sneered with pleasure. "If that's your game, Freeman, then I'll personally join in the efforts to dismantle the Fulbrights."

"I'm not after the Fulbrights," corrected M. "I want John Doe —"

Lawless's smile dropped and he grabbed M by the neck, lifting her off the ground. He gritted his teeth and hissed, "The only way I'll let you near Doe is over *your* dead body."

Struggling, M pulled her gloved fist out of her pocket and brought it down hard. A powerful ripple from her magblast thrust Lawless aside and shattered all the windows on the first floor of the house.

"How's that for a signal, guys?" M coughed as she felt her neck to make sure it was intact. Then she held out her gloved hand to Merlyn. "I'm sorry I wrecked your life, but we need you if we're going to stop Doe. Are you with us?"

Merlyn stumbled backward and fell to the ground, wincing as if he thought M might magblast him, too. "Get out of here!" he screamed. "I can't help you anymore, so just leave before you really hurt someone!"

"Merlyn, wait —" Before M could finish, her left hand was lashed by something cold and metallic. A force jerked her around and M relented, feeling her arm almost detach from its socket. It was Mrs. Eaves, and the zipper from the back of her expensive-looking dress was now a whip digging into M's flesh.

"Sounds like the playdate's over, young lady," she said from halfway down the steps. "You've worn out your welcome."

Foley and Zara flew into the room, crunching over the shards of glass that covered the ground like the debris of a shimmering accident.

"Let her go!" screamed Evel as he ran into the room and reached through the staircase slats from behind, grabbing Mrs. Eaves's ankles and pulling. The attack caught her off guard and her whip uncoiled from M's wrist as she fell to the ground, hard. The walloping sound startled Evel. "Sorry, ma'am!"

But as soon as she landed, Mrs. Eaves lashed her whip back at him, trapping Evel's legs and pulling him down, too. He writhed like a fish caught on a line. But M conjured a magblast that gently shoved Evel out of her grip and to safety.

That's when the others arrived. There were ten of them from all sorts of Lawless School cliques, but these weren't students. These were adults, hardened criminals, who all had an axe to grind with M. They entered through the broken glass windows. *Great,* thought M, *I'm glad I made way for their war-path.* She took aim at the nearest target when Foley reacted first, firing a series of deep-freeze stunners that knocked three of the thugs out immediately. Then Zara launched into Mrs. Eaves while a home alarm went off, triggered by Mr. Eaves, most likely. M magblasted the others, but that merely shoved them back into the forest surrounding the house. It would only buy her a few minutes.

Meanwhile Merlyn scampered off through a door that slammed shut, followed by a second metal door that dropped down like a guillotine, severing M's chances of rescuing her friend.

"Did you really think Merlyn would abandon us?" Dr. Lawless had regained his composure. He stood up and brushed glass from his suit, chuckling. "You have no idea how powerful the Lawless family is."

"You like games, don't you, Lawless?" M asked. "Let's play a game. Truth or dare. You go first."

Lawless began pacing around M. He seemed willing to play along, especially after seeing what her magblast was capable of. "Truth: You knew this was a trap, didn't you?"

"Yes," answered M as she matched his steps, keeping him in front of her at all times. "Truth: You really need that cane, don't you? Someone beat you up?"

"Yes, but you should see the other guy," taunted Lawless. "Truth: You trust everyone in your little group?"

"No, I don't," said M. "Dare: Shake my hand and you'll never see me again."

"It's been a dishonor and misfortune ever meeting you in the first place, Freeman." Lawless spat as he shoved his left hand forward. "Double dare: Shake my hand and you'll wish you'd never met me, either."

M held out her left hand, then used her magblast to pull Lawless right to her. The move surprised the school principal and he instinctively raised his right hand to block her. As soon as he did, M snatched Lawless's glove off his hand and was floored by what she saw.

Lawless's hand was no more than a fleshy stump with four fingers missing. The sight stunned M as strongly as if a lightning bolt had shot through her.

"Four fewer fingers, yes. But four more reasons to hate you, Freeman," snarled Lawless as he unsheathed a blade from his cane and kicked her furiously in the stomach. M flew back as Lawless slashed down with his sword. Luckily, she caught the blade with her own glove.

"You!" she exclaimed as he leaned over her, pushing the blade lower with all of his might. "You were the Fulbright . . . you killed Jones . . . you gave me a shot . . . made me forget . . . everything . . . everything that happened."

"Oh, my dearest." Lawless grinned as he loomed above her. "I'll never know what he sees in you."

"What *who* sees in me?" M felt the tip of the sword inch closer to her own beating chest.

"Our fearless leader, of course," snapped Lawless. "Or don't you know?"

The whites of M's eyes flared and she felt a ripping sensation in her right arm muscle. Without the rest of her suit on, she could not hold the sword back from its target much longer.

"Oh, you *don't* know," said Lawless, in an almost giddy tone. He eased off his sword and M's arm deadened into pins and needles. "Here's one more truth for you to take to the grave: John —"

The stylish house suddenly rattled as if it would shake to pieces. Lawless dropped the sword and clutched his head in agony. But he wasn't alone. M felt it, too. She *heard* it. A low, gnawing tone that made it feel like her brains were being scooped out like ice cream from an almost-empty container. It was ten times worse than the wall of sound she'd suffered through while saving Jules. The ground swelled and shook as if the atoms that made up the entire world were separating to swallow M whole.

And just as everything in her field of vision was going white, a set of oversize earmuffs clasped over her ears and as suddenly as the sickening racket had started, it was silenced. M gazed over the now soundless room. A crowd of panicked faces tried to fight against the inescapable noise that surrounded them like waves crashing over flailing swimmers in a hurricane.

Merlyn, in another set of earmuffs, helped her up and pushed her toward the door.

"I'm not leaving you!" M yelled at him.

But Merlyn shook his head and pointed toward the door again with wholehearted hysteria. Then he held up a scribbled note that read *Go or die!* M paused and grabbed the paper and pen. She wrote two words and held it up. *Find Sercy.* Then M crumpled the note and pulled Merlyn in for a hug one last time, realizing this was possibly the last time she would ever see him. Then she punched him square in the nose.

He flopped backward as his earmuffs flew off his head and skipped across the floor. M marched over, picked them up, found Zara scrunched in the fetal position, and placed the earmuffs on her. Together, the two girls grabbed Foley and Evel, then dragged them back to the van outside.

Zara jumped in the driver's seat and tore off down the driveway. Then, swerving into the road, she rocketed away from Merlyn's house as fast as she possibly could.

The whole time Jules waved her arms and her lips moved frantically, but no sound came out. At least not until M removed her earmuffs. "What happened! What's wrong with Foley and Evel? Where's Merlyn?! M, tell me what's going on!"

The boys were doubled over in the backseat, whimpering and moaning. Even the minute or two that M had suffered through the loudspeakers had rewired her insides and she was still having trouble pulling her pieces back together.

"It was an ambush," M panted, catching her breath. "Dr. Lawless . . . waiting . . . Merlyn . . ."

"Where's Merlyn?" pressed Jules. "We can't leave him there."

Her voice was so loud, M winced in pain. She couldn't imagine what Jules's voice must have sounded like to the others who had been trapped in the sound waves longer.

"I knocked him out," admitted M.

"You what!"

"It was the only way to save him," M said, almost shocked at her own brutal logic. "He risked his life to save us. His mom, his dad, Dr. Lawless, he turned on them to help us escape. I couldn't just leave him there."

"But you *did leave him there*," snapped Jules.

"She left him there as a hero who tried to stop us from escaping," clarified Zara from the front seat. "That bloody nose proves he's on their side. So quit jumping down Freeman's throat. She barely escaped Lawless this time."

The dark shadows in the forest outside were deep and mysterious, but they were nothing compared to the murkiness that M was sorting through right now. Dr. Lawless in a Fulbright costume, working with John Doe — it could mean only one thing. It was unthinkable, irrational, and insane. But when the impossible has been ruled out, no matter how crazy it seems, what's left must be the truth. "The Lawless School and the Fulbrights aren't fighting each other anymore."

"What are you saying?" asked Zara.

"I'm saying that the game has changed. The Lawless School and the Fulbrights are working *together*. And we're the last ones standing in their crosshairs."

CHAPTER 16

THE OCEAN BETWEEN THE WAVES

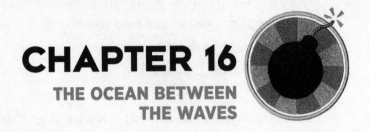

With nowhere else to go, the crew drove to a deserted campground tucked away in the mountains. Zara and Foley worked quickly and robotically, peeling a giant black sticker wrap off the van to reveal a forest green color underneath. They switched the license plates, too. Madame V had trained them for these moments, where a few misdirections could buy them just enough time to escape.

The evasive maneuvers did little to make anyone feel safer, though. A fresh coat of paint was little comfort when the Fulbrights were involved. Add Lawless to the mix and the group would be foolish to ever sleep again.

Evel and Jules helped Keyshawn out of the van and propped him up against a mossy tree. M leaned in and took his pulse. A weak smile spread across his face as he tried to talk, but the poor guy could still barely breathe. His words were little more than wheezes that clung to his lips, hollow and thin.

"It's okay." She tried to put him at ease. "We just need to regroup and refocus. And you need to rest and get better. Think of good things. What about your family? You saved them, right?"

Keyshawn shook his head and it rolled weakly to the side. "I ... made ... my ... choice ... I ... saved ... you ..."

The weight on M's shoulders grew like a hundred-pound anchor. "I'm sorry," she apologized.

"Don't ... get ... sad ..." he breathed. "Get ... even."

M nodded and, as if by her permission, Keyshawn finally closed his eyes and fell asleep. At least, she hoped he was only asleep.

The others in the group joined them, some sitting cross-legged on the ground and others lying down as if they'd just finished a marathon.

As the clouds pulled back and the stars rolled out above them, M knew that she owed the group as much of the truth as she knew. In the quiet of the forest, she described what had happened during the last night in her house. How she'd been summoned there by John Doe, the leader of the Fulbrights. And how she'd watched her friends sit trapped in a deep freeze as they were carried away one by one to the chamber that would steal their skills. By Professor Bandit.

"No way," cried Zara. "That no good, double-dealing ... What was he doing there? How could he —"

But M held up her hand. "It gets worse." She continued her story with her escape from Doe and finding the passageway hidden in the basement, where she was attacked by a masked Fulbright soldier. She fought and bested the soldier only after her friend Jones had been killed. "That Fulbright was Dr. Lawless."

In the moonlight, M watched the color drain from the group's faces. Everyone went silent, processing what they'd just learned.

"So what does this all mean?" asked Evel.

"Here's my theory," started M. "Zara told us a story in France about a man named Jonathan Wild. He was famous in London during the sixteen hundreds for being the head of the police *and* the leader of the criminal underground. And this may seem crazy, but he started both the Lawless School and the Fulbright Academy."

"That's impossible," said Zara. "Wild was executed for his crimes way before these two schools started."

"It gets worse," said M.

"You keep saying that," said Evel. "I hate it when you say that."

"Wild is still alive."

"Now I know you're crazy," said Foley with a laugh. "How does someone alive in the sixteen hundreds survive all the way until now?"

"I don't know," admitted M. "But we all know him by a different name. He's John Doe."

M stretched her legs and stood up. She opened the van door and pulled out the yearbook. "This used to have a picture of Jonathan Wild in it. He was the founder of the Lawless School. In the photo, he looks exactly like John Doe."

"Shut the front door!" said Jules as she grabbed the yearbook to study it.

"And you're telling us this now?!" Zara's whisper barely contained her fury. She marched over and pointed her finger at M, almost touching her nose. "*You* knew *this* the whole time and you're telling us now!"

"I wanted proof," said M. She snapped a small branch off a tree. The crack nearly made the others jump out of their skin. She whiffed the stick through the air like a sword as she paced around the outside of the circle. "Without that missing page, no one's going to believe me."

"I would have believed you," said Jules. "You know that, right?"

M smiled slightly at hearing that from her friend. "I let you down again, Jules. This is the last time I do that."

Jules extended her hand to M, almost like they were back in the Box the first time they'd met, and M took it.

"Okay, super-happy-fun-time is over," said Zara. "I hate to be the bearer of bad news, but if what M says is true then we're probably at the top of the most wanted list for both groups. Madame V is in the wind and we have nowhere else to turn."

"Zara's right." M scribbled lines absentmindedly in the dirt with the branch. "Lawless can tell the underworld that I attacked him and technically he'd be right. Doe can tell the Fulbrights that I attacked him and technically he'd be right. That's the only part that people will hear and believe."

Another moment went by and the woods began their nighttime banter. Soft rustling in the underbrush, branches lifting with the gentle hush of waving leaves. It was all background music on the sinking ship that M and her friends were struggling to keep afloat.

Then Evel spoke up. "What if there were a group of people who didn't like either the Fulbrights or the Lawless School?"

"That's what Madame V is," Zara told him. "If I could just get in touch with her . . ."

"No." M's voice was little more than a whisper.

Foley moved forward. "What's going on, M? Do you have any other secrets we should know? You've been steering Zara away from Madame Voleur all night. You wouldn't let us try to find her at the cabin. And now you won't even let Zara mention her name without shutting her down. What happened to her back there?"

Zara joined Foley's side. "Yeah, M. You obviously have trust issues. Look, we're your friends . . . sort of . . . but we're the only friends you've got right now. What's going on?"

M held her breath and exhaled. "I lied." Her hands shook and her throat went dry. The words felt like bile in her stomach.

Zara stepped swiftly up to M, like a rattlesnake uncoiling to strike. "You lied about what? And think real hard about what you say next."

"Madame V . . . she was . . . in the fire." It was all M could force out. The rest of her words choked somewhere in her chest, her voice caught between her heart and her lips. The girls stared at each other. It was the first time M could remember silence settling between them.

Then Zara shoved M. Hard. M fell to the ground, and Zara leaned over her. She was fighting back tears and her mouth turned down into an ugly sneer. "Now I know why your mother left you." Then Zara marched off into the thick trees that rose all around them. Five steps in and she had disappeared.

"Zara!" M cried out before Foley held up his hand to block her.

"Let her go," he said angrily. "You've done enough damage for one night. You can't keep lying to your friends. We don't stand a chance if we can't be honest with one another."

"But how could I tell her something like that?" asked M.

"It's Zara. You just tell her," Jules chimed in. "She's the toughest person I know. But lying to her and then surprising her with the truth later probably made the truth hurt that much more. You gave her hope, M. Then you took it away."

M wondered if hope really was so dangerous. She'd held on to hope so many times in her life. Hope that she'd save her mother from the Fulbrights. Hope that her father may be still alive. Hope that she held the key to solving whatever mystery tied the moon rocks, a meteorite, and the *Mutus Liber* together. But right now, all of that hope had fled into the woods with Zara.

Evel stepped into the group circle again. "As I was trying to say, you know someone else who hates both the Fulbrights and Lawless. Ronin, like me. We were rejected and made invisible. We were kept under constant surveillance, sent away from our families, and told that we were worthless by the groups that ruined our lives. We wanted to rebel, but we've never known how. You saw how the Fulbrights attacked us. Now we have a chance to strike back. Let us help."

Jules nodded. "'The enemy of my enemy is my friend.' It could work, M."

"We have resources, you've seen that," continued Evel, as he became more excited about the idea. "I have the finances. Sercy can be our digital eyes, ears, and voice."

"I don't like it." Foley had a look of scorn on his face.

"Why not?" M asked.

"There's a reason people become Ronin. Am I the only one who remembers that? They couldn't cut it at either school. They're not special like us; they're average at best. So why in the world would we want to put together an army of outcasts and losers?"

M had never heard Foley sound so negative before. "Yeah, but Foley, welcome to the club. We're outcasts and losers." She waved her hands around to show him. "Jules is a plain old kid. Evel flunked out of the Fulbright program. I've basically been kicked out of both schools. And maybe it's hard for you to see this in your new life, but neither the Masters nor Dr. Lawless seemed especially pleased to see you alive and on our side."

Foley snatched the stick from M's hand and broke it over his knee. "You know what that is? That's exactly what the

Fulbrights are going to do to us if we walk into a war with Ronins on our side. That snap you heard, it wasn't a stick. It was your spine."

"Well, at least she's not spineless," said Jules. "Like some people here."

Foley growled in frustration, spun, and threw the sticks into the forest. He ran his fingers through his hair, then breathed deeply to calm down. "It's not that I'm spineless, okay? But I am trying to keep us alive. There has to be another plan, a better plan. What if we found your mother, M? She'd know what to do next, right? And that would fall into Madame Voleur's original operation that we were already working toward, yeah?"

"We're not the only people looking for my mother," said M. "You saw what just happened when we tried to save Merlyn. And no offense to him, but finding my mother won't be as easy as driving to her house. What happened to Madame V should only drive my mother deeper underground. She's going to vanish in a way none of us can track."

"How do you know that?" asked Foley. "Seems like you barely knew your mother at all."

"I know it because that's what I'd do." M stepped right up to Foley. Their noses almost touched, but there was nothing tender about the moment. She could almost feel the static bouncing back and forth between them. "She's turned into a drop in the ocean and you want to find her in the waves. Good luck. She'll slip through your fingers and evaporate into the air before you know how close you were to her. So no, we're not going to just pick up and look for her. She'll find us when she's ready."

M moved to the edge of the woods and stared in the direction that Zara had drifted. "If you really want to help, go find Zara. She needs a friend right now."

Foley breezed past M in a huff, nudging her shoulder along the way. And he had every right to be upset. M had already witnessed what the Ronin were willing to do to not be Ronin anymore. But they had axes to grind . . . and M had a feeling that she would need some axes on her side sooner rather than later. "Evel, get in touch with Sercy. Fill her in on what's happened and have her reach out to Merlyn. He deserves to be part of this, too. Then tell her we need to get a message out to all Ronin."

Evel made for the van to use the computer but stopped short. "What's the message?"

"That we're at war."

As Evel ran to make the call, Keyshawn coughed and raised his arm to get M's attention. "It's . . . not . . . right."

M kneeled down next to him. "What's not right?"

"Any of it," he answered slowly. Keyshawn struggled to speak and his voice was little more than a whisper. M leaned close to listen. "John Doe is devious and cold-blooded in his schemes. He's toying with us. If he wanted you gone, then you'd be gone."

The words were made of steel and pierced M's confidence like a knife.

Keyshawn continued. "Which means we *do* have something he wants. The answer? Did Zara retrieve the answer from the safe house?"

"Yes," M said. "But what is it?"

Keyshawn's head flopped forward and then he pulled it back up, smacking against the tree trunk. He sucked in air through his teeth as if he were in serious pain. "Do you remember the Chaucer book you found in my lab?"

"How could I forget that clunker?" M's laugh made Keyshawn grin. The giant book had been about Chaucer's obsession with a tool called an astrolabe.

"You need to find the . . . Chaucer . . ."

"The what?" asked M.

"It's part of his plan," whispered Keyshawn. "Part of the answer. The poison is the cure."

M shook her head and steadied Keyshawn's shaking hands with her own. "I'm sorry, but you're not making sense. Tell me again, what am I looking for?"

"The moon wasn't always the moon. The earth wasn't always the earth. Time is man-made, but we don't understand it. Time changes, time passes, time waits for no one. And then your time is up." Keyshawn was rambling now, incoherent sentences spilling out of his mouth. His eyes unfocused and stared beyond M into the shadows behind her. This was more than

Rex's knockout punch. Something else was happening to Keyshawn. And it was shutting him down.

M checked his pulse again, and his heart was racing. "Jules! Get Zara and Foley. Keyshawn's not doing well. I think it's bad."

Jules bolted into the woods before M could even finish.

"Stay with me, Keyshawn." M tried to hold his focus. "Tell me more about this Chaucer."

"Stars, course, can't, tell, Chaucer, pen, entire." Spittle was foaming around the corners of Keyshawn's lips as his body went into shock. His arms jerked and spasmed while his legs twitched in soft kicks like dying bugs that don't know they are dead yet.

"No, no, no," comforted M. "You don't get to leave me twice, Keyshawn. Just wait, Zara will be here and she'll know what to do."

Evel ran over to M's side with a bottle of water. "Is he okay? I mean, he doesn't look good."

"Chaucer," Keyshawn muttered.

"He's good," lied M. She didn't need Evel to break down, too. "He's going to be okay. Did you get ahold of Sercy?"

"Yeah, the message was heard loud and clear," said Evel. "It should be in every encrypted in-box by tonight. A call to arms by M Freeman — that's going to cause a stir."

"Don't want to cause a stir," said M. "I want to stop one from happening."

Evel opened the bottle and poured a drip of water into the cap. Then he held it up to Keyshawn's parched lips for the old man to take a sip. "So I guess this is the calm before the storm?"

"There's nothing calm about this," said M. "This is just the open sea and we're adrift. Like the ocean between the waves. Hopefully we're building a seaworthy ship."

Suddenly the sound of underbrush being kicked and trampled erupted around them. They looked up in alarm only to find Jules, breathless, scurrying out of the forest and tripping along the way.

"No . . . no sign of those two," she wheezed as she bent over and placed her hands on her knees.

Then, quietly, a set of red lights lit up the world around them and cast Keyshawn in a plastic glow. M turned in time to see the van's brake lights blink and hear the vehicle roar to life. She leapt up and ran over to the driver's-side door, where the shadowy outline of Zara stared back at her with Foley in the passenger seat. M grabbed the door handle and tugged, but it was locked.

"Don't, Zara!" she pleaded. "Don't do this, we need you. I need you."

The window rolled down a crack as Zara glanced at her, separated by a sheet of bulletproof glass. "Sorry, Freeman, this is where we part ways. I trusted Madame V, and she told me to trust you. Now she's gone and you lied to me. That's not what team leaders do. So I'm pulling rank."

"When was I the leader?" begged M. "Please get out of the car. We need to talk about this."

"Talk is cheap," taunted Foley. "See you at the end of the world."

The rear tires of the van skidded on the dirt and peeled out, sending clouds of dust through the campground. Evel and Jules covered their faces, but they still practically hacked up their lungs. M fell to the side of the path and watched as her hopes drifted into the distance, a set of taillights growing smaller and smaller and smaller until they were gone. She'd lost almost everything. In fact, she could just barely catch her own breath.

CHAPTER 17
BLIND SIGHTED

"At least they left your suit," said Jules.

M stopped in the middle of picking up the essentials that Zara and Foley had left for them and shot a glance at Jules. "I'd hardly call two bottles of water, a compass, and my suit a silver lining. We're still stranded in the middle of nowhere and we've lost the two most important members of our team."

The clouds rolled back in as the choir of the night buzzed, clicked, and rustled to life again. M flipped open the compass, looked at it, then flipped it shut and handed it to Jules. "You're the guidance counselor. Which way can we head that doesn't lead to our doom?"

"I don't think Zara and Foley were the most important," Evel said quietly.

"Excuse me?" M put her fist up to her chin in a mock-deep-thought pose. "Hmmm, let me see, Zara almost certainly knows more about the plan that's unfolding than we do, and she might just know how to contact my mom. And Foley is a heavily trained Lawless student who survived a close encounter with John Doe. How could they not be important?"

"Because they're not you," said Evel more forcefully. "And they're not Jules and they're not Keyshawn and they're not me. We're the only ones that are important now because we're the only ones here. I've spent my entire life being told that I wasn't important, that I wasn't living up to expectations. Well, look at me now. I just ordered a call to arms to take down the craziest people in the world. Jules stayed by your side even though you called her a completely average kid . . . which you're not, by the way," he added, turning to her.

Jules smiled and her teeth almost beamed in the night. "He's right, M. Listen, you said it yourself. Your mother will be found when she wants to be found. And the only side Foley wants to fight for seems to be whatever side Zara's on. He wasn't prepared to play nice with the Ronin, and we need the Ronin on our side."

"I handled things wrong, didn't I?" M asked.

"It's not the first time you've messed things up," teased Jules. "Probably won't be the last, either. But that's why I stick around. Don't want to miss what happens next."

"Plus, if Lawless is looking for a group of kids in a van, they'll never find us now." Evel smiled. "I'd say things are looking up."

"Isn't it cute when he tries to be optimistic?" snickered Jules.

M stared them down as the two friends exchanged glances and tried to hold back their laughter. "You are both very odd people with a poor grasp of what makes a positive situation.

But I'm glad you're here with me. Now, if only they'd left us a phone, we'd be in business."

"We could always night gaze," suggested Evel. "I hear it does wonders to clear the head. Isn't that comet supposed to be visible to the naked eye this week? The reports say it's going to pass pretty close, like right between Earth and the —"

"Your suit!" Jules interrupted. She pointed to Keyshawn, who still lay against the tree, drooping like a toy animal with the stuffing knocked out of it. "There's a link through the suit Keyshawn built. Use it! Call Sercy and let her know we need a lift."

"Duh," said M. "Jules, you're a genius!"

She unrolled the suit and put it on. The back opening clasped together as M pulled the mask down. Again the suit's familiar fabric tugged and settled into place all over her like an extra layer of muscles molding to the outside of her skin. The sensation was still so strange that M wasn't sure if she'd ever get used to it. It was comforting, supportive, and imprisoning all at once. As the power surged through the wires, M realized that she had no idea how to use the suit to call anybody. Merlyn had always been a fawning fan of Keyshawn's suit and would talk for hours about the interface and how user-friendly it was. *It practically knows what you want it to do before you realize you've asked it to.* As Merlyn's voice echoed in her memory, M tapped the side of her mask, hoping to spark an obvious answer. But she wasn't connected to an operator. Instead a video began playing through the mask's goggles.

M watched as lights whipped by overhead, seen through a murky shade, like a glass window. Then the audio kicked in and M could suddenly hear deep, frantic gasps. The effect was startling. A hand reached into the frame and pressed against the window. It was *her* hand, wrapped in coiled wires that glowed red.

The suit! It had recorded her time trapped in the escape pod on that fateful night. M listened and watched as the old M was stripped of her memories. Then with a sudden jolt the escape pod stopped moving, and it nearly made her lose her balance as she watched. The recorded breathing steadied and M found herself matching the audio of her own breaths now. It calmed her.

"What's going on, M?" asked Jules. "Are you all right?"

"Yeah, there's a video," she explained, "playing through the mask. It looks like a video of the night I escaped from Doe. Only now I'm watching everything that happened after I blacked out."

Through her mask M watched the recorded shadows of tree branches wave above her like witches conjuring up a spell. The sound of her breathing had relaxed, and it was the only sound . . . until there was a *click*, and a crack of light in the shape of a door appeared. The hatch was opening. An arm reached in and pulled up M's limp body. The view tipped and tumbled, and the forest ground came into view, along with a set of feet in dress shoes.

"Well, you weren't supposed to be alone," a man's hushed voice said. "And what's this?" M could hear the stranger searching through the pod. "A yearbook? *Tsk, tsk.* Your father was supposed to have destroyed this little piece of evidence."

The voice, she'd heard it before. It was the same hurried voice from the video the Fulbrights had showed her. The one of her father in the photo booth, leaving her a message while a voice warned him that people were on their way.

This man had been a trusted accomplice of her father's. But who was he?

There was a sound of pages being turned, and then a gentle ripping. He was the one who'd removed the missing page. The tearing sounded slow and unearthly in the recording, like the sky itself was being slit apart and something more sinister would be revealed. "I'll keep this safe. They find this on you, young M, and they'll kill you on the spot. But then your father never was one for thinking about the consequences his actions would have on the rest of us."

The stranger finally rolled M over and stared directly into the camera. It was Professor Bandit. "Oh, the things we do for our dear deceased friends." His colorful eyes swelled like alien storm clouds, gazing back at M as if he were right there in front of her, standing next to Jules and Evel in the same upstate New York night. "Can't have this tech falling into the wrong hands. I'll leave the suit here for you, in the pod. Bandit's honor. And when you find it, heaven help the poor fools who get in your way." Then the feed ended and the mask went black.

M struggled to see anything more, but the video was over. Slowly, the dark night of the present returned, washed out and blurry at first, but then forming into solid shapes. Jules and Evel were huddled around Keyshawn. Beyond them there was something else moving in the forest. She tried to track it, but the mask kept the intruder fuzzy, like walking fog.

"Your mask won't work on me," the intruder said. "Take it off. We don't have time for games."

M ripped back the mask as the real Professor Bandit stepped forward. Jules and Evel scattered away in a panic. Bandit bent over Keyshawn and gave his shoulder a small pat of approval. "He kept you alive this far; that bodes well."

"What do you want?" Jules demanded from a safe distance. "Come to cash in on the bounty?"

"Like I need blood money, Ms. Byrd." Bandit smoothed his suit and refused to look in her direction. "I've saved you once already. A repeat performance comes at a hefty price for all involved. Much more than what Lawless would pay me for your hides."

"He's here to help," said M.

"But he was at your house with John Doe," said Jules, confused. "He locked me in that casket. He's a traitor! Little more than a pallbearer at old Jules's funeral."

"No," M disagreed. "He was punching us in the face, just like I punched Merlyn. He did it to save our lives."

"Technically that was to save everyone-on-Earth's lives," Bandit corrected. "But Ms. Byrd gets points for having a good memory. We weren't sure exactly what Doe's experiment would do."

"Where's Doe now?" demanded M.

"You're in no position to dictate any orders to me, Ms. Freeman." Bandit's eyes flared red, but his stance remained relaxed. "If I knew where he was, of course I'd tell you. But I rather had my hands full after your shenanigans that night."

"Doe sent you out to find me," said M, "but you were working for someone else."

"Ah, you want to hear me admit it, do you?" Bandit nodded. "Your father made me promise, years ago, to watch over you if our paths should cross. And the safest thing for both of us would have been to have you expelled from Lawless, but that didn't take. Now we find ourselves in the deep, dark forest."

He motioned to the group. "Remember. You are the fugitives." Then he motioned to himself. "I am still the big baddie."

"Don't believe him, M," said Jules. "He's got a trick up his sleeve."

"I'm sure he does, but he's telling the truth about my father," said M. "I saw it with my own eyes. My suit has a camera ... somewhere. It taped the night everything went wrong, and I just watched the footage of Bandit stashing my suit. What did you do after that?"

"Set you on your merry way, of course. If I had found you, well, I wouldn't be here chasing you now." Bandit's logic was dizzying, but M had spent a year with him as a teacher. His language was his best defense. Words that spiraled until the conversation didn't even know what it was about.

"You ripped a page out of the Lawless yearbook," M noted. "Why?"

"I can't have the Lawless School learn the truth about John Doe, can I?" Bandit's smirk shone even in the darkness. "The truth was never part of the deal. Just the living, keeping you alive."

"Then are you here to save us?" asked Evel.

"Evel Zoso, how surprising. Does your sweet little sister know that you're hanging around with the wrong crowd?" Bandit rubbed his pointer fingers together in a *tsk-tsk-tsk* motion before bringing them both up to his lips. "*Shhhhhhhhh.* Your secret is safe with me."

"Quit scaring the rookie, Bandit, and get to the point," said M. "We're burning precious moonlight."

Blllleeerrrp. Bandit, any sign of the targets?

Bandit was wearing a communicator on his wrist. He brought his finger up to his lips, motioning for everyone to keep quiet. Then he spoke into his communicator. "No van here. Moving to the next location."

He looked back up at the kids, who were frozen with fear. "What? There isn't a van here...I didn't technically lie to those fools."

"But you were sent out here to hunt us, weren't you?" said Jules.

"You didn't think I was here out of the kindness of my heart?" Bandit laughed. "You should have guessed by now that I have no heart, only obligations."

"Just help us already, please," said M.

Bandit pulled out a phone and tossed it to Jules.

"What's this for?" she asked.

"That, my dear ex-students — and you, Evel — is called a *phone*," Bandit said with a heavy dose of sarcasm before getting serious again. "It's untraceable. Use it wisely." Then he turned and walked into the woods.

"That's it?" M pressed. "That's your best knight-in-shining-armor effort?"

Bandit stopped and turned his head slightly over his shoulder, giving the others a view of his sharp facial features silhouetted in shadow. "Don't be confused by any help I've provided you. I am not on your side, Ms. Freeman."

"Then whose side are you on?" asked Jules.

"I'm on my own side, of course," he said. "If that is all, I still have a black van to find. Remember, you don't have to go home, but you can't stay here. Maybe there's another museum in your future?" With that, he walked out of sight.

"What was he talking about?" asked Jules. "A museum?"

"I have no idea," admitted M. "Bandit's a wild card."

Jules handed Evel the phone. "I guess you should call your friend, then."

Evel turned it on and dialed Sercy's number but was met

with empty air when he put the phone to his ear. He tried a second time, but the phone still didn't work. "No good. This thing must be a dud. Your not-friend is playing with us."

M's first instinct was to run and track down Bandit. How dare he play with them like this? For all they knew, he could have handed them a bomb and they'd just activated it themselves! The muscles in her arms and legs burned, ready to leap forward, but Jules stopped her.

"Wait, let me see the phone." She flicked through to the settings and smiled. "It's an international phone. It looks British. You need to dial internationally to call a US number."

"Weird," said Evel. "Wonder why he wouldn't just give us a regular phone?"

"Jules, you're a genius!" said M. "Evel, call Sercy. Tell her we need to get Keyshawn to a hospital first. Then we need to get to London. Fast."

CHAPTER 18
WOBBLY BRIDGE

The London skyline spoke to M, but it didn't have anything good to say. Standing on the Millennium Bridge, she felt the world moving all around her. The clouds in the sky, taxis, cars, pedestrians, bikes, dog walkers, even the muddy waters flowing underneath her — London was on the move, but she was stuck in a different time. This was the city where she'd become a true criminal. This was the city where she'd been deceived by her mother, by Cal, and by Cal's mother, Ms. Watts. The city that looked exactly the same, like nothing had changed. But it had. Everything had changed. *No thanks for the memories.*

Evel and Jules leaned over the bridge's wide-winged suspension wires that opened up like the palm of a giant's hand.

"What now?" asked Evel. He looked cagey, as if London were a trap he'd walked right into.

"We wait," said M. "According to Sercy and Merlyn, our contact will meet us here on the bridge. Better to connect in an open, public area than a dimly lit back alley. Whoever we're meeting was smart to choose this location."

"Smart, maybe, but I don't like hanging out for too long in one place," said Jules. "Maybe it's my circus blood."

"Or maybe it's your spider sense," said M. "I don't think you're wrong to worry, but Evel's bringing too much attention our way. He looks like he suspects every person that walks by of being a secret agent."

"And how do you know they're not?" Evel stared down a tour group. Their guide held up a tall baton with a stuffed panda at the end. The stuffed animal had seen better days. Its eyes were gone and its fuzzy fur was matted into clumps from months of rain-soaked trips between St. Paul's Cathedral and the Tate Modern Museum.

"Because they're all staring back at you," answered M. "And probably a little freaked out that some random kid on a bridge is trying to burn a hole through them with his eyes. You need to relax."

"I knew I should have stayed back in the States with Sercy," Evel said nervously. "I'm not built like you guys."

"Sure you are," said Jules. "Two arms, two legs, one brain that's telling you to run as far away from this situation as possible."

"You mean, you're nervous, too?" Evel's death grip on the railing loosened.

"Definitely," said Jules. "M?"

"If you're not scared, you're not paying attention," M said as she casually flipped her hair in the wind to study the crowd.

"These people here aren't scared. They're just living their lives, seeing the sights. Honestly, I'd rather be them."

Another tour group shuffled through. That made five. By her calculations, each group took about five minutes to cross the bridge. Which meant their contact was almost a half hour late. M knew they couldn't afford to wait much longer. There were cameras everywhere in London. Cameras with facial recognition software and a million digital back doors that Lawless and Fulbright hackers could enter at will to conduct their own manhunt on the British government's dime.

"Five more minutes and then we're on our own," said M.

As the crowd opened up, Jules spotted someone running from the other side of the bridge. The kid had a backpack and shaggy hair. He stumbled several times, almost tripping even though there was nothing in his way. "This guy's in a hurry."

"Jules, why does this kid look familiar?" M asked warily. He was awkward, he was struggling, and worst of all he was late. Not a great start to uncovering and stopping John Doe's master plan.

"Because we know him!" said Jules. She ran over and gave Ben Downing a huge hug.

"Sorry, sorry, sorry," Ben said. He looked exasperated, sucking in air and pulling at his sweat-soaked shirt. Gone was his trim haircut and soldier's build. Civilian life had softened him up — it looked like he'd had one too many trips to the fish and chips shop.

"Someone's chasing you, aren't they?" Evel asked with distress. "You doubled back, took a different route, lost them for a while, but now they've found us."

"No," exhaled Ben. "No, I just got really, really lost. This city is *massive*."

M put her arm on Ben's shoulder. "I'd ask if this was your first time in the city, but I know it's not. It's good to see you again, direct."

"It's good to be seen," he said. "But it's not good to be seen too much. Follow me. I know a great place to eat around here."

Ben started walking toward the Tate Modern, then stopped, circled around, and headed in the opposite direction. "Blast, it's that way. I'm a right mess, all turned around like the A23."

The others stared at him blankly.

"Oh, yes, you're all Americans," said Ben. "The A23 is a road that runs through . . . ah, never mind. This is the way. Let's go."

Evel looked at M. "This is our contact?"

"Yep," she replied. "Don't worry, he's always been bad with directions. He was a Fulbright, after all."

"What's his story?" Evel asked.

"My story," Ben said as he wheeled around, "is basically this: joined up with the Fulbrights, met M after two years of service, led her in a special task force made of Lawless students to uncover a missing book, and was promptly double-crossed by John Doe and the Fulbright Academy that I had sworn to serve. Dishonorable discharge. What've you done recently, pip-squeak?"

"Relax, Ben," said Jules. "Evel's cool."

"I don't do cool," sniped Ben.

"Without Evel we wouldn't have our link to the Ronin," explained M.

"Is that who Merlyn is working with?" asked Ben. "I hate to say it, but it was good to see his face again. Thought Doe might have melted it off. When he told me what happened in those chambers..." Ben's voice drifted off as he let out a shudder. "Sorry, Jules."

"I'm getting used to it," she said with a shrug.

On foot, the streets of London spun out in a million nooks and crannies. Turn after turn, M began to feel like she was back in the Fulbright Academy's maze of hallways. But there was a sky above her, the air was crisp, and the stone buildings that had survived for centuries surrounded them like history they could touch. Gradually the streets became narrower and narrower until they could physically reach out and touch the walls on either side. M traced the smooth stones and felt the vibration of the city.

"It's buzzing," she said to Ben.

"Yeah, it's the tube, beneath us." He motioned to a sign that marked a London Underground station entrance. "It's like a dragon under the city, isn't it? The beast lumbers past and the day goes on like everything's normal."

"But what happens when the knight comes?" joked Evel.

"People go home," answered Ben. "Most trains stop running at midnight."

"No, it was a joke," explained Evel. "What happens when the knight comes, like K-N-I-G-H-T."

Jules snickered. "Don't give up your day job, Evel."

"I don't know what you guys are talking about," said M. "That joke *slayed*!"

The group erupted in a fit of giggles and M smiled brightly. The joke was dumb, but they needed to laugh. Evel already looked calmer, and just for a moment, Jules seemed like her old self again.

"This is the place." Ben opened a plain red door and ushered the others inside. Most of the chairs were still upturned on the tables and a woman was mopping the floor. She was older and looked sloppy with the mop, like she was in a hurry to get the place opened.

"Any seat you want, loves," she said and motioned to the room. "A bit behind today, but the place is open. Looks like it's all yours, too."

"Cheers," said Ben as he took a chair down from the table in the middle of the room.

It was a coffeehouse by day and a pub by night from the looks of the room. The furniture was made of heavy wood and the walls were covered in green wallpaper with a floral print that roped all the way up to the white ceiling. There was a bar with stools in front and mirrors on the wall behind it. A few cans of paint sat on top of the bar, their lids cracked open. M could smell the slight odor of paint fumes, but she couldn't see what had been painted. In the mirror, she watched the waitress's reflection pass through a swinging doorway into the kitchen carrying the bucket of dirty water.

"So, let's get down to business," said Ben. "Merlyn caught me up on your lives, but I don't know what brings you to London."

"Neither do we," confessed Jules. "This is all based on a hunch M had when the cell phone that —"

M interrupted her before Jules could say Bandit's name. "The cell phone that we stole off a Fulbright. It had a British number, and I thought it would be worth a visit. So how did Merlyn find you?"

"Me?" Ben pointed to himself. "He didn't. Some girl named Sercy did. And when she rang the alarm, I came to help."

Jules coughed and cleared her throat as Ben finished talking.

"You okay?" he asked.

"Yeah, it's just dusty in here. I'll order a glass of water when the waitress comes back." She grabbed a paper napkin from the bin on the table and blew her nose. At the same time, she looked off to her right, where the waitress had been cleaning up.

"How'd you find this place?" asked Evel. "It's so . . . British."

"Is it?" Ben's eyes traced the space. "Looks normal to me."

"Of course it does, you're British," said Evel.

"How'd you find this place today?" M repeated innocently. "There were a lot of turns we made getting here and you seemed to be tracking it like a hunter. We must have passed fifty other shops that we could have stopped in."

"Can I take your order?" The waitress appeared at the table with a small notebook in one hand and a pitcher of water in the other. She placed the water on the table and pulled four cups out of her apron. "Today's specials are pork pie, steak and kidney pie, and black pudding that's to die for."

"We'll need a few to look at the menu, love," chimed Ben before exchanging a smile with the waitress. Then he poured water for each of them. Evel took a deep gulp as soon as his cup was filled.

"Whoa, thirsty, huh?" Ben refilled Evel's cup. "So seriously, what's in London? You're not the only ones in town, I hear."

"Really?" asked M.

"Word is something's going to go missing soon," said Ben, and he tapped the table. "I may not be in the game anymore, but I keep my eyes and ears trained for oddities."

Jules coughed again and grabbed a second napkin. This time M followed her eyes. The tile floor was a total mess of grungy footprints from the night before. All except for the one area where the waitress had been mopping something up. Small shards of glass lay underneath a nearby table, untouched, right next to the cleaned area. Either that waitress was really bad at her job or . . . "Ben, can you tell me what happened that night with John Doe?"

"I'd rather not," said Ben. "It's a lot to relive, you know."

M let his answer hang in the room. She knew that sometimes the best way to get someone talking was simply to wait.

"I just, you know, saw an opening, had a chance to get out of there, and I didn't even know what was going on because I think my mind had shimmied off. Next thing I know, I'm back in Brighton, Mum and Dad putting a washcloth to my forehead, telling me they'll do their best to fix it."

"Fix what?" asked Jules.

"Fix it with Doe and the Fulbrights." He said it in a hushed whisper, crowding over the table as if there were microphones hidden everywhere.

"And how's that going for you?" M baited him.

Ben glared at her, then smiled. It was a different smile than M remembered from when she first met Ben in the Glass House. But it was familiar in another way. "It's not working at all. Can't you tell? I'm here with you. So please, for the third time, what brings you to London?"

"Chaucer maybe?" The room fell silent around Evel's two tiny words. "Yeah, the other night in the forest, I heard Keyshawn tell you something about Chaucer and the stars. Does that ring a bell, M?"

It did. It rang a bell that couldn't be unrung. "He was out of it." M tried to cover up the clue. "Keyshawn might've had a concussion that night, not an answer. I wouldn't hang my hopes on anything he said."

"Keyshawn's alive?" asked Ben.

"Maybe, we're not sure. We dropped him off at a hospital before we came here. He was in a — what do you call it — a coma," said Evel. "Coe-maa," he repeated, drawing out the word as if it fascinated him. Then Evel turned to M with a dazed look in his eyes. "And actually, he sounded pretty sure of himself. Like he was struggling to get everything out in the open before he slipped into that coma. And Jules, I don't think you like me very much."

"What?" blurted Jules.

"You look at me and I think you see my sister." Evel was on a roll. "And I can understand that, but I also think you don't like me because I was a failure and now I'm here and partially, a little, your life depends on me and you're worried that I'm going to blow it somehow. But I'm not. I don't think. Maybe I would, but at least I wouldn't blow it on purpose."

"Okay, Evel, it's all good," said M. "There's no need to get so chatty. We're your friends, not your therapist."

"You, M. I think you keep me around because of my sister." Evel's speech was starting to slur and his arms went rubbery as he tried to point at M and then back to himself. "Like you think she won't hurt you if I'm on your side. But she will. She'd shove me into a pit of angry snakes to get a crack at you."

"No, Evel, I asked you to come because I trust you," said M, trying to calm him down.

Then Evel knocked over his empty glass and it shattered on the ground. "Oh my gosh!" he gasped. "I am sho shorry. Lest me clean mit ups."

Flump. Evel passed out.

M and Jules both glanced at their full glasses. Small flecks of white dust floated near the bottoms. They turned to focus on Ben, who didn't seem at all surprised by what had just happened.

"Is your friend okay?" he asked with a bizarre note of sincerity.

"I think we're ready to order now!" M hollered without looking away from Ben. "And could we get it to go?"

Simultaneously, M and Jules splashed Ben in the face with their water, then ducked under the table and flipped it over. A second later, a sonic boom erupted, pulverizing the table to smithereens.

The kitchen door swung open to reveal Cal in his Fulbright uniform, unmasked, clenched fist raised, standing beside the waitress. M and Jules were shaken, covered in wood slivers and dust, but they knew what was coming next. Wherever Cal was, his mother wouldn't be far behind.

The waitress reached to the back of her neck as if she were going to undo a necklace, but instead she pulled off her face. The thin mask peeled away with a sickening sound, like the tearing of actual skin. With the mask gone, she shook her blond hair out, then flashed her green eyes. The same green eyes as Cal, her son. Ms. Watts was back.

CHAPTER 19
BAD BLOOD

"Hello, Ms. Freeman." Ms. Watts glared at her, then motioned for Cal to lower his magblast. "May we sit and talk? There's so much to catch up on."

"Take a rain check, you old cuckoo bird. It's time for my friends and me to leave." M had nothing to say to this woman. She was the one who had admitted to killing her father, who'd manipulated her, and attempted to kill her. Talking was not an option.

"You can try to leave, but no one gets out alive until we have our one-on-one." Ms. Watts shrugged.

"You dosed Ben, too, didn't you?" accused Jules. "With that hypnotic Lawless junk."

"Oh, and Calvin told me you were the average one," said Ms. Watts. "Cal, were you pulling my leg?"

"No, Mother." Cal's voice sounded flatline. If it had been in the hospital, the doctors would have declared it DOA.

"Yes, dear Ms. Byrd, I gave Mr. Downing a taste of Lawlessness. The poor boy does have a soft spot for you and M, though. Calvin convinced Ben that you were in trouble and my, oh my, did he come running."

"Right into your trap," said M. "And Evel . . . I'm guessing truth serum in the water."

"You never did disappoint, Ms. Freeman. Except for that one time when you let the Fulbrights destroy the Lawless School." Ms. Watts made an ugly face, turning her lips into a sneer and wincing. "Though that was as much my mistake as it was yours. I never should have given that meteorite to —"

"Dr. Lawless, I know," M interrupted. "He's working for the Fulbrights. Bad move on your part, then. But thanks for telling me. I feel a little less guilty."

Ms. Watts clapped her hands together slowly in approval. "Someone's been learning on her adventures. So you know that we want the same thing."

"And what's that?" asked M.

"The same thing your father and I used to want: to destroy John Doe." Ms. Watts's green eyes widened with glee at the thought.

"My father didn't want that," countered M. "You said so yourself. He wanted to *expose* Doe. You were the one out for blood."

"And what are you out to accomplish?" Cal spoke up. His mother held her smile, but the emotion in his voice seemed to surprise her.

"We're going to stop him from hurting anyone else . . . maybe everyone else." M's heart beat harder seeing Cal. He'd grown taller and looked stronger than before. His shaggy hair was unkempt and fell almost below his chin. And M couldn't wait to knock *his* block off. He'd found his mother, just like he planned. But here he was, standing by her side like a faithful son, threatening M's mission for his own selfish revenge. "So are you two working together again? The last heist you pulled, your mom left you to drown in a frozen river. Is that all water under the bridge now?"

"Isn't that cute, Calvin? Your friend is trying to drive a wedge between us," Ms. Watts said.

"She's not my friend," said Cal coldly. "Just a means to an end. Infiltrate the Fulbright Academy, kidnap Dad, and get out alive. Mission accomplished."

Cal's words shouldn't have hurt M, but they did. The sharp-edged statements rattled in her head and tore at her memories of Cal. The boy in the water. The patient in the infirmary. The prisoner in the glass house. The double-dealing thief in the library. The disappearing partner who had reappeared with a weapon aimed directly at her.

Not her friend.

"We've got what the experts call bad blood," said M, and she spat on the floor. "So this is the end of our visit. I hear the guards at Buckingham Palace are a sight to see. I'm sure they're more interesting than watching the two of you playing house."

"So we're clear," said Ms. Watts. "If you don't want to help us, we'll have to place you on the disabled list. It would be a shame to bench your talent."

M flexed her right hand behind her back. The magblast glove from the suit she was wearing underneath her clothes obeyed and clasped into place.

"Then let's not waste one minute more." M fired a cyclone magblast that knocked Cal and Ms. Watts together. Cal was back up in no time, but Jules grabbed the paint cans from the bar and heaved them at him. Cal instinctively raised his hands to block the cans, but the paint splashed all over his magblast glove. He tried to fire another attack, but the device was jammed.

"RUN!" screamed M as Ms. Watts jumped up and pulled out a weapon of her own. The baton was silver and began to glow red. M wasn't going to stick around to find out what it did, though. She grabbed the dazed Ben's elbow and dragged him through the front door while Jules yanked Evel off the ground and followed.

Once outside, M used the magblast to mold the door shut by warping the wooden frame. She heard a muffled scream of "Get them!" from inside the restaurant, and they scrambled down the alley before the door blew off its hinges.

Evel stumbled and tripped over himself, keeping Jules from running fast. "It's not going to work, M! We need to face them."

"No," said M as she shoved Ben down next to Evel and Jules. "I need to face them."

"Wait!" yelled Jules, but it was too late. M sent a magblast that cradled her friends and lifted them up off the ground.

Holding the weight of three people set M's arms on fire, or at least that's what it felt like. Her elbow shook under the effort it took to move them slowly and safely. For a second, M thought her arm might snap in half, but then the suit kicked in and fortified her weakest point, just like Keyshawn had designed it to do.

Jules stared down at M, shaking her head and smashing her fist against the invisible sphere that guided her higher into the air.

Once her friends were deposited on the nearest rooftop and out of harm's way, M pulled her arm to her chest and fell to one knee. The magblast tech burned white hot against her knuckles and the pain in her elbow pounded like it had its own heartbeat. Still, M knew what was coming. She tried to collect her wits and plan her next move. She had made it back to the narrow alleyway. It was as good a place as any to make a last stand, she supposed, if she could use it to her advantage. She stretched her arms out and touched both walls with her palms. Maybe she could magblast herself to the roof with the others. She placed her fist to the ground and prayed it would work . . . and not tear her arm off.

Click.

It was the hollow sound of an empty chamber as the hammer connected with nothing. Her magblast wasn't going to save her now. She'd used too much energy saving the others.

Cal came roaring around the corner first, sword in hand slashing down at M. She kicked from wall to wall, climbing up above his attack as the sword whiffed the air underneath her. Then she landed and kicked Cal hard in the back before unsheathing her own sword from her suit. The small pieces slid into place and combined with a clicking that sounded like a hail of bullets striking a metal sheet.

Cal recovered faster than M had hoped. Crashing against the wall, he kicked off and landed like a puma ready to pounce, sword extended. With his free hand, he shot out a whip that snagged M's sword. She wrenched it back toward her, and both the sword and whip exploded into bits of the suit's programmable matter, which scattered across the ground like technological ants.

As Cal charged, M quickly formed a shield. His sword landed this time, clanging sharply and bringing the two nose-to-nose.

"Work with us, M," Cal rasped. "It's the only way."

"Never." The word had barely escaped her lips when her body convulsed with electricity. Her mouth tasted like a battery, and the wires lacing her suit glowed white and contracted, squeezing her body like a fist wringing water from a towel. M crumbled to the ground.

Ms. Watts loomed over her with the silver baton in hand. "Oh no! How could this have happened . . . ? That's what you must be thinking right now. I told you we needed to talk, Ms. Freeman. You used to confide in me, remember? So let's try this again. A part of you knows exactly why you're here in London."

"You . . ." M struggled to speak. "Need to leave. Take the *Mutus Liber* and go. If Doe gets his hands on it . . ."

"Full of predictions, just like your father, aren't you?" said Ms. Watts. "No, I think we'll stay. I'm beginning to like it here. I've got my boy, I've got my husband, and I've got you. Next I'll get John Doe. Who said a woman can't have everything in life?"

"Cal . . . you know I'm right," M pleaded. "Leave London."

"You heard her!" Ben's voice echoed from above them. He was no longer under Ms. Watts's spell. "Get out before I come down and kick you out on your lousy, evil bums."

"Ha!" scoffed Ms. Watts. "You and whose army, you Fulbright surplus reject?"

"Me and that army," he called back.

A crowd appeared in the alley, surrounding Ms. Watts and Cal. First from one side and then from the next. They were different ages, different builds, different nationalities. M even recognized some of them from the roving tour groups that had crossed the bridge earlier that day. Sercy and Merlyn had done their job. The word was out and the troops had assembled.

"Ronin aren't big fans of you, Ms. Watts," said Ben. "We are many and you are few. Two, to be exact. So I'd take M's advice."

Cal retracted his sword and nodded to his mother. "We should go. These are just kids. Not a part of what we're after."

"They're all a part of what we're after," said Ms. Watts. "The in-the-way part."

She charged her baton and aimed at the children, but Cal moved between them. "Stop it. We have an idea of what we're after now, Mom. This isn't a necessary fight."

Ms. Watts flipped the baton to rest on her shoulder while looking at Cal, then she studied the Ronin behind him. "You're right . . . and you're wrong. I'm letting them live today. But only because slaying these misfits would raise a red flag, and that's not the grand entrance I'm looking to make."

With Ms. Watts under control, Cal guided her away, but the Ronin held their ground, blocking the exit. The kids looked scared to death, but still they wouldn't budge. One could almost hear their hearts thumping in their chests over the silent standoff.

"Please, don't be stupid," warned Cal. "M?"

"Let them through," M ordered weakly from the ground as her suit let go of its strangling grip. "They're not worth it."

The Ronin stood aside and formed a path for Ms. Watts and Cal, who shoved their way through and disappeared around a corner.

A door flew open and Jules came bounding to M's side, helping her friend up. "M, are you okay?"

"A little trash-compacted, but I'll live." M stretched her arms and legs after she stood. It was like her own skin was a size too small.

"Good, now I don't feel bad saying this," said Jules. "You totally deserved to get beaten by those two. You were lucky this time and you know it. M, there's no way you can handle this on your own. So stop trying."

"But you didn't have a weapon, Ben wasn't himself, and Evel was loopy. I didn't have a choice," pleaded M.

"Hey, I'm a big girl. I know what I signed up for by coming here," said Jules. "Back there, you took my choice away and made me powerless. That's not what a leader does, M, so don't ever do that again. As my friend, you've got to promise to let me help."

"I'm sorry, I didn't . . . I didn't see it that way," said M. "And I promise, next time, I'll fight alongside you."

Ben and Evel joined the crew as the Ronin army stood hunched with bad posture and general confusion. These were not well-trained recruits ready for a war. They were slackers and scrappers who, like Evel, had spent their entire lives being told that they were powerless. That they didn't make the cut, were missing the right stuff to be either good guys or bad guys. But through her, they were going to be the ones to help take down the good *and* the bad. They were the last hope of saving the world.

"So what's next, guys?" asked Ben. "Am I wrong in guessing we have some sightseeing to do?"

M hugged her friend again and pulled Jules next to her. Around them the Ronin kids had started watching one another. They jostled nervously, then one kid shoved another. "You want to go, you criminal failure?" Another kid pushed in and yelled, "You Fulbright wannabe! Get your paws off him or I'll show you how it feels to be beaten bad!"

"Stop it!" yelled M. "Stop it, all of you!" Then she beckoned the Ronin to come closer. Her hands shook as she waved them over. "You're used to being on different sides of this war. You probably don't trust each other at all and I don't blame you. But that's what they want. If you keep fighting each other, you'll never realize who the real enemy is."

"And who are you supposed to be?" asked the Fulbright Ronin. "Why do you know so much?"

This was the moment she'd rehearsed for. The speech that had been growing inside her, turning in her throat since the very beginning of her adventure, tumbled out. "Hello. My name is M Freeman and I always knew I had a purpose. Now you have a purpose, too."

CHAPTER 20
A BARD'S TRAIL

"*The* British Museum," said Ben Downing as he held a foam double-decker bus at the end of a stick high in the air, "is the oldest national museum in the world. Founded in 1753, it was designed to serve all those who were 'studious and curious' . . . and I can tell we've got a quite of few of you on this tour today!"

The group following Ben chuckled and lifted their cameras, vying for the best picture of the museum's massive entrance. Flanked by giant columns that stretched from the foundation to the sky, the museum's façade looked like it should be the home of Greek gods on Mount Olympus. Ancient relics and art from every human civilization were displayed inside, spanning two million years' worth of human existence in over eighteen acres of rooms. And breaking in was easy, because it was free to anyone who wanted to visit.

M, Jules, and Evel were not part of Ben's tour group. They filtered into the courtyard and shuffled through the crowd of tourists taking in the majesty of the building. The entrance was set back while either side of the museum extended forward, pulling people in as if with an oddly warm embrace. Many famous monuments around the world had the same effect, from Versailles in France to St. Peter's Basilica at the Vatican to the Taj Mahal in India. All were extraordinary feats of architecture built in different worlds at different times but said the same thing to all who passed by: *You are drawn to me.*

"Do we even know what we're looking for?" asked Jules. "This place is huge."

"No," admitted M, "but we've got a hint, thanks to Evel blabbing when he was on the truth sauce."

"Again, I was thirsty," Evel said with exasperation in his voice. "You can't stay mad at me because I was thirsty."

"I'm not mad," said M as she playfully punched him on the arm. "Just don't take drinks from strangers anymore, okay?"

"I'll try," said Evel. "But what did I say? I can't even remember."

"You said a lot of things," said Jules. "Like a verbal faucet that sprang a leak."

"Chaucer," said M. "You mentioned Geoffrey Chaucer. I'd forgotten what Keyshawn was mumbling back in the forest, but he mentioned Chaucer, too. Plus, he had a book by Chaucer back in his lab at the Fulbright Academy."

"I wish we could just call Keyshawn and ask him for clarification," said Evel.

"Coma patients can't shed a lot of light on much, but we can work with what we know," said M.

"So what do we know about this guy Chaucer?" asked Jules.

"He was a writer, so we'll start with any famous books they might have here," explained M.

"Ugh, not another library," complained Jules. "My knees still hurt from climbing through the last one."

"I have a feeling this place is going to be different." M breathed in the cool morning air, then casually touched her hand to the side of her head as if she were brushing hair out of her face. "Okay, Ben, take everyone inside. Remember, have them cover every exit, two per door, and keep watch for anyone or anything suspicious. Over."

Across the courtyard, Ben waved the tour group on. "And now, ladies and gents, let's go get cultural. Each of you pick a partner and stick together. This lovely museum is full of surprises lurking in every nook and cranny. So prepare to have your eyes set to 'stunned.'"

As the Ronins walked inside, Evel looked at the sky. It was a clear, sunny day. Beautiful by any standard. "The sun is out and the world is happy. So why do I feel like it's all going to fall apart?"

M punched him playfully on the arm again. "Because you're smart. Clear skies mean that Fulbright helicopters can see for miles. Crowds at the museum means that anyone could be a Lawless thug waiting to steal the same thing we're after, whatever it is. Plus, Ms. Watts and Cal are in the city and they would love to play tie-you-up-and-throw-you-down-a-bottomless-pit with all of us."

"Can we go inside already or are you guys not finished stalling yet?" asked Jules.

She was right, they were stalling. M didn't want to admit it, but even she was scared. She had a lump in her throat over what they would find behind those Greek-revival museum doors. But that wasn't going to stop her from going inside. She'd already survived a black hole. It was hard to imagine anything worse, though she knew John Doe was capable of anything.

Inside, the museum felt expansive and endless. There was a gigantic central room, known as the Great Court, that served as a welcoming area. Its roof was made of glass panes, and the sunlight poured in from above, casting spiderweblike shadows over the walls. It was like walking into a piece of graph paper. M was measuring the connecting lines, plotting points to find the fastest means of escape and the areas of greatest possible danger.

"If we live through this," said Jules, "remind me to come back and take my time touring this place. It's incredible."

"I'll add it to the top ten things we should do together if we don't die today," M said with a chipper lilt in her voice. "So, to the library?"

"This way," said Evel. "It's the big oval room in the middle of everything."

He started walking and M grabbed his arm to pull him in another direction. "Wait, let's not be so direct. We're being watched."

Sure enough, there were three adults dressed in black turtlenecks positioned around the room. They were all talking on phones ... and the phones were all the same brand and model. They reeked of Fulbright undercover operations. The way they stood out in the crowd, staring daggers at people — that's how M knew they were trouble. Unlike a Lawless operative, a Fulbright was meant to be seen, because like cockroaches and mice, if you saw one in your house, you could bet that there was an army of them just out of sight.

M and Jules guided Evel to the Egyptian Room. It was filled with ancient sarcophagi, mummies, broken pieces of pottery, obelisks, and more.

"Whoa, look at this!" Evel leaned closer to a glass display that enclosed a heavy piece of stone.

For a second, M's mouth went dry. "Tell me it's not another meteorite."

"Meteorite? No," said Evel. "Groundbreaking, codebreaking discovery, yes. This is the Rosetta Stone! It's the best key researchers have ever found to help them understand and decipher Egyptian hieroglyphics! Without it, all those drawings and etchings would have been nothing more than fancy wallpaper. But this helped us know what the ancient Egyptians wanted to tell us!"

Jules stared at it, then stared at Evel, whose eyes were wide with excitement. "How did this rock help?"

"See those symbols inscribed in the rock?" asked Evel as he pointed to the markings etched into the stone. "Those say the exact same thing in three different languages: hieroglyphic, demotic, and Greek. People knew how to translate Greek, so by reading this stone, we could finally read hieroglyphics, too."

"So what's it doing here?" asked M.

"Being awesome." Evel was beaming being this close to history.

"I mean in England," said M. "Why not keep it in Egypt if it's part of their history?"

Then she found a floor map and studied the layout, room by room. Egypt, Assyria, Greece, Africa, North America, China . . . these historical pieces had been taken from all over the world. Taken and collected, just like the Lawless and Fulbright students. Just like thieves steal artwork and just like authorities capture criminals. But this was meant for a greater good — to provide a chance for people to visit and learn, to become enlightened by the beauty, wonder, and mystery of the world. There were too many thoughts clouding her head. M tried to focus.

"We should make our move now," she said. Then she spoke into the commlink sleeve again. "Ben, we need a distraction in the main room. Three guys, you'll see them right away."

As M, Jules, and Evel emerged from the Egyptian room, a group of security guards were questioning the black turtlenecks.

"Yes, sir, I saw all three of these men using *flash photography* in the museum!" accused Ben irately.

M smiled and gave him a wink as she walked into the center Reading Room. The walls were covered with books on shelves that circled up and up far overhead. Reading tables emanated from the middle of the room like rays from the sun, and nearly every seat was filled. Bright windows ran all around the curved walls and allowed a deluge of light into the room. There wasn't a place where the sunlight didn't reach. It was like being inside of a church, where an air of respect and appreciation merged with the sense that the world is bigger and grander than just the people in it. That and it was so quiet that M could hear the blood pumping in her own body . . . along with the occasional flap of turning pages.

In the middle of the room, there was a small information desk. M walked up to it and said, "Excuse me, but I would like to see a book by Chaucer. Geoffrey Chaucer."

The woman at the desk smiled. "Yes, I assumed you meant Geoffrey Chaucer, miss. We don't get many people in here asking about any other Chaucer, but I'm afraid you'd be better off visiting the British Library . . . or any bookstore in the world."

"No to the library . . . I've already tried them," said M. "I'm looking for a very specific book."

"Specific how, miss?" the woman asked.

"Ummm." M paused. "Specific to the British Museum?"

"Real smooth," joked Jules. "Please excuse my friend. What's she trying to get at is that we're playing a scavenger hunt game for school and one of the clues was Chaucer at the British Museum, so naturally we came to the Reading Room first. We just need to take a quick pic and send it back to our teacher to get the next clue. Can you please help us?"

"Oh, wow, that sounds brilliant," the woman said, "but we don't have any of Chaucer's books here."

M's face dropped. "Oh."

Then the woman typed something into the computer before nodding. "I thought I remembered this. We don't have any books in the Reading Room, but it looks like we do have something in the Medieval Europe section. Room forty on the map."

"Excellent!" cheered Jules, a little too loudly. A wave of *shushes* rose from the readers. "Is it a famous book, then?"

"No, afraid not," said the woman. "Says here that it's an astrolabe, whatever that is."

M, Jules, and Evel stared blankly back at the woman. Even surrounded by a collection of some twenty-five thousand books, there were no words for what the three of them were thinking. Like stepping on a land mine and hearing the *click*, they forced themselves to stand stone still, trying to stave off the explosion for as long as possible.

"Oh dear, did I pronounce it wrong?" asked the woman.

"You all look gobsmacked. As-tro-labe? Astro-la-be? A-stro-lab-eh?"

"As-tro-labe," corrected M. "You said it right the first time. In room forty? That's outstanding. Thanks so much."

As the crew ran back down the aisle, M whispered orders. "We split up, each person going a different way, then we'll all meet up at the target."

"Then what?" asked Jules.

Stepping back out into the grand hallway, M turned to her friend. "We hope it's still there. And if it is, then we do what we do best. Take it."

CHAPTER 21
TIME'S UP

M's path took her up a set of stairs closest to the gallery where the astrolabe was supposed to be found, but she didn't head directly there. The museum had filled with patrons and now there was a steady flow of onlookers stopping and admiring the works. Foot traffic was great for the museum, but horrible for M's bad guy radar. Any of these people could be with Lawless. A dad with a toddler on his shoulders, a mom quickly grabbing her child before he touched a precious statue — in any other world they would be sweet and frazzled parents. But here and now, M filed them under *maybe*. And the *maybes* were everywhere.

Before she knew it, M found herself in the Greek and Roman gallery. Handmade water jugs, cups, and urns had stood the test of time and now waited out the rest of their existence safely behind glass. The detail in the design and painting on the pieces was truly amazing. To put this much effort into things designed to carry other things — water, wine, ashes — seemed truly foreign to M. Most of her cups at home had been plain old plastic or glass, while these each told a story. And most of them told a story with familiar elements: women, children, war, and hope, all artfully rendered into these everyday, common tools. M found she could relate.

She turned a corner and saw a display of war helmets. These were actual pieces of protective armor worn by the Romans and Greeks of distant times, crafted as a mixture of delicate edges, ornate designs, and rugged practicality. They floated in the exhibit, staring back at M — only they couldn't stare. They were empty on the inside. No one was wearing the helmets. They had all died. Maybe in battle and maybe after a long life, but they were gone now and all that remained were those helmets. She shifted her neck, wrists, and ankles, suddenly aware of the suit she was wearing underneath her own civilian clothes. Would her suit be in a museum one day, too? And if so, where would she be?

On the other side of the room, there was a very different artifact. It was a small, creepy-looking, faceless doll. M never would have called it a doll herself, but that's what the plaque said. It had been made of cloth stuffed with rags and papyrus. Its arms and legs dangled limply. Its tobacco-brown stains and moth-eaten holes gave it a sense of age, making it look more like a mummy than a plaything for a child. But it had belonged to a child and it had been loved. M imagined the girl or boy curling up with this doll at night after their parents had tucked them in to whatever Greek and Roman kids slept in.

And now here was M. Somewhere between the doll and

the battle helmets, and probably two rooms away from a lynchpin in John Doe's scheme. She couldn't help feeling like the Greeks and Romans had it easy compared to her.

She pushed on, inching closer to the Chaucer exhibit, while still casually viewing the sights, though she began to think that once she'd seen one mosaic, she'd seen them all. Finally she moved into a room with a disturbingly familiar sound. Ticking. M's first instinct was to look for a bomb, but the ticking was coming from every direction. Clocks. She had wandered into an entire display of rare and fanciful clocks from all around the world. The sound of each clock over-lapped and M was transported back to Keyshawn's vertical maze, the room with the cuckoo clocks. The memory was diz-zying, but M kept herself steady. She didn't have the luxury of taking a tumble through memory lane right now.

"Got the time?" slithered a familiar voice.

M turned. Leaning against the glass that held an oversize clock was Devon Zoso. Her hair was longer now, her severe bangs hanging just above her eyes. But her smile, that was just as sharp and cutting as M remembered.

"There's got to be a clock around here somewhere for you to check," M said.

The two enemies circled each other casually as the crowd of sightseers moved around them. "I know the time, Freeman," said Devon. "Just want to make sure you know it, too."

"How kind of you," said M. "So is this where you tell me my time's up?"

Devon looked slightly defeated. "Well, yeah, but you weren't supposed to know my line. And it sounds so corny when you say it."

"And how would you have said it?" asked M.

"I don't know, more menacingly, I guess," Devon mused. Then she added, "I finally got my own suit, by the way."

"Did you?" M smiled as they stepped close together and pretended to look at the fancy clocks. To the people around them, they would look less like mortal enemies and more like old friends running into each other at the supermarket. "Is it everything you wanted it to be?"

"Not yet," said Devon. Then she leaned over and whispered, "Because I wanted it to end you."

"You know how to make a person feel wanted, Devon," said M. "So what brings you to the British Museum at this time of day? Isn't there a Fulbright class on lying, cheating, and generally being an awful person in the name of justice?"

"That class was pass/fail," said Devon. "I passed. And now I'm spending a year abroad. Felt like getting out of the house and slipping into something more cultural. What about you? What have you been up to? It feels like years since we've talked."

M stopped next to a bizarre clock in the shape of a maritime ship made of bronze and gold. Black cannons stuck out of the sides of the ship, which appeared to be sailing into battle. Every hour, the cannons would pretend-blast at the threats around it. "Strange way to tell time."

"So is waiting for your shoulder to mend." Devon smiled again. "Or for your hair to grow back. Time has a funny way of reminding you that it takes forever to pass . . . then, when you're ready to have a *good* time, it races by you like a roller coaster."

"Are we having a good time?" M asked.

"We're going to," promised Devon, "as soon as you tell me why you're here. We know about your little Ronin buddy, Ben Downing. He was running that operation downstairs. Now you and your other cronies . . . who are they, now? No doubt your pesky partners in crime, Jules and Merlyn."

"Guilty as charged," admitted M. *Let her keep talking,* she thought. *If Devon doesn't know that her brother is here with me, what else doesn't she know?* "But if I knew why I was here, would I be walking around aimlessly?"

"Did Dr. Lawless put you up to this?" asked Devon. "Yeah, I know he's back. I thought we'd be lucky and he'd be on the other side of that little black hole we started."

"*You* started," corrected M. "If I was working for Lawless, would you take me in? Read me my rights?"

"You don't have any rights as far as I'm concerned," snarled Devon.

"Well, I'm not working for Lawless," said M. "Especially because he's working for John Doe and the Fulbrights."

"Very funny, but I'm not biting." Devon followed M into room forty.

The Chaucer astrolabe was somewhere in here. M's heart beat in her chest. She was thankful that Devon wasn't wearing her mask yet, because she would have known that something was off if she could get a reading of M's vitals. "No lie, it's true. Actually all of Lawless works for Doe. I don't think most of them know it, any more than you knew it. Remind me, that's, like, your job to know this kind of information, isn't it?"

"A rat on a sinking ship will say anything to save her own life," rationalized Devon. "I was sent here by Doe himself to stop you, just like he sent me to hobble Lawless."

"Oh good, then maybe you know what to stop me from getting," said M. "That would make my mission so much easier. This place is *huge*. It'd be great to narrow it down to one cursed object, or hidden secret code, or whatever it is."

"I should lay you out right here and now." Devon's voice was a tight, forced whisper filled with venom.

"So Doe didn't tell you what you're protecting," said M. "Sounds like he really trusts you to get the job done. Wait, no it doesn't. It sounds like he wants you to stop me, so he can steal the whatever-it-is for himself."

Zoso's fists clenched. M knew she had about a minute before Devon actually took a swing at her.

"You're on the wrong side of this, Devon," insisted M. "As much as it pains me to tell you this, you're being played. If you don't believe me, ask the guy behind you."

Devon whipped around to face her brother, Evel. "What are you —?"

But Evel stopped her with a big hug. "*Sis!*" he boomed, then mouthed to M: *Behind me.*

And there it was, just over Evel's shoulder: Chaucer's astrolabe. It was smaller than M had imagined, probably five inches across and flat like a compass. She could easily slip it into her back pocket, no problem. And no one was paying attention to it. The crowd passed it by, instead drawn by a large knight's suit of armor that held a mace aloft in the corner. Everyone seemed to be posing for selfies with it, blowing kisses or making fake screams. The moment was right . . . if it wasn't for Devon and Evel's family reunion.

"Evel, you idiot. Are you with *her* now?" accused Devon.

"I am and you should be, too," Evel answered. "She's saved me multiple times. And there's an evil at work here that's bigger than all of us. It's, like, an ancient evil."

Devon sent chilling stares M's way and shoved Evel aside with so much force that he crashed into the suit of armor. "You think you can use my brother to convince me to turn my back on Doe? Ha! You're dumber than I gave you credit for!"

So much for keeping quiet.

M ducked in the nick of time, as the heavy gust of a magblast whooshed over her back, smashing the glass case that held the astrolabe. People began screaming and running in all directions at the commotion, swarming Devon and blocking her view. M used the opportunity to reach in and grab the object. She shoved it into the neck of her suit. The metal was shockingly cold against her skin.

"She's got it!" yelled one of the would-be sightseers. "It's an astrolabe!"

He was a thin man, one of the selfie-takers from earlier, and he was fast. He slipped through the crowd and threw a punch at M, but she was able to block it. *Poor fighting technique, blends in, must be Lawless*, thought M. She pummeled him with a magblast, but now the room had cleared and she was face-to-face with Devon. And Zoso had her dead to rights.

Then a trio of Fulbrights rushed in and one of them spoke to Devon. "Stand down, cadet. We'll take it from here."

"I'm no cadet, soldier," Devon fired back. "Freeman's mine to deal with. Pick up the other trash in the corner."

"Cadet," the Fulbright replied, "we have orders to not engage if it risks damaging the astrolabe. If you attack her, we will take action against you. Now stand down."

"The astro-what?!" said Devon. She didn't take her eyes off of M. "Soldier, did Doe tell you what Freeman was looking for?"

But Devon never got her answer. Instead one of the men jumped her from behind while the other two wrestled with M. They were strong! They forced her down, but M struggled. She looked over and saw Devon was fighting to get free, too. And Evel was standing over them with the mace from the suit of armor held high. Next thing M heard was a muffled thud as the Fulbright was knocked clear off of Devon.

Zoso leapt to her feet and sent a magblast that crashed into one of the Fulbrights holding M, sending him toppling into another exhibit. Then M magblasted the Fulbright who had been doing all the talking, thrusting him up against the ceiling.

She held him there, too, while Devon and Evel came to her side. Evel helped M up, but Devon stared at the chump pressed above them.

"He did tell you, huh?" said Devon. "Well, send him a message from Devon Zoso. No more Ms. Nice Gal." Then she knocked M's arm down and sent the Fulbright slamming to the ground.

"There's more Fulbrights like him here," said Evel.

"And there's us, too." A blast of wind caught M, Evel, and Devon in a hale of force that drove them right through the solid wall and out onto the white floor of the Great Court. M cushioned their fall with a magblast, but she couldn't mask her shock when Ms. Watts and Cal stepped out from the rubble and looked down at them from the second-floor landing.

"Give it to us now," said Ms. Watts, who was holding Jules over the edge. "Or we'll see if Ms. Byrd can really fly."

"Don't!" screamed Evel. "Just stop — it's not worth hurting anyone else." Then he pulled out a second astrolabe from his jacket and held it above his head. "Here."

Using the magblast, Cal retrieved the astrolabe. It flew back to him like a trained falcon. He looked at it and nodded to his mother.

She sneered down at them and repeated Evel's final word. "Here." Then she tossed Jules from the second floor, but Devon caught her with a magblast, while M shot another blast at the Watts team. Cal blocked it easily.

"You get what you deserve," Cal yelled at M. "Remember that."

As Cal and his mother disappeared through the hole in the middle of the museum wall, another team of Fulbrights had taken control of the first floor. M, Jules, Evel, and Devon huddled together as the soldiers advanced. They were surrounded.

"Is this how you planned it?" Devon asked M.

"Not exactly," admitted M. "But this is how my plans usually end up. I guess you take that side." She motioned to the twenty men advancing from the left. "And I'll take this side."

But then a dull, repetitive thud clapped from above them. M looked up and could see a lone helicopter through the glass ceiling. *The glass ceiling.* "Everybody, cover your heads!"

M rocketed a magblast upward and a monumental smash sounded out, like a tidal wave crashing against a shore. The ceiling above them was obliterated into a billion shards of glass and rained down on the plain-clothed Fulbrights.

She braced herself for the downpour of minuscule particles of glass, but she needn't have worried. A cocoon had formed around the group of friends — a cocoon made of the programmable matter of Devon's suit. M reached over and clapped Jules and Evel on the back to let them know it was okay now.

Then she turned to Devon and said, "Now that's what I call a plan! Feel like catching a helicopter ride?"

Devon pulled on her mask and looked up at the copter that still hovered in the sky, unfazed by the destruction. "That's not a Fulbright-issue vehicle."

"I have a suspicion who it is," said M. "Now, use your suit and let's get out of here before they make us pay for this damage."

M took Jules's hand and magblasted them off the ground. Her legs and arms flailed like she had jumped from a tall building and was plummeting down, but instead, she was falling in reverse. The next thing she knew, M was perched on the helicopter's landing skid with Jules in tow and she waved to the pilot, her mother. And this time, her mother opened the door to let M inside.

CHAPTER 22
REUNION

The beating blades of the helicopter weren't any quieter on the inside of the cabin. Instead they made a different kind of white noise that rattled the riders. M felt like she had stepped into her own skull, and the memory of her mother was driving. But it was all real. Mrs. Freeman gave her a slight nod, then started to pull away from the museum. M clutched her mother's shoulder and shook her head no. "Not yet! More friends coming!"

She looked out of the side of the helicopter and watched as the Fulbrights surrounding the courtyard swept forward to collect the survivors. Devon leapt right into their midst and started brawling. From this high up, it was like watching a video game. Devon's skills were unquestionable. She was whupping real-deal soldiers like they were cardboard cutouts. But there were more coming. There were always more. And from this vantage, M could see that Devon was losing the battle. She was fighting with anger, not her wits.

M's mother twirled her hand in the air, a signal that meant *let's wrap this up before we have company*. So M took aim and blasted the next wave of Fulbrights charging at Devon . . . and Devon got the message. Devon grabbed Evel and flew straight up, like superheroes taking flight and jumping right out of a 3-D movie screen. Behind and below them, the soldiers were gathering and turning their attention, and weapons, toward the getaway vehicle.

When they landed, the helicopter tipped sideways. M grabbed Evel and pulled him in while Devon created a shield to deflect the Fulbright attacks. Mrs. Freeman shifted the heli-copter to the right, leaving the museum behind them. Devon climbed in and shut the door behind her, airtight, and sud-denly all the noise of the engine was gone.

"Is that everyone?" asked Mrs. Freeman.

M was stunned, but managed to get an answer out. "Yes." Then she added, "Isn't it conspicuous to fly a helicopter that close to a national building?"

"Only if they can see you, dear," said her mother as she flipped another switch. M watched as the reflection of the heli-copter in a midtown building's windows shimmered, then disappeared. "You can't find what you can't see."

Jules leaned forward. "Mrs. Freeman, I'm Jules Byrd. It's nice to finally meet you."

"Hello, Jules. It's always nice to meet M's friends," her mother said in a chipper voice. "Come to think of it, I haven't met that many. Hmmm, you may even be the first."

The helicopter cruised over the city. As M, Jules, Devon, and Evel looked down, the blue lights of police cars flashed through every street. London didn't know what had hit it. M watched the skies for Fulbrights, but there were none. The only other eyes in the sky were police and reporter helicopters, looking for a great shot of a great story. They flew by them, sometimes incredibly close, but didn't seem to notice the invisible vehicle.

Her mother continued on, leaving the city behind and heading toward an airier England, with lush green countryside fenced off by stone walls, bushes, and forests. Finally she landed near a small cottage.

"Okay, we're here," she announced as she pulled off the set of headphones she had worn during the flight. "Careful getting out. We're still undercover . . . and stepping off an invisible landing is harder than you think."

The others shuffled out, leaving M and her mother in the cabin. "I'm still mad at you, you know."

"I know." Mrs. Freeman sat down across from M. Her hair was pulled back and flawless as usual while M's was an untamed pouf of cotton candy. "You look . . . frazzled, but healthy."

"And you look perfectly put together, as always," said M. "I'm still mad at you."

"You said that, dear," her mom reminded her.

"Because you didn't let me finish. I'm still mad at you, but I missed you." M let her shoulders sag and felt her body relax at telling the truth. There was a black cloud between her and her mother, charged with enough energy to create bolts of lightning . . . natural wonder and natural destruction. But that's what families can do to one another. "Are the moon rocks safe?"

"They're safe."

"Do you have any other secrets I should know about?" M asked. "Because we've had enough secrets between us."

"We have." Her mother reached back, pulled her hair down, then messed it up so that it matched M's hair nest. M laughed and her mom smiled. "Do you know why I keep my hair back all the time? It's because your father hated it up. See, when my hair is down, it looks exactly like yours. Wild, tangled, free. He loved that about my hair and he loved it about yours, too."

"Dad loved my hair?" asked M.

"He loved everything about you," her mother said, and her smile turned down at the corners, just slightly. "After the accident, my hair reminded me so much of him that I tied it up. Hid it. Did my best to forget it was there in the first place because losing my hair was easier than admitting that I'd lost him. I may have done the same thing to you, M. I'm sorry."

Tears welled in her mother's eyes and M gently reached over and touched her knee. Then M said three magic words. "I forgive you."

They sat in silence for another few minutes. Resting in the truth they had finally shared. M imagined her mother as a young woman in love, a young mother in hope, and a young widow in loss. She'd thought for her entire life that her mother had been cold and calculating, but that wasn't the case. She was frail and breakable, so like fine art, she put herself behind glass.

M pulled out the Chaucer astrolabe. "Well, at least we got away with this. Thanks to some quick thinking on Evel's part."

"What is it?" her mother asked. "What does it do?"

"That's exactly what we need to find out. Because both Lawless and the Fulbrights are after this thing." M stepped through the door and felt the ground come up to meet her. She stumbled awkwardly, but wasn't hurt. Devon, Evel, and Jules were sitting on the grass outside.

"I'm glad you're here, Devon," said M as she kneeled down and showed her the astrolabe. "Why is this important?"

Devon stared at the gold disc, then shook her head. "No idea."

"It's not time to be tough, Devon, it's time to tell the truth," demanded Jules.

"She's not being tough," said Evel. "I mean, she *is* tough, but she's being honest about the astrolabe. I don't think she's ever heard of it in her life."

"How can you be so sure?" asked Jules.

"Because she's my sister," said Evel. He looked at Devon, but she stared off in another direction. She was angry and had every right to be. John Doe had hung her out to dry. "I mean, sure, she threw her big brother into a five-hundred-year-old artifact to get a shot at M. But she didn't know what she was protecting. If she had, we wouldn't have it right now."

Devon's face shifted slightly from angry to annoyed. "The others knew what to protect," Devon said, "but they were supposed to be reporting to me. How can someone lower on the totem pole know more than their leader?"

"Because they were going to steal it, too," insisted M. "Like I was trying to tell you, Devon. You thought you were double-agenting Lawless, but Doe pulled one over on all of us. He's leading both factions."

"That's insanity, Freeman. Did I bump you on the head too hard or something?" said Devon.

"It's true," said Mrs. Freeman. "I can tell you more, but let's get inside first before we draw too much attention."

As soon as M set foot inside of the cottage, she felt haunted. Or maybe she was the one doing the haunting. Rustic, sparse, and open, the small house was unnervingly similar to the one Madame Voleur had lived in back in the States. The house she had died in. The floors even let out similar creaks as they walked through. A shiver ran down M's spine.

Her mother closed the door and locked it. As if one dead bolt was going to keep the bad guys out. Everyone found a seat and Mrs. Freeman began speaking. "M's father was a double agent. He discovered the truth about Doe years ago. And he gave his life searching for a way to prove it."

"He did a bang-up job," said Devon as she peered outside around a closed curtain. "Because no one seems to know this little tidbit of trivia that would have been life-altering to everyone involved."

M's mother nodded in agreement. "He never found a convincing way to prove it. He needed to find the smoking gun to put Doe and Lawless away. He was close. We knew he was getting close when Lawless and Doe both began to chip away at his reputation. People who used to be our friends left our lives . . . or even tried to kill us. One person succeeded."

"Mom, it's okay," said M. She knew her mother was talking about Ms. Watts, but her mother clearly didn't know the whole story. "Dad did have proof. He hid it in our house, and he told me where to find it. It was an old yearbook for the first Lawless School class."

Mrs. Freeman paused. "M, we need that proof. Hard, undeniable proof. Where is it?"

M shook her head. "I don't have it anymore. Bandit took the page that showed Jonathan Wild as the founder. He's John Doe. I don't know how it's possible, but it is. I saw it with my own eyes!"

"Well, this just gets sadder and sadder, doesn't it?" said Devon. "You're lucky I'm in a bad mood, or else I'd turn you all over to the Fulbrights."

Evel reached over and put his hand on Devon's shoulder. She didn't pull away. M knew how much that meant. The sister who had given up her choice in life to save the family for Evel's decision was now treating him like a brother again. He smiled.

"If it helps," Evel said, "I've seen both sides try to take out M and her friends. They're scared of her. And I'm backing anything that they're scared of. You should, too."

"They should be scared of *me*," hissed Devon.

While they were talking, a door somewhere moaned open slowly. M and Devon trained their magblasts on the direction the sound came from. "Mom, it's an old house, but doors don't open by themselves."

"Hold your fire," Mrs. Freeman said and she stepped in front of the girls. "I have guests. And you might not like seeing them, but they were the ones who convinced me that you needed help in London."

A hand stuck out from behind the door and waved a white flag made out of cloth tied to a stick. "Easy, easy, M. You don't want to blast your old roomie, do you?"

Out stepped Zara and Foley. Foley was holding a box with both hands.

"You." M spit the word out of her mouth like phlegm. "Ditch me and run back to my mom?"

"Sure, it looks bad, but we were in a bad way back in the forest," sputtered Zara. "And you were getting into some weird ideas. Using the Ronin to fight, I mean, c'mon."

"Except it worked, Zara," said M matter-of-factly as she pulled out the Chaucer astrolabe and flashed it to the others. "Ronin helped us steal this."

Foley's eyes lit up. "Is that what I think it is?"

"If you think it's a six-hundred-year-old device that can map the universe, then yeah, it's exactly what you think it is," said M. "Now, what's in the box?"

"Moon rocks," admitted her mother.

"The moon rocks from Dad's old hideout?" asked M. "And you gave it to them?"

"For safekeeping," said Zara. "Look, I was wrong to abandon you guys . . ."

"It's behind us now." M surprised the room by letting Zara off the hook. "Why didn't you ever tell me about the astrolabe?"

"I've never heard of that thing before," said Zara. "Honest. You figured this one out on your own."

"But you still sent my mom to help us?" M asked, suspicious.

"The underground lit up," said Foley. "We could tell that something was going on, we just didn't know what. But it had M Freeman written all over it."

M lifted the astrolabe to study it against the ceiling. She tried to remember how Keyshawn had described the anatomy of the astrolabe. Twisting the latch on the back, M removed the three main pieces. The outermost one was thin and ornate.

"That's called the rete," mumbled Foley.

"It tells the position of the stars in the sky, doesn't it?" said M.

"Yeah, that's right." Foley sounded surprised. "How'd you know that?"

"I've been paying attention." M flipped the next disk over in her hands. Swiping lines blossomed out, etched into the heavy metal. "This is the plate. It represents the position of Earth. And this" — she held the back piece where the plate nested —

"is the mater. The question is, Foley, why do *you* know so much about astrolabes?"

"I was a geek in a previous life," he joked.

"News flash, you're a geek in this life, too," said Devon. "So what makes this astrolabe so valuable? They were all built the same, right?"

"They're similar enough that the other astrolabe I grabbed fooled your friend Cal. I found that one on my way to room forty, but it's at least a couple hundred years older than Chaucer's."

"Nice work, Evel," Jules said, beaming. "Looks like M is rubbing off on you."

"They're similar, but not identical," argued Foley. "The rete, the plate, and the mater are all usually pretty alike. But the key is on the back of the mater. If you look, there's another set of etchings. Those are scales for calculations involving the sun. But they're specific to the location of the person who used the astrolabe. Someone in London would have a different scale of where the sun rises and sets than, say, someone from California or Russia."

"And these scales were created by Geoffrey Chaucer," said M as she rubbed her hand over the astrolabe's back. "But that still doesn't tell me why it's important. I mean, this plus the *Mutus Liber*, it's all unsolvable."

"Maybe it's a map?" suggested Jules. "Maybe the astrolabe and the book are supposed to be used together to lead us to a . . . um . . . a treasure?"

"A treasure?" echoed M. "I don't think so."

"Let's take it one step at a time," suggested Mrs. Freeman. "Start with the astrolabe. What does it do?"

"Tells time," said M.

"Maps the sky," said Foley.

"Predicting." M put the pieces back together and slid them around with her fingers. Then she looked up at the others. "Predicting, that's it. This predicts the position of the sky. Sunrise, moonrise, and where the stars will be at any given time of year."

"So how does that help us?" asked Zara. "Explain a little more — we're not all living inside your head, M."

"What if," started M, "there was a celestial event that happened during Chaucer's time — say, a comet that passed through space? Once the comet became part of the night sky, it could have been mapped."

"There are always comets and asteroids in space," said Devon. "How would this Chaucer guy know the difference between it and a star, or an airplane in the sky?"

"Well, there were a lot fewer airplanes in the thirteen hundreds," said Mrs. Freeman.

"And don't comets have paths, or orbits, that they travel?" asked Jules. "Like Halley's Comet, it passes Earth every seventy-five years. Astronomers had been noting it since, like, 239 B.C."

Everyone stared at her. "What? I have a lot of time on my hands since Doe stole my abilities. And I lived in a traveling carnival. The night sky was my ceiling, so after enough stargazing I did a little reading. It's not like M owns all the rights to knowing random facts."

M shrugged. It was true.

"Anyway," continued Jules, "people didn't realize that there was a pattern to the comet's approach until some guy named Halley in the seventeen hundreds. I think the comet has even appeared in an old tapestry of a battle. Apparently comets were seen as a sign of change or disaster back then. I mean, it must have looked like a broken star to people who didn't have telescopes. Like the sky was falling."

"Wait," interrupted Evel. "Comet? There's a comet that's heading past Earth right now."

A sick feeling rose in the pit of M's stomach. "Comets can make meteors as chunks fall off. What if this comet hurling our way was the source of the meteorite that caused the black hole that destroyed the Lawless School?"

The room fell silent until Foley broke the spell. "That comet is thousands of miles from us in deep, deep space. The chances of a chunk of it breaking off and landing where Doe could get it are slim to none. It's completely laughable. I think we're spiraling down a delusional path, which is exactly what Doe wants. What if that astrolabe doesn't do anything? What if he's just sending us in circles, tying us up with meaningless mysteries while he's making bigger moves?"

Again, M held up the astrolabe. "He doesn't want to get a chunk. He wants the whole thing. You don't know this guy, Foley. He's crazy. He's smart and he's insane. Doe created the good guys *and* the bad guys, and I have no idea why. But I can make an educated guess about what he wants. If he had this astrolabe, he'd know the path of the comet."

"So he'd know the comet's path, whoopty-doo," argued Foley. "What good would that be to him?"

"If he knows the path, he knows the trajectory," explained M. "And if he knows the trajectory, he could try to alter its course."

"How?" asked M's mother. "What on Earth could cause a comet to change direction?"

"A missile?" suggested Jules.

"A satellite?" said Devon.

"A laser?" added Evel.

"A magnet?" guessed Zara.

"No," M said slowly. "A black hole."

CHAPTER 23
THE RESURRECTION MEN

"You are all officially crazy," snapped Foley. "I mean, listen to yourselves. Black holes, comets, trajectories, what do you know about any of this? I'm telling you, this has misdirection written all over it. You're falling into Doe's trap."

M tucked the astrolabe back into her suit. The birds were chirping outside and the sun was beaming across the grassy meadow. Hearing those birds reminded her of being on her first assignment at the Lawless School, while she was hiding in the woods waiting for Foley, of all people, to get out of his class so that she could plant the deep freeze on him. Then she remembered the secret underground tunnel that she chased him through, and the underground hallways at the Fulbright Academy.

"It's always been a trap," said M. "All of it. Doe's trap. The Lawless School, the Fulbright Academy, they've trapped us all into thinking that we're on different sides. We've been fighting one another instead of focusing on the real problem."

"Recruit them young," said Zara with venom pulsing in her voice. "Teach them to hate one another. One group follows orders while the other breaks the rules. We've been brainwashed."

Mrs. Freeman nodded. "It's not something we could just tell people because it's not what people want to hear. M's father, Madame Voleur . . . we needed proof."

"Seems like your need for proof has cost a lot of lives," said Devon.

"No, she's right," said Evel. "Without concrete evidence, it would seem like another trick. Another trap. It's genius. Disgusting, but genius."

"But none of this helps us if we don't know Doe's next move," said M. "What does he need?"

"If it's a black hole he's after, he'll need more of that meteorite," said Zara. "But we destroyed it all."

"But what if you didn't?" asked Jules. "What if he has more?"

"No, I stole the last chunk from him," M said confidently. "The way he reacted when I took it, it was like I ripped his soul away from him. If there's more of that meteorite out there, then it's hidden where he can't find it."

"One thing isn't sitting right with me," said Devon.

"One thing?" said Foley. "How about everything?!"

"Can it, Foley, and let her talk." Zara's face was deadly serious. She'd worked a long time and lost a lot to get to this point. Everyone had. Zara motioned for Devon to continue.

"Who's hiding this stuff?" Devon's question was one that M hadn't considered. She'd been too busy searching for these cursed trinkets to stop and consider the history behind each hiding place. The cane from Scotland Yard. The buried *Mutus Liber* in Prague. Maybe even the moon rocks from around the world that her father had destroyed. They were all hidden, and that meant someone other than Doe knew their value.

Before anyone could guess at an answer, a shrill ring cut through the tense discussion. Everyone froze.

"Has that phone ever rung before?" M asked her mother.

"I didn't even know it was working," she said. "I'm certainly not paying any phone bill."

"Looks like someone really wants to talk to us," said Zara as she reached out and answered the phone. "Secret undercover ops residence, how may I direct your call?"

A smirk spread across her face. "Big surprise, M, it's for you."

All eyes fell on her as she took the phone from Zara. "Hello?"

"It's Merlyn," the voice on the line said.

M smiled. "How did you get this number?"

"I just answered that question, weren't you listening?" he said buoyantly. "It's Merlyn. *That's* how I got this number. And I had some help from Sercy. Well, a lot of help from Sercy. She can leap sprawling mainframes in a single hack. Listen, we've got another major flare-up over here. My parents are on their way to London."

M's smile faded just as fast as it had appeared. "Why are they doing that?"

"There's something going down at another London museum. The Hunterian Museum. Tonight. My parents usually don't go to these things, but it's going to be crawling with Lawless grads. You should go, too. It's a swanky high-society deal, though, so you'll need to get dolled up and carry a big stick. I promise you're going to need it."

M nodded into the phone. "I get it. Contact Ben, let him know where we'll be." Then without waiting for a good-bye, she hung up and pulled the plug out of the wall. "That was Merlyn. We don't have much time. There's another target in London, at a party of some sort. Get out your credit card, Mom. We need to go shopping."

The limo pulled up in front of the Hunterian Museum promptly at eight p.m. M could not stop fidgeting with her outfit. The black lace dress left her arms exposed, the ballerina flats had a slick bottom, and the silver clutch couldn't fit anything she really needed inside it. If they weren't walking into a trap, M was sure dressed in one. Still, her mother had convinced her to play the part. Devon, on the other hand, had needed no convincing and was perfectly suited for black-tie attire. Her silver cocktail dress shimmered under every streetlamp they passed and her black hair looked flawless. Zara also seemed quite at home in her dress, a royal-blue satin piece with wraps and straps, while Jules wore a ruby-red dress with ruched, airy fabric that floated around her. The boys wore tuxes, though Evel was struggling with his tie as if it were an assassin trying to choke him.

Just before the door to the limo opened, M realized that this might be as close as she would ever come to a normal life. It was like they were going to prom, instead of a mission. And then the cameras began to flash.

Photographers were outside of the car, calling out to the kids. "Who are you? Who are you? Who are you wearing?" Luckily Mrs. Freeman was posing as their publicist. She told the press that they were American interns for Doctors Without Borders. That called off the photo hounds, who quickly moved on to the next, more glamorous guest arriving behind them.

Inside, the guests were impeccably dressed and every bit as bubbly as the champagne the waiters served alongside a nonstop buffet of appetizers. Their mingling voices mixed with the quartet of musicians playing classical music. Nothing out of the ordinary there — it was just as M imagined a black-tie charity event would be. Boring.

But the real shocker was the museum itself.

Bones. Everywhere, there were bones behind glass, human skeletons of every size, animals sliced open and pickled in jars, even veins, arteries, and nerves splayed out and pasted onto wooden boards and displayed like art.

"What is this place?" asked Devon.

"The Hunterian Museum collection was established by John Hunter, a doctor who advanced modern surgery techniques and anatomical education by leaps and bounds in the eighteenth century," Jules read off of the pamphlet one of the staff had handed to her as she entered. "The charity event tonight is celebrating his contributions to medicine and raising money for medical organizations around the world."

"A surgeon's museum? What would Doe want here?" M whispered before addressing the others. "Okay, here's what we know. There's something here that Doe wants. Should we have spent more time researching this museum than getting dressed for the event, yes, but hindsight is twenty-twenty and at least we fit in. Let's split up and see what stands out. Meet back here in twenty minutes; this place isn't the Louvre, we should be able to make the rounds by then."

The team scattered. Mrs. Freeman was on door duty, watching the guests arrive and looking for anyone suspicious — or anyone she recognized from her former double life. Jules grabbed a mini lamb chop with a mint glaze from a passing waiter but couldn't even take a bite. She and M walked into a display called the Crystal Gallery. It was filled, wall-to-wall, with a gruesome A to Z of anatomy. Fetuses floating in jars, severed spines with nerves still attached, every organ of the human body, bleached and preserved and put on display.

Jules handed the lamb chop back to another passing waiter. "Ugh, I think I just went vegetarian."

"Not your average run-of-the-mill museum," agreed M. "So what could be valuable in here? Is there a secret code etched into one of these . . . things?"

Jules peered closer to study a human skull that was misshapen due to a tumor growth. "Doe has a weird concept of what makes something valuable. I would have stolen gold."

They continued on through a gallery that showcased the history of surgeons' instruments. Scalpels, clips, retractors, and scissors through the ages, designed to open, hold, and slice into the human body to cure it. To pull out the evil inside and fix what was broken. The tools reminded M of the sick bay at the academy, when Cal had been stitched up. She shook at the memory of the cold metal instruments clattering on the floor and the creepy collection of eyeballs hidden under the cabinet. But slowly a connection was starting to form. There was a link here somewhere, M knew it.

In the art gallery, a group of professors and doctors were chatting about John Hunter. M and Jules faked being interested in a piece of art to listen to their discussion.

"I disagree," said a gray-haired gentleman. "If the Irish Giant wanted his remains buried at sea, then he should have been buried at sea. Not living out his afterlife as a bone display."

"But great things came from his remains," argued a woman in a burgundy dress. "And while the lengths Hunter went to in procuring the remains were highly illegal by today's standards —"

"Highly illegal!" the man barked. "I should say so. The Resurrection Men were a disgrace to the sanctity of our profession. Glorified tomb robbers is all they were."

"Still, there was no other way to gain access to cadavers during Hunter's time," the woman continued. "Even criminals were off-limits."

M's mind was racing now. Criminals, surgeons, museums — her seemingly random world was suddenly growing smaller and smaller. "Excuse me," she interjected. "I couldn't help but overhear your discussion. Would you mind if I asked you a few questions?"

"Of course not, dear," the woman said.

"You mentioned the Resurrection Men. Who were they?" asked M.

"Well," began the woman, "when Hunter was practicing back in the seventeen hundreds, people were not willing to donate their bodies to science. So a group of people saw an opportunity to make money. They would procure bodies after people had passed and sell them to Hunter for his surgical experiments."

"Procure!" The man laughed. "That's a kind way to say 'dig up bodies from the grave and sell them without the families' consent.' Here, follow me."

They moved the conversation out of the art gallery and stopped in front of a giant skeleton. It was almost eight feet tall and kept a creepy watch over the rest of the room.

"This gentleman is Charles Byrne, also known as the Irish Giant." The man crossed his arms and shot a look at the woman. "Mr. Byrne knew full well that Hunter wanted his bones as a trophy. But he'd spent his life being gawked at, and he wanted some peace in death. He expressly wrote in his will that he wanted to be buried at sea. And yet here he is, thanks to the Resurrection Men."

"Ah, but it's only because Mr. Byrne is here that we're able to understand and treat the medical anomaly that causes this type of giganticism," countered the woman. "Without him, we would never be able to help those who suffer from the same issue."

Sensing a rekindling of their argument, M changed the subject. "You mentioned Hunter's experiments. What were they like? Was he operating underground, in private?"

"Oh goodness no!" both the woman and man agreed.

"Hunter's surgeries were akin to the performance of a Shakespeare play," said the woman. "He always had an audience. The idea was to record and share the information from the surgery with the world. Every procedure led to a better understanding of the art of saving lives."

"Thank you," said M suddenly. Then she grabbed Jules and the two made their way back to the meet-up point.

"What's going on, M?" asked Jules.

"*The Anatomy Lesson of Dr. Nicolaes Tulp* by Rembrandt!" M rushed to try to connect the dots for Jules. "It's a painting of surgeons dissecting a corpse. That corpse was a criminal named Aris Klindt. And that painting used a technique called the *umbra mortis,* the same name of the black hole created by the Fulbrights. And now we're here, in a surgeon's museum, filled with the remains of people, many of whom may have been criminals, or may have been stolen by criminals . . . It's all connected somehow. We're missing a clue and I'll bet it's right in front of us."

"Oh no," gasped Jules and she jumped back as if she'd seen a ghost, nearly crashing into a waiter. But Jules didn't notice the waiter. Her eyes were glued across the room and she pointed over M's shoulder with a shaky hand.

M turned to see what was waiting behind her. Her blood turned to ice, like she'd been submerged in the Hamburg River again, and her legs grew rooted to the floor. People were moving around her like a river and she was a rock, holding her ground yet lost at sea.

A skeleton stared back at her: the *last* last remains that she would have expected to find on display in a museum.

Devon was the first on the scene. "What's the deal, you two?"

Zara and Foley came next. "Nothing out of the ordinary to report . . . Well, you know what I mean. What's up with M and Jules? They seem more haunted than they usually do."

"Those bones," said M. "That's what . . . I mean, who . . . I mean, what Doe is after."

The plaque beside the display read: *Jonathan Wild, Thief-Taker.*

"But Jonathan Wild is the founder of both the Lawless School and the Fulbright Academy. He's John Doe. I was sure of it," said M. "This can't be him."

M felt an arm clasp around her neck.

"Stop it, M," said Foley. "I told you it's impossible. He's dead. His bones are right there."

She tried to shrug him off, but Foley's grip was painfully solid.

"Hey, Foley, what gives? Let her go, this is big news." Zara tried to push him away from M, but Foley knocked her clear across the room with his free hand. She crash-landed into a group of adults, spilling drinks and shattering a plate of food. All around the museum, a tense quiet arose. Everyone had quieted down to see what was going on.

"No, Zara," said Foley. "*This* is big news."

Devon, Evel, Jules, and M's mother rushed forward to help M, but strangers in the crowd grabbed them.

"Merlyn *did* tell you that this was a Lawless-inspired event, didn't he?" Foley's mouth twisted in a malformed laugh. "It's always good to be prepared."

"What are you doing, Foley?" screamed Zara. "This isn't you!" She turned and kicked, and the men holding her back fell moaning to the floor. Zara stepped over them and kept her eyes trained on Foley.

"It's the *new* me," he sneered. "I think you'll grow to like it in time."

As Zara advanced, a hissing sound came through the air vents, followed by puffs of yellow gas. The non-Lawless guests started screaming and running for the exits, clawing and pushing one another out of the way. But then they stopped. A calmness came over the guests, and M watched in terror as the crowd became zombie drones under the power of the Lawless gas.

Even Zara was overpowered. She slowed her purposeful march across the room and then just stopped. Likewise,

Devon, Evel, and M's mother all stood casually in place as if nothing out of the ordinary was happening. The men holding them back released their grips but no one moved. A pair of the Lawless thugs still secured Jules, who remained conscious. M was still alert, too.

"Why isn't the gas affecting us, M?" asked Jules in a panic.

"Because you've both received such a high dosage of it in the past, it doesn't work the same way on you anymore," answered Foley. "Same goes for me."

"You don't have to do this, Foley," pleaded M.

"And what do you think I'm doing?" he asked.

"Doe's not worth it. Whatever he's offering you, he's lying." M grimaced as Foley dug his fingers deeper in her neck. She went to swing her arms, but his grip was immobilizing, like he had her nervous system on lockdown.

"Oh, I think he's worth it, M." Foley smiled and whipped her around to face him. "See, I've invested my whole life in him, so he'd better be worth it."

"What are you talking about?" demanded Jules. "Let her go!"

Foley obliged and M dropped to the floor. She tried to stand, but her legs wobbled out from underneath her. The blond-haired boy left M and circled Jules.

"Do me a favor, Jules," said Foley as he grabbed her cheeks and cradled her face violently. "Don't call me Foley anymore. Foley's dead. He died that night in Hamburg when you scatterbrains left him behind. Isn't there a rule about never leaving a teammate behind? Wait, is that a Lawless rule or a Fulbright rule? I could never remember."

"So what do you want us to call you . . . Doe?" M hadn't finished the sentence before she launched herself at him, but she was tackled savagely by two of the zombies: her mother and Zara. They looked at her through dead eyes.

"Oh, don't call me Doe, either," he said. "That name has worn out its welcome, hasn't it? Let's try my old name back on for size . . . I hope it still fits. Call me Jonathan. Jonathan Wild. Thief-Taker. And that's what I intend to do."

Wild pointed with his left hand. "You, bring me that," he commanded, and another guest smashed open a glass display to get a bottle, which he carried over to his master. "Isn't it just like a doctor to keep chloroform out in the open? With kids around, even. Tsk, tsk."

He uncorked the bottle and poured its contents onto a cloth napkin. Then he covered Jules's mouth. Her legs kicked in defiance and then went limp. Wild let loose a sick grin that really didn't belong on Foley's face.

"How?" asked M. "How are you still alive?"

"I'll admit it wasn't easy at first." Wild paced back to M and waved to zombie Zara and Mom to let her up. "I was caught, sentenced to death by hanging, but I was rather attached to my neck. So I took a potion, a special elixir that I'd gotten my hands on."

"It was the gas, wasn't it?" said M.

Wild only smiled. "Then I lived out my life on the run. Took on a few lives here and there, until it was time to die a nice, natural death. And naturally that wouldn't suit me, either. So I began working with the less scrupulous surgeons and doctors. They became my own Resurrection Men. Together we kept my body cobbled together with spare parts. And when those parts gave out . . ."

"You found newer and younger parts to replace them with," finished M. The thought made her sick to her stomach. "So why the fake bones in the case?"

"Simple. They aren't bones at all, they're pieces of the meteorite. And thanks to your parents hoarding those moon rocks, I now have everything I need to finally complete my lifelong work."

"You used Zara to get to my mother. To steal the rocks," said M. She glanced at her mother and Zara standing side by side right at that very moment. But they were lost to the gas. "You convinced her to leave me in the forest, didn't you?"

"I burned Madame Voleur down with the cabin, too. But that was her fault for living in firewood." More and more of Wild's mannerisms were coming out and more and more of Foley disappeared. He was mere skin and bones now. A costume that a madman had stolen. "Madame V and her bratty crooks dogged me for years. Hiding the Rembrandt paintings. Leaving a trail to my death cane in the Black Museum. And hiding that copy of the *Mutus Liber* was a feat, too. But you handled all those missions for me, M. So you can see why I had no choice. I needed to teach Madame Voleur a lesson once and for all. And I made sure she knew that I was the teacher before she went up in flames."

M felt Zara's grip loosen on her arm. Could she be fighting the gas? M needed to buy more time. Then her father's voice sprang into her head. *The more you know about the people around you, the more you know about the situation you're in.* "All these years," she started, "you've been waiting for the comet to return."

"That blasted thing travels a dreadfully long orbit," Wild said with exhaustion. "What was I to do but wait?"

"How does that explain creating the Lawless School and the Fulbright Academy?" M could now move her right arm. Zara was coming to, slowly but surely. "And why would you destroy —?"

Wild laughed. "Killing time, M. I was only killing time by doing what I do best. It was fun to make a mess of this place. Like playing with toy soldiers . . . only mine were real. I created an entire reason for families to live! A team for them to root for, a legacy for their children to follow. The parents were so proud. The graduates felt like they had earned their future, while the Ronins suffered through utter failure and rejection for the rest of their lives. And for what? Tell me, did you know how long your father had the Lawless yearbook that I so vainly allowed my name to appear in? Oh, he found that years ago. Makes you wonder why he didn't share it sooner."

"I'm sure he had his reasons," said M.

"I remember now," said Wild. "It's because I told him I'd kill you and your mother if he ever let my secret out. Must feel good, knowing that your father cared more about the two of you than the rest of the world."

"Because he knew I'd find it," said M with sudden confidence. "He knew I'd finish what he started."

"Well, you are a smart cookie, Ms. Freeman. A chocolate chip off the old block! But tell me, are you a fortune cookie, too? What do you think lies in your future?"

Stopping you.

That's what she would have said if Jonathan Wild hadn't choked her with chloroform. And the roomful of strangers turned off like a light.

CHAPTER 24

THE MOON IS NOT THE MOON

The black hood was heavy and thick with M's own breathing. She felt damp sweat roll into her eyes and down her cheek. It was uncomfortable and claustrophobic, but it meant she was alive. A parched moan escaped her as she felt the outside world take form around her. It was cold and hard. Pushing her hands against a marble floor, M gently lifted herself up to her knees and pulled off the hood.

She studied the room. It was dark, but she could make out two other hooded figures slumped across from her. M called out but her voice was raspy and dry. "Hello?" The slight whisper echoed like a ghost in what had to be a gigantic room.

One of the other prisoners flinched to life and slowly pulled off her hood. It was Jules. "M?" She coughed up phlegm and spit it out.

"I'm okay," she replied. "You?"

"I've been better," groaned Jules. "Chloroform headache. Ugh, and I can still taste it in the back of my throat."

The third figure began to roll around on the floor and sat up. A muffled scream came from under the hood, as the prisoner's hands went to his face and patted it as if to make sure his head was still intact. Then he ripped the hood off and gasped for air.

"Merlyn?!" Jules was shocked to see their old friend here. "But how?"

"Jules?" he answered hopefully, then he turned to see M in just as much trouble and hung his head low. "You're here, too? This isn't good."

"It's my fault," said M. "I told Foley we were working together after you called."

"Huh?" Merlyn looked confused. "Why would Foley send a team of Fulbrights after me? They swarmed my house and shot me with a tranquilizer dart." He touched the back of his neck gingerly where the dart must have struck its mark. "I've heard of holding a grudge, but we put him in that deep freeze, like, years ago."

"Foley's not really Foley," explained M. "He's John Doe. And Doe is really Jonathan Wild."

"What?" asked Merlyn. "I think that dart is still messing with me 'cause you're not making any sense."

"I'll explain it after we escape," M said.

Merlyn grinned. "Same old M. Hey, you remember that time we escaped the Box? That was cool."

"I don't think we're in the Box anymore," said M. As her eyes finally adjusted to the darkness, she examined the room, which was huge. It had a cathedral-style ceiling with gorgeous, stained-glass windows built in directly above them. Two sets of marble staircases rose up on opposite sides of the room and candles were lit all over the ground.

M tried to stand up, but she bumped her head against something invisible. She pressed hard against the air. "There's some sort of force field around me."

"Me, too," said Jules as she clubbed the ghostly surface.

"Where are we?" asked Merlyn.

"Don't you young scholars recognize the Library of Congress when you see it?" asked Foley — Wild — from the top of the staircase. "That's right, friends, welcome to Washington, DC, and the largest library in the world."

He was wearing his own special Fulbright suit with the mask slung behind him.

"What are we doing here?" asked M, still groggy from the trip.

Wild clapped his hands and spoke with pure enjoyment. "You three are going to help me achieve my ultimate goal! It's been years in the making! Tonight, children, we are going to destroy the world . . . and the universe, if my calculations are correct."

"You . . . you'll never get away with this," said M. "You can't destroy the universe. That's just . . . plain stupid for one thing."

"Not to mention impossible," said Merlyn.

"So was setting off a black hole on Earth," snapped Wild. "And I managed that."

He walked down the stairs toward them and raised his

265

hand to draw attention to his neck. "See, I've had a long time to come up with this plan. A. Long. Time. When the police finally caught me, I was sentenced to death by hanging. And let me tell you, the entire population of London turned out to watch that evil Jonathan Wild get what he deserved. I'll never forget their joyful cheers when the rope went tight. Have you ever heard a crowd of people cheering at your very breath being taken away? Well, I have. I still hear them, even through Foley's ears. Not one person on Earth cried for me. Now they'll know how it feels."

"But those people are long gone!" cried Jules. "No one deserves this!"

"That's where you're wrong," Wild snapped. "I have watched humanity for centuries and found them wanting. Wars, crime, death, unspeakable evil. There's no hope here."

"You can't give up hope," begged M.

"I didn't give it up, Freeman," Wild said. "It was stolen from me. Now, that's my story. But let's go further back. Have you ever heard of the Big Bang theory? Sure you have, the one where a ball of nothingness squeezed so tight that it caused an explosion that built everything ever in existence?"

"No," Merlyn gasped. "You can't be ... You're not considering —"

"The opposite theory?" Wild finished. "I am. Oh, Merlyn, you are the smart one! Care to explain it to your friends?"

Merlyn threw his head back and turned it slowly, deflated by whatever he was about to say. "It's called the Big Crunch.

Some scientists believe that eventually the weight of the universe will become so unbearable that it will collapse in on itself, crushing everything ever in existence back into nothingness. But even if they're right, that won't happen for a long, long, long, long, long, long time."

"And I do hate waiting," snarled Wild. "So let's move things along. If my favorite comet were to ever come in contact with your only moon, well, that should make the black hole to end all black holes. It would swallow everything and cause the universe to fold back in on itself. Good-bye, Earth. Good-bye, life. Hello, uncreation."

"You're crazy," said Jules.

"Tell me something I don't know, Byrd!" snapped Wild. "Many great thinkers were called crazy in their time. I consider it a compliment."

"Most of those great thinkers didn't want to end all of life," said Merlyn.

"Well, then they weren't thinking big enough, now were they?" said Wild.

"Why are we here, Wild?" said M.

"What can I say, I'm a reader," said Wild as he jumped up and paced toward a door. "And did you know that the Library of Congress has a version of one of my favorite books of all time, the *Mutus Liber*?"

With a snap of his fingers, Wild summoned Devon and Evel from the shadows. They each held a book, and their eyes were empty. M knew they were still under the influence of the gas.

Zara came in from a third side, holding a third book in one hand and dragging Keyshawn on a hospital gurney with the other. The wheels creaked eerily in the large room, echoing like in a horror movie.

"Keyshawn!" yelled M as she strained against her force field.

Then each of Wild's zombies flipped the books open to the same page, and placed the books together between M, Merlyn, Jules, and Keyshawn. The books made three sides of a larger square on the ground in the middle of the room.

"No," said M, hoping to buy some time. "I meant why are *we* here? You could have gotten rid of us easily back in London. Wiped out our minds again. And Keyshawn is in a coma."

"I love an audience, but you four are much more than that." Wild sat down and crossed his legs, then leaned back on his elbows. "Do you know what we all have in common?"

"Nothing," said Merlyn.

"We've all been dosed with the gas," said M.

"Correct," said Wild, "but there's more. Guess what else happens over time? Life and families. Oh yes, families grow and grow and grow."

"Are you telling us that we're . . ." Jules said with a pause to try to stomach the last word. "Related?"

"Forget about Merlyn — you're the smart one, Byrd!" A crooked smile creaked over Wild's face. "What, no love for Great-great-great-great-great-times-ten-grandpa?"

"I'm gonna be sick," gagged Merlyn.

The thought made M severely uncomfortable in her own skin. She suddenly felt as if every muscle, bone, and blood vessel in her body belonged to someone else. But there was one important part of her that Wild could never own. Her will. "The future fixes the past's mistakes," she said.

"Well, that's why I'm wiping out the past, future, and present." Wild jumped up and stood over the three books that lay open on the floor. "As you can see, I need one more copy to complete my collection. A copy that dear Mr. Calvin Fence has in his possession. When I told him I had you, M, it wasn't long before he came running."

Dr. Lawless entered the room, shoving Cal ahead of him. Both were fully suited and a haze of smoke came off of them. The smell of burning metal hung in the air. Lawless tossed the final copy of the *Mutus Liber* in front of Wild.

"It wasn't much of a fight," bragged Lawless.

"Did you beat him with four fingers tied behind your back?" snarked M.

Wild came forward and picked up the book. He examined it closely then grinned. "You've done well, Lawless. It's a perfect match."

"C'mon, Cal!" Merlyn yelled. "You brought the real book with you to save us? Why not bring a fake?!"

"I'm sorry, guys." Cal's face was already bruised and red with scrapes. "The plan made more sense in my head."

Wild let out a howling cackle at that. "This is precious, Calvin Fence. You disappointed your father. You disappointed your mother. And now you've disappointed your only friends in the world. I'm beginning to like you more and more."

Wild slapped Cal playfully on the cheek and gave the book to zombie Devon. She used it to complete the square in the middle of the floor. Then Devon pulled out a knife, followed by a five-inch gold circle that she laid over the center of the newly formed square. Tracing the circle with a knife, Devon cut away at the original books. When she was finished, she handed the four cut pieces back to Wild.

"Thank you, Devon, my perfect little soldier." Then Wild held aloft the Chaucer astrolabe. "Do you know why we don't use astrolabes anymore? It's not because we have computers now. No, the astrolabe died out a long time before computers existed. It was replaced by the invention of the sailor's astrolabe. See, sailors realized that they didn't need the entire night sky to tell time or direction. Therefore they didn't need the whole circle of the astrolabe. Instead, they broke the sky down into quadrants, so I've done the same."

He fanned out the four pieces of paper cut from the *Mutus Liber.* Then he kneeled down and held the pieces over one of the candle's flames. Slowly, writing began to appear on the pages. "During my first lifetime, I became casually obsessed with the night sky. Especially the rumors of a deadly comet. It was said to carry an evil spirit that would annihilate everything in its path. But while those rumors were eventually dismissed by all sorts of scientific minds as unbelievable fiction to scare children, I knew it was true."

When all of the writing had surfaced, Wild lifted the papers to his lips and blew on them. They bent with his breath. "So I tracked the comet through history and I discovered its path. Then I drew up the coordinates on the edges of these famous books. When I was caught, I had some of my henchmen hide the books for safekeeping. Turns out, though, that some of them didn't want the world to end. They wanted to keep the books away from me, to save the world, I suppose. So they hid them; they even made more copies to try and fool me, but you can't keep a good man down. I mean, if I've proven anything, I've proven that."

Wild took the four quadrants and formed a complete circle, which he placed in the Chaucer astrolabe. "And yes, the comet has made a few passes during my long life, but tonight will be the first pass when I have pieces of the moon! Now I have the exact information I need to set off another black hole on Earth to knock the comet just a touch off course. Toward the moon."

"Wait, what?" asked Dr. Lawless. "You are going to do *what*?"

"Comet hit moon, go boom," said M. "What did you think he needed the book for, you moron?"

"No, Wild, I won't let that happen!" Lawless pulsed a magblast, but Wild swept the attack aside with his own magblast and lifted Lawless high in the air.

"I don't remember asking for your permission, Doctor," said Wild.

M watched as Lawless drifted up toward the stained-glass windows above them. There was something odd about them and it wasn't just that Dr. Lawless was about to smash into them. The colored panes were vibrating ever so slightly. She caught Cal's eye and knocked against her force field. "He's holding us down with a magblast. Up on the ceiling."

"Thanks," he whispered back.

"You knew we gave you the wrong astrolabe back in London, didn't you?" she asked.

"Yeah," he murmured. "But I needed to flush Doe out."

"So this is actually part of your plan?" said M.

"Well, not *all* of it."

But their conversation was cut short by a scream and a heavy thump on the ground. Dr. Lawless lay there between M and Cal. He moaned and moved his legs. In the suit a fall like that wouldn't do too much permanent damage, but it would definitely sting.

Wild stepped over Lawless and held Chaucer's astrolabe up to calculate the coordinates hidden in the *Mutus Liber* pages. He smiled and entered the numbers into a handheld device. From the ceiling above them, M heard the sounds of heavy machines shifting into a different position. Then M, Merlyn, Jules, and Keyshawn were moved to different parts of the room by the force fields like pieces on a chess board.

"Okay, friends," announced Wild once everyone was in position. "Our time has come to an end. If you will each take a meteorite and place it in front of your favorite contestant."

Devon and Evel carried a pile of bones — the phony bones of Jonathan Wild's fake skeleton. Then they set them in front of M and her friends. Legs, arms, ribs, and more were splayed across the floor in stacks.

Once the bones were passed out, Zara brought around the moon rocks. She handed each of the rocks to the prisoners, reaching through their force fields and trapping the stones inside with them. When she reached M, she handed her the final piece. And winked. *The answer,* she mouthed.

M took the rock in her hand. It looked just like the others, only slightly darker, less bleached out. As she held the chunk, she thought back to one of Keyshawn's murky statements from before. *The moon is not the moon.*

Suddenly the bones in front of her began to rearrange against the force field, forming into a small cage that wrapped around her. The same thing was happening to the others. The bones were drawn to the moon rocks! As the rocks began to shimmer, everyone screamed. M backed away from the building light. She knew what came next. A deep, sucking darkness that would swallow them whole. M watched in horror as a black halo formed over Keyshawn, then over Jules, and then over Merlyn. Then the halos started to churn, faster and faster, spinning into more halos as the ground started to shake.

"Yes!" screamed Wild from above them. "This too shall pass!"

"You said you'd let them go if I brought you the book!" yelled Cal. He raised his glove and fired a blast at Wild, but the magnetic force fizzled out. It was nothing next to the twisting gravity of the budding black hole.

"No one here gets out alive!" Wild roared. Then Devon and Evel turned on Cal, knocking him down and holding him in place.

Wild raised both hands and formed the most powerful magblast that M had ever seen. It scorched with intensity, like a handheld tornado. "Now, young Calvin, you must learn that you cannot make deals with the devil!"

The magblast attack was furious, fighting its way past the growing black holes and heading straight for Cal. But before it could strike, another force shoved Cal, Devon, and Evel out of its way. Standing there with a fierce-looking metallic staff was Cal's mother, Ms. Watts.

"You don't get to kill my son, Jonathan Wild." Ms. Watts sneered with the same cold hatred that Cal had shown when he was talking about his own mother. "You unmade me. Turned me against the man I loved. Turned me against Calvin's father. And then turned me against my own son . . . all on a whim. Now I get my revenge."

"My death is yours," said Wild. "If you can earn it."

Ms. Watts swung the staff around her head and hurled a blast at Wild. Chunks of the marble burst where the attack hit and were sucked into the growing black hole oblivions.

Meanwhile, Zara scrambled to check on Cal, Devon, and Evel. The siblings had finally been jolted awake. Evel climbed over to Devon and hugged her. "I'm so glad you're okay!"

"Me, too," she said as she hugged him back. "Me, too."

"We need to get them out of here!" Zara yelled to Cal over the gushing wind. The floor itself buckled underneath them and Cal looked up at the ceiling.

"I can do this!" he said.

He jumped up and shot a magblast at the stained-glass windows above them. The glass exploded and so did the engines behind them that had trapped M and her friends.

With the force fields gone, the skeleton cages collapsed into the glowing moon rocks and accelerated the process. M, Merlyn, and Jules scattered out of the way in time, but Keyshawn was violently thrown from his gurney. M ran to Keyshawn's side, but they were now out in the open and caught up in Ms. Watts and Jonathan Wild's battle.

Ms. Watts wielded her staff like an outer space samurai, connecting hit after hit on Wild. She used the building wind around her to channel her attacks, flipping through the air as if gravity didn't apply to her anymore.

Cal ran over to M's side. "Come on, let's go!"

"We can't leave Keyshawn!" cried M.

Cal moved to pick up the old man when something made him freeze. M leaned forward to grab him, but before she could, Cal was drawn violently backward.

Wild had caught him in a magblast. "Decision time, Lady Watts! Me or Calvin!" Then Wild flipped Cal toward the largest black hole.

"Calvin!" screamed Ms. Watts as she dove into the air and caught her son. She threw him back to M, who grabbed his ankle and held on for dear life. Cal watched as his mother was shredded left and right in the warped wind tunnel, screaming with pain and anger. Then Ms. Watts plummeted into the black hole deeper and deeper until she disappeared.

Cal screamed. Wild cackled. His plan was going to work.

But the moon rock M had held suddenly glowed white. She looked up and saw that the halo nearest to her was not black at all, but a brightness that defied color. The halo grew and grew, quickly taking over the room. It swallowed the other black holes and crushed them flat. M's hands burned holding Cal and keeping him from flying into the mess, but watching the power that emanated around her, she clutched him tighter, like she was holding life itself in her hands.

"No, no, no!" bellowed Wild as he ran up the stairs. "What is happening?"

As the bright rings swirled outward, the moon rocks and bones lifted into the air, dissolving into dust until a powerful explosion of light erupted in the room, forcing everyone to take cover. And then, it disappeared.

"Where is my ending?" shrieked Wild. "What have you done?!"

"The moon is not the moon." M fought to stand up and face the madman. "And you are not a threat anymore."

He marched toward her with a murderous gleam in his eyes, but paused when he heard Keyshawn finally speak.

"She's right." His hoarse voice sputtered. He clutched at his stomach, but his white teeth cut into a smile. "The moon wasn't always the moon, you fool. It's a chunk of Earth that broke off eons ago. And just like Earth, the moon is made of different elements in different places. Mother Nature is a funny thing, Doe, or Wild, or whatever your name is. She decides the way to destroy herself and the way to reinvent herself. I found the one thing you didn't bother to look for. The one thing M's father was searching for. A piece of the moon that was elementally different from the other fragments that created your *umbra mortis*."

Wild twisted his neck and redirected all of his anger at Keyshawn. A brutal shudder disturbed the air around him. Then he unleashed the blast. It sent the old man flying off the ground. Keyshawn smacked into the back wall like a fish hitting the butcher block, then landed awkwardly and didn't move. His eyes didn't even blink.

"I'm not a threat, M," heaved Wild. "I'm a promise."

Cal fired another magblast, but Wild held it at bay with a shield. He was wearing two magblasts and knew how to use them. "Oh, Cal, we could have been so good — or bad — together. Maybe there's hope for you yet. Let me finish my discussion with M first, then we can talk about your future."

"We don't have a future," gritted Cal, pushing to break through Wild's hold.

"Then have fun watching your friends die, knowing that there's nothing you could do to stop me," Wild taunted. Then he aimed his right hand at M.

She ran, but Wild tracked her like a hunter through a scope.

Thwack!

M felt a shudder of wind rush by her, but Wild's blast had missed. Looking up, she watched Wild's blast careen off of a magblast shield that was protecting her. Then someone helped M up off the floor. "Better late than never, I suppose."

Vivian Ware was dressed in her uniform and glowing hot red. She shrugged at M and held up another suit. M's suit. "A gift. Right where Sercy said I'd find it."

As helicopters swarmed the hole in the ceiling and search-lights swept the ground, M felt the familiar embrace of her suit as it closed around her and booted up. "We started this together, Vivian. Let's end it together."

Fulbrights came flying down on ropes like angry bees, blasting everything in sight. In the chaos, Wild broke off and retreated behind his soldiers. The haze of battle took over, as M, Vivian, and Cal plowed into the throng, taking down attackers from every angle. The Fulbrights had expected to battle a few kids, but they had no idea that an army was on its way.

CHAPTER 25

RONIN

The doors to the library blasted open and in marched Ben Downing, leading a full battalion. "Ronin!" he yelled. "Attack!"

Like a flood, the Ronin washed over the Fulbrights, moving forward as one cohesive unit. The Fulbright cadets fell back and looked to their leader to give them orders, but no one was there. They'd been abandoned. Some dropped their weapons right there and surrendered in defeat, freeing up enough Ronin to climb up the dangling ropes to the helicopters, where they secured the airspace above the combat.

M couldn't believe her eyes, seeing everyone working together to defeat the Fulbrights, and that's when she got clocked. The hit came from behind her and forced her to the ground. Still, she flipped back up and dodged the next blow. The Fulbright pulled down his mask. It was Dr. Lawless.

The room went quiet as far as M was concerned. The war around her was wiped away and only one man stood before her.

"I knew you were going to be fun, Ms. Freeman," sneered Lawless as he flicked out his saber. "Looks like Wild ran with his tail between his legs. That makes me the next in command. And since I never had the honor of slicing up your father, you'll make a suitable substitute to carve."

Lawless moved first, striking at M, but she shifted out of the way.

"Are you sure you wanna fight me, old man?" teased M. "Wild roughed you up back there. Lucky you've got that suit to protect you."

The doctor slicked back his sweaty mat of red hair and came at her again. This time M batted down his sword in one smooth motion with her forearm, then shoved him into a wall.

"You're a slippery one, aren't you?" barked Lawless. "Must run in the family."

M flicked out the sword from her suit and waved for Lawless to attack again. With a battle cry, the man charged with all his might and, to his surprise, M charged, too, directly toward him. Their swords connected in a spark that shattered the arm of Lawless's suit, revealing his wounded hand. He grabbed M around the neck and dragged her off the ground, but she found footing against another Fulbright and jumped off, flipping Lawless over and onto his back where she clutched him into a crushing chokehold.

"I'm not like my dad, Lawless," she whispered in his ear. "I'm not a ghost you can walk right through. Remember that when you wake up next week." M quickly unzipped the back of his suit and pressed her palm against his back.

The magblast sent shockwaves through the room, knocking

down the several other Fulbrights that had foolishly surrounded her. Lawless lay slumped and ready to collect dust on the cold slab he'd made for himself.

With Lawless out, M scanned the room for Wild and caught a shadow, darting between the fighters. M moved to follow it, but sensed someone approaching her from behind. She wheeled around to throw a hard punch and stopped an inch away from Cal's nose.

"Happy to see you, too," he said without flinching. Then he looked beyond her and M turned back. Wild darted up the stairs, making a break for the roof.

"It's him," said M.

"He's mine," said Cal.

"No arguments there, but let me tag along for old time's sake." M could finally read the look on her friend's face, a pure mixture of determination, vengeance, and something like satisfaction. All these years he'd been searching for a target and tonight he'd found it.

The two of them magblasted into the air, leaving the battle buzzing below as they landed on the roof where Wild was waiting.

If he was surprised to see them, he didn't let on.

"The most important thing to remember when you're making a plan is to prepare for the worst," he said as he backed away toward another section of the rooftop that was hidden from view by air-conditioning ductwork. "Step one: Have a getaway plan in case the situation blows up in your face. And you blew it up, all right. But don't worry, my comet will come around again."

"But you won't be there to see it," yelled Cal as he fired a magblast.

Wild caught the attack, easily crushing the swirl of wind with a clap of his hands. "Step two: Have backup at the ready."

Another Fulbright emerged in the moonlight. It was Bandit. With a stinging zap, he tied M and Cal together with a whip-like rope. Then his entire suit glowed an electric blue and a terrible rush of power surged through the two children. Their own bodies flared up until the wires woven around them cracked, popped, and died out. The red glow of their suits washed out and the shape went slack. Their magblasts, their suits, and their programmable weapons were all gone.

Bandit smiled and slowly reeled them closer. His eyes flashed neon yellow in the night.

"Step three: Leave no witnesses." Wild walked around a corner and Bandit joined him. Three more gas chambers like the ones from the night at her house, the night Jules, Merlyn, and Keyshawn had been eaten alive, were waiting for them like empty dinner plates on a set table. "You remember these, don't you, goody-two-shoes? I've been soul-searching ever since you two ran away from me and I haven't been able to find adequate replacements. And now thanks to your tenacity, it seems I won't have to. Come home to Wild."

M and Cal kicked and struggled, but the dead suits now weighed a ton. It was like wearing a lead blanket. The three doors to the chambers opened with a sickening *hush* that sounded like a parent easing their child into a bad situation. *Hush, this won't hurt a bit. Mr. Wild is only going to drain you.*

"You can't do this!" M screamed at Bandit.

"My dear," he answered. "I can do anything I want. I told you to leave the Lawless School. I warned you not to trust Zara. I've done all I can. There's only so many burning buildings I'm willing to run into to save you before I realize that you just like running into burning buildings."

Then Bandit tossed them inside the chambers like he was throwing bags of trash into a bin. He wasn't enjoying himself like Wild was. He looked, if anything, bored to be the one to finally close the door on M. She listened to Cal's muffled and distant screaming followed by the *thunks* of what must have been his kicking against the chamber walls.

M searched the lining, grasping for some safety latch to open the hatch, but there was nothing there. A wide window above her faced up into the night. The helicopters from earlier must have landed on adjacent buildings because nothing was above her now except for the sky with its shimmering stars, also muffled, distant, and screaming in their own beautiful way. Then, through the glass, Wild gazed down at her and tapped the window.

"People have always told me that it scares the itsy-bitsy fishies when you tap on the glass of the water tank," said Wild. "And I've always responded, *Why yes, that's the point.*"

Then he slapped his palm on the window, causing an awful bang that rattled inside with M. He left his palm there, as if he were waiting for M to place her hand against his. But she didn't. She only stared past him into the darkening space. Anger swelled inside of her. This wasn't over. This wasn't the end. No matter what this maniac stole from her, he would not steal her hope. And she would channel that weapon to stop him from ever seeing his plan through.

Wild peeked over his hand and his lips cracked into a demented smile. "Sleep well, M Freeman. And when you wake up this time . . . Oh, I can't lie to you after we've been through so much. You're not going to wake up this time. When you see your father, tell him: Nice try."

M pushed herself up to the window in time to watch Wild hop into the third chamber. Bandit shut the door and threw a switch. The metal walls around her came to life, vibrating so fast that M could feel the roots of her teeth. She clenched her entire body as tight as she possibly could, trying with every last bit of energy to hold on to whatever essence in her Wild was after. Holding on to her soul.

And then the walls stopped vibrating. It was over. M's heavy breathing sounded metallic against the chamber walls. She could hear her heart thudding as well. It sounded ragged in her chest, fumbling and beating in a new rhythm that sounded out of time with the rest of the world. M touched her face, then her arms, and on down, making sure she was still in one piece . . . and not soaked up inside of Foley. Then M caught her reflection in the window. She was still herself. She closed her eyes, saying "Thank you, thank you, thank you," over and over again, though she wasn't sure who or what she was thanking.

As the door opened, M's suit suddenly sparked back to life. The heavy wires became light as air again, but she was hesitant to get out of the chamber. Carefully, M raised herself up. Cal was climbing out of the chamber across from her and between them Bandit stood, keeping watch over Wild.

A shaken and disoriented Cal tried to find his footing. He was woozy and could barely stand up straight. Even his suit couldn't right him. Finally, he powered up his magblast and took aim at Bandit. "It didn't work."

"It did work, Cal," M warned as she stumbled over and batted down his arm, then swept him into a hug. She held him once again like she'd done underwater in Germany, but this time she was the one who felt like she was drowning. "It worked. It worked, but not the way Wild wanted it to work. This is Bandit's play."

The night around them had become quiet. The war below was over. Footsteps carried over the gravel as Zara arrived.

Bandit shifted to face the kids. "Don't come over here. I don't want you to see Foley like this."

"Don't you mean Wild?" asked Cal.

"No, I mean Foley," Bandit said sadly. "Wild's gone."

Zara's face twisted into a quiet agony. She stepped forward, but M reached over and pulled her into a hug, holding her back from seeing Foley. M realized that Zara's feelings for Foley had been honest and real. Zara had loved him. Zara's arms crushed and clawed around M's back, but instead of pushing away, M only held on to her tighter.

Then there was a sudden kicking in M's suit, like an itch to attack. She jerked back from Zara and turned to Bandit, who nodded a confirmation that something was wrong. "Take it off, Cal," she demanded. "Take off your suit right now!"

"That would be a good idea," said Bandit. "I don't fully understand how this contraption works, but I did my best to reset the directions. I channeled Wild into you ... or rather your suits, once I'd freed up the space, so to speak. Now those suits are cursed with his ghost, and that's a strand of evil wires that you can't control."

M and Cal both slithered out of the suits and kicked them aside. It was like climbing out of quicksand. They had been so tight that M could still feel the suit coiling around her even when it was off.

Then, awkwardly, the slack sleeves folded over and the legs slid across the ground until both empty suits lifted themselves up. Bandit trained his magblast on them, but one of the suits shot first, freezing him in place. Then the other suit took aim at M, who braced for what came next.

"Get down!" screamed Jules from behind them. M, Cal, and Zara all dropped to the roof as Jules flicked two knives at the suits, puncturing both magblast arms and trapping them against the nearby wall. The suits struggled to get free, but Jules pulled two more knives and struck the other arms. The empty suits were splayed out, helpless.

"I told you I could get it back," said Jules. "Now blast those creepy things to kingdom come."

Bandit obliged, firing a furious hit. One minute the suits were lumps of cloth, the next they were pulverized into dust that caught on the wind and blew away.

"You saved us," said M.

"Maybe you saved me this time," admitted Bandit. "This was the opportunity I've been waiting for, but you made it possible."

"And now?" M let the question dangle in front of Bandit.

He sighed heavily. "I've kept my promise to your father. You are alive. But now you should keep your distance, M. Go back to your life and have the childhood he would have wanted you to have."

"What about you?" she asked.

"This isn't the moment where I realize the error of my ways," he admitted. "I'm too old to change, or rather, I don't want to change. I'm a criminal. I'm a teacher. Those are both powerful callings. The Lawless School may have been destroyed, but schools can always be rebuilt. I'm sorry if you thought this would end differently."

Above them a stealth plane hovered without making a sound. Ropes came down and Bandit hooked them up to Foley's chamber.

Zara stepped forward and said, "Bandit, wait. I'm coming with you."

"Zara, no, please. Stay with me," M begged. "You can live with me and my mom. We can give you a normal life. Well, as normal a life as we can make after all of this. It's a chance for something beyond a life of crime."

"Thank you, M," said Zara as she wiped the tears from her eyes. "I'm not cut from a normal cloth, though. You and I both know that. I'm staying with Foley and leaving with Bandit."

M nodded. "You know this means someone will have to stop you."

"Someone, yes," said Bandit. "But I do love a worthy opponent. Farewell, Freeman, Fence, and Byrd. Until we meet again."

Bandit handed Zara another rope and she stepped into the bottom loop. Then they all lifted into the night, Zara, Bandit, and Foley, and disappeared.

New footsteps raced toward them. It was M's mother, who swept her up in the strongest hug she had ever felt in her life. "You're safe, you're safe, you're safe," she repeated between kisses to the top of M's head. Then M's mother began to sob. "I thought I'd, I'd . . ."

"I'm okay, Mom," said M. "Remember, we're Freemans. Safe, smart, and special. Nothing can change that. Not even the end of the world."

"Is it over?" her mother asked. "Is it finally finished?"

"Yes," said M. "And no. It's not over. It's different." She paused and looked at her friends around her and the dark sky, which suddenly felt so far away. "It's better."

EPILOGUE
ONE YEAR LATER

Sunlight broke through the slit in the curtain at just the right angle to cut a path straight down the middle of M's bed and directly into her eyes. She groaned and rolled over, pulling the covers tighter around her. She'd been meaning to fix that curtain for a while now, to show it who was the boss. But she never did. There were worse things than being woken up by the morning sun.

Chirp, chirp, chirp, chirp.

Like her alarm, which for some reason she had decided to switch from the standard bell chimes to a bird audio file. "Go back to the nest, you little devils," said M as she reached for her phone to hit snooze. Unfortunately, she batted it off the side table and it skidded under her bed. "You win, world. I'm up."

M slid onto her soft-carpeted floor and reached under her bed to silence the phone. She used the desk to pull herself up and gave a sideways look at the bright-teal-and-burnt-orange chevron drapes. "If you weren't so cute, I'd snip you into paper dolls."

She made her bed with its silver sparkle duvet that was

lighter than air. When she flipped it up, the blanket looked like a jellyfish softly landing all around her mattress. M loved doing this every morning and was surprised at the simple thrills a clean room could give her.

She looked in her full-length mirror. The bruises were almost gone on her arms. Survival class yesterday had threatened to knock the wind out of her sails. Photos still framed the mirror, tacked and taped around the edge. All of her best friends stared back at her: Jules, Merlyn, Devon, Evel, Ben, Vivian, and Cal. So did her father, M Freeman, and so did Jones. And lastly, there was a blank piece of paper with only one letter written on it: Z.

M shuffled downstairs like a zombie. "What is that smell, Mom? Don't tell me you tried to cook."

Her mother had thrown out the kitchen table as soon as they moved into the house in Harmon and commandeered the space as her new art studio. Apparently the lighting from the bay window was to die for. Michelangelo should have been so lucky.

"I did, M," answered her mother, whose hands were covered not with flour or sugar but pastels. "You should be proud! I made toast."

"Toast?" repeated M.

"With butter!" Her mother handed M a plate with one mangled piece of toast. It had been mashed down to within an inch of its life, though sharp peaks of cold butter still raised high above it.

"Thanks, Mom," said M. She took a bite and heard the

audible crunch of burnt bread. "I think you're getting the hang of this whole chef thing. Just warn me when you're moving on to casseroles."

"Everyone's a critic," her mother said as she went back to her easel and continued work on her new piece. Over the past year, her mother's art had really come into focus. It was odd at first because M had only known her mother to be a copy artist or restorer. But apparently, her mother was much, much more. She even had her own gallery opening in a few weeks of all original works.

As M ventured a second bite, the side door opened behind her. "I've got the newspapers!" cheered Jules.

"And I've got the latest details from Sercy," said Merlyn as he joined them inside.

"Hmmm, all I brought were some biscuits and bagels," said Cal.

M tossed her plate, uneaten toast and all, into the sink. "My hero!" She dove into the bag, grabbed a biscuit, and pulled it apart. Steam rose in the air and the room filled with doughy-scented goodness. She handed one half to Cal, who smiled, then took a huge bite.

Cal's father brought up the rear and shut the door behind him. He held two coffees and offered one to M's mom. "That piece is really coming together."

"All right, everybody," said M. "Let's get to work." She unfolded a copy of *El Pais*, a newspaper from Spain, and began to skim through every article.

"There's a postal stamp auction at Christie's in New York coming up," said Merlyn.

"Nah, not their style," replied M as she flipped to the next page.

"Oh, I've got one," said Jules. "A tech startup is joining a private space firm to launch a satellite to beam selfies to a galaxy called EGS-zs8-1. It's more than thirteen billion light-years away."

"Catchy name," admitted M. "And clearly the best place to send all of Earth's selfies. Plus it's got all the calling cards of being just weird enough. Have Sercy look into it."

M had almost closed *El Pais* when she noticed a small piece about one of Pablo Picasso's most famous works of art, *Guernica*. "Wait, guys, listen to this: A giant robotic machine that took tens of thousands of microscopic shots of Picasso's antiwar masterpiece has gone missing from a museum in Spain. It has lenses so strong that it can find air bubbles and scratches that were previously undetectable. One scan showed so much depth that you could actually see Picasso's mistakes, which still exist under the artwork."

The room fell silent.

"That's the one," Cal agreed. "No doubt."

M breathed deeply and steadied herself. It had been a year since Bandit and Zara saved her life ... possibly even the entire universe. A complete year of total silence.

But the Lawless School couldn't stay quiet forever.

ACKNOWLEDGMENTS

Thank you, reader, for making your way through the Lawless School, the Fulbright Academy, and beyond. It takes dedication to finish a trilogy, and I appreciate you sticking with this story to the very end—unless for some reason you've just now flipped to the back of the book to start with the acknowledgements. That's just weird. What kind of a person does that? I mean, besides you, the person who did it. You know who you are.

Thank you, Scholastic, for giving M's story life. Thank you, Nick, for working with me, believing in this trilogy, and pushing it further along whenever M ran into walls, plot holes, and things that go bump in the night. Thank you, also, to David for giving me a chance.

Phil Falco designed all these nifty covers and made me swear that I'll eventually watch the Battlestar Galactica reboot.

Thanks to Brooke Shearouse, my excellent publicity contact, and thanks to Annie McDonnell for proofreading each of these books. They needed it!

Thank you to Josh and Tracey Adams for being the agents who made these books into actual, real books and not just voices in my own head.

Thank you, also, to my uncle, Rick Salane. He won't finish this trilogy, but his spirit is in every word.

I have to thank my Mom and Dad, not because it's manda-tory, but because they actually deserve a never-ending supply of accolades, kudos, and applause for teaching me how to dream.

Thanks and congrats to my brother, Matt, and his wife, Ashley, for being in love.

To my Lawless daughter, Wren, thanks for being yourself.

To my Fulbright son, Dez, thanks for being yourself.

And to Adrienne, thanks for joining me on this adventure and letting me be a part of yours.

ABOUT THE AUTHOR

Jeffrey Salane grew up in Columbia, South Carolina, but moved north to study in Massachusetts and New York City. After spending many years playing in several bands, he now works as an editor and writer. He lives with his wife and kids in Brooklyn, New York. The author can prove his innocence at www.jeffreysalane.com.